PEGASUS

AND THE FLAME

Also by Kate O'Hearn

Pegasus and the Fight for Olympus
Pegasus and the New Olympians
Pegasus and the Origins of Olympus

Valkyrie

SHADOW OF THE DRAGON
Part One: Kira
Part Two: Elspeth

Other titles published by Hodder Children's Books:

Far Rockaway
THE STONEHEART TRILOGY
Stoneheart
Ironhand
Silvertongue
Charlie Fletcher

Ice Angel
Otto and the Flying Twins
Otto and the Bird Charmers
Otto in the Time of the Warrior
Charlotte Haptie

PEGASUS

AND THE FLAME

KATE O'HEARN

*Hodder
Children's
Books*

A division of Hachette Children's Books

First published in Great Britain in 2011
by Hodder Children's Books

14

A Catalogue record for this book is available from the British Library

ISBN 978 0 340 99740 6

Typeset in AGaramond Book by Avon DataSet Ltd,
Bidford on Avon, Warwickshire

Printed and bound by
CPI Group (UK) Ltd, Croydon, CR0 4YY

The paper and board used in this paperback by Hodder Children's Books
are natural recyclable products made from wood grown in
sustainable forests. The manufacturing processes conform to the
environmental regulations of the country of origin.

Hodder Children's Books
a division of Hachette Children's Books
338 Euston Road, London NW1 3BH
An Hachette UK company
www.hachette.co.uk

As always, without the support and love of my family, my wonderful editors Anne and Naomi, and my fantastic agent, V, this book would never have seen the light of day. Thanks, guys, you're the best! (OTB will never die.)

I would also like to dedicate this book to all the horses everywhere; especially those who suffer under poor working conditions and horrific abuse. I wish Pegasus would come to rescue you all. Without him, it will be up to us to make your lives better.

My dearest reader, please help whenever and wherever you can. Abused horses everywhere await your love and assistance.

Prologue

War came to Olympus.

There was no warning. No clues that an unknown enemy was building an army against them; an army whose only goal was complete destruction. One moment there was peace, the next they were fighting for their very existence. It was bloody, brutal and totally unexpected.

But for one Olympian, it was the perfect opportunity to fulfil a dream.

Paelen ducked behind a marble pillar and watched the best Olympian warriors gathering to take on the invaders. Jupiter was leading the attack with his thunder and lightning bolts in hand. His wife Juno stood on his left, grave-faced and ready. On his right, Hercules was looking strong and prepared, as were Apollo and his twin sister Diana with her bow. Mars was there, and Vulcan with his armoury full of weapons. Standing behind them in his winged sandals and helmet was Mercury, the messenger of Olympus. All preparing to fight.

Paelen's gaze trailed over to Pegasus. The stallion's eyes blazed and wings quivered as his golden hooves pounded the ground in anticipation of the upcoming battle. Further back gathered more Olympians, all there to defend their home.

But Paelen had no intention of fighting. He wasn't a warrior. He was a thief with plans of his own which didn't include getting killed in a battle they couldn't possibly win. War was everyone else's problem. He was too busy concentrating on how best to profit from it. With the defenders occupied in the struggle against the Nirads, a thief would be free to enter the palace of Jupiter and take whatever they wanted.

But Jupiter's treasures weren't what interested Paelen. What he desired most was the shiny gold bridle worn by Pegasus.

Everyone in Olympus knew the bridle was the greatest treasure of all. It alone held the key to possessing the powerful winged stallion. With Pegasus under his control, Paelen could go anywhere he wanted and take whatever caught his eye, with no one able to stand against him. This was the true prize, not the silly jewels or gold coins that could be found in the abandoned palace.

As Jupiter called his fighters forward, Paelen crept closer to listen to his desperate speech.

'My children,' he said gravely. 'We are in our darkest hour. At no other time in history have we faced such terrible danger. The Nirad fighters have breached our borders. Even now they are making for the Flame of Olympus. If they succeed in extinguishing it, all our powers, all we have ever known, will be lost. We must stop them. That Flame is our very existence. We cannot let them succeed. If we do not make our stand against them now, then everything we have known will be destroyed.'

Paelen listened to the murmurs of the crowd and felt the tension growing. His eyes were still locked on Pegasus. The stallion shook his head and snorted, causing his golden bridle to give out an enchanting tinkle that no other forged gold could ever make.

Hearing the bridle's song made Paelen's fingers itch to reach out and snatch it from the stallion. But he controlled himself. This wasn't the time to make a move. His dark eyes were drawn back to their desperate leader.

'We who never die, now face our destruction,'

continued Jupiter. 'But it is not only our world we must defend. All the other worlds we guard will fall if the Nirads defeat us. We fight for them!'

Jupiter raised his lightning bolts in the air and their ferocious booms echoed throughout all Olympus. 'Will you join me?' he cried. 'Will you rise against these invaders and drive them back to where they came from?'

Paelen's eyes grew wide at the sight of all the Olympians raising their arms to Jupiter. Pegasus reared on his hind legs and opened his wings in salute. Battle cries filled the air.

'For Olympus!' howled Jupiter as he turned and led his warriors into battle.

1

Emily put her hand on the window and felt the glass shaking from the heavy peals of thunder cracking overhead.

All day the radio had been reporting on the unexpected and violent storms raging up and down the east coast of the United States. Where Emily lived, in the heart of New York City, the storm was at its worst. Sitting alone in the apartment she shared with her policeman father, she never imagined that a simple thunderstorm could be *this* bad.

She clutched her cellphone and felt guilty for lying to her father. He'd just called to check on her.

'All the police have been summoned in to work, honey,' he explained. 'We're doing double and triple shifts. The city's a madhouse because of the weather and they need everyone on duty. Do me a favour, will you? Keep away from the windows. There are lightning strikes all over the city, and our top-floor apartment is at particular risk.'

Yet, despite his warning and her promise to keep away, Emily sat in the large window seat and watched the raging storm. This had always been her mother's favourite spot. She used to call it her 'perch': her special place to sit and watch the world moving around twenty storeys below. Since her death, Emily found herself sitting there more and more often as though it could somehow bring her closer to her mother.

But not only that, from this vantage point Emily could see the top of the Empire State Building and watch it suffer the storm's onslaught. Her father had once told her that the building itself worked as a giant lightning rod to protect the other buildings around it. But as more and more forked lightning struck its tall antenna, she wondered how much more it could take.

Emily hugged her knees to her chest to keep from trembling. She'd never been frightened of thunder when her mother was alive. Somehow, they'd always found ways of making foul weather fun and exciting. But now, all alone with her father at work, Emily felt her mother's loss as acutely as the day she died.

'I wish you were here, Mom,' she whispered sadly as she gazed out the window. As they had done countless times before, Emily's eyes filled with tears that trailed down her cheeks.

Suddenly there was an ever louder peal of thunder and brilliant flash of lightning. It struck the Empire so hard, the antenna at the top of the building exploded in a flash of electrical sparks and flying debris.

Emily could hardly believe what she had just witnessed. She wiped the tears from her blurred eyes as all the lights in the tall building blinked out. Immediately after, the lights in buildings around it went out. The darkness spread like a grape-juice stain on the carpet, as the city was hit with a blackout.

Emily followed the progression of the blackout as she peered up Broadway. Block after block was going dark. Even the street and traffic lights were out. It wasn't long before the power outage reached her block, plunging her apartment building into darkness. She leaned further against the glass and tried to see where the blackout ended. It didn't. The whole city was in darkness.

She jumped as her cell burst to life. With trembling hands she flipped it open and read her father's name on the small view screen.

'Dad,' she cried. 'You won't believe what just happened! The top of the Empire just blew up!

Lightning hit it and it exploded. Pieces went flying everywhere!'

'I just heard,' her father said anxiously. 'Are you all right? Did anything hit our building?'

'No, everything's fine,' Emily replied, hiding the fact that she was far from fine. She was actually starting to get very frightened. 'But the power's gone out. From what I can see, it's dark all over the city.'

Emily heard another voice in the background. Her father cursed before speaking to her again.

'We're getting reports that the blackout has spread to all the boroughs and is now hitting New Jersey. This is a big one, Em. And from what I've just been told, it's not going to be fixed anytime soon. I need you to go into the bathroom and fill the tub with water. Then fill whatever you can in the kitchen. We don't know how long this is going to last and we'll need that water.'

'I will,' she promised. Then before she could stop herself, Emily asked weakly, 'Dad, when are you coming home?'

'I don't know, honey,' he answered. 'Hopefully soon. Look, do you want me to call Aunt Maureen and ask her come over to stay with you?'

Emily loved her aunt, but she didn't want to

sound like a baby. She was thirteen, after all; certainly old enough to take care of herself. 'No, thanks, Dad, I'm fine.'

'You're sure?' her father asked. 'I'm sure she could use the company.'

'Yeah, I'm sure,' Emily said. 'The storm's just got me a bit freaked. But I've got lots to do here. Besides, it's too dangerous for Maureen to come over in all this and then have to climb twenty flights of stairs. Really, I'm fine.'

There was a hesitation in her father's voice before he said, 'All right. But if you need me or anything at all, I'm just a phone call away. Understand?'

'I do. Thanks, Dad,' Emily said. 'Now I'd better go before the water shuts down.'

Emily ended the call and used the light from her cellphone screen to guide her into the kitchen. She quickly found the emergency flashlight and crossed to the bathroom.

This was the standard operating procedure for blackouts. Fill the bathtub with water and anything else that will hold it. One of the downfalls of living in a tall building during a blackout was the pumps sending water up to the apartments soon stopped. If they didn't store all the water they could, they would quickly find themselves in a lot of trouble.

She began to fill the bathtub, and then the pots and pans in the kitchen. Just as she finished filling the last big soup pot, the pressure behind the water flow started to weaken. It wouldn't be long before it stopped completely.

'Well, it's better than nothing,' she sighed aloud as she shut off all the faucets.

While she worked, Emily had managed to forget about the storm for a few minutes. But with the water off, the sound of the rumbling thunder and police and fire sirens from the city took over as the only sounds in the apartment.

Just outside the bathroom window, Emily saw another burst of lightning and heard more thunder. The lightning was so bright it left her seeing flashes, even after she closed her eyes. There was no pause between the light and sound, which meant this latest strike was very close.

As the thunder rumbled angrily, Emily moved away from the window. This time she would follow her father's advice and stay well clear of them. The storm was now directly overhead – and getting worse by the minute.

2

Paelen stared in shock at the destruction around him. He had never seen anything like it before. The palace lay in ruins, as did every other building around it.

He had tried to keep up with the defenders, but they had left him behind. Now in the far distance, he heard the constant booming of Jupiter's thunderbolts and saw the flashes of lightning in the sky. The violent battle was raging, but far from this area of devastation.

Paelen's heart lurched as he saw Mercury on the ground. The messenger was lying on his side, a spear sticking out of his chest. Blood matted his fair hair and his face was covered with bruises. Paelen bent down to see if he was still alive.

Mercury weakly opened his pale blue eyes. 'Paelen,' he gasped, 'is it over? Have they extinguished the Flame?'

Paelen wondered if he should call for help. But there was no one left to call. From what he could see, everyone around him was either dead or dying. 'I believe it is still lit. I saw the others heading towards the temple.'

'We must stop the Nirads!' Mercury reached for Paelen's arm and tried to rise. 'Help me up.'

Paelen helped Mercury get to his feet. As he stood, the messenger pulled the spear from his chest. His wound opened and the bleeding increased. His legs gave out and he crumpled weakly back to the ground.

'The war is over for me. I am finished,' Mercury gasped.

'No, you are wrong,' Paelen said fearfully as he knelt beside the messenger and cradled him in his lap. 'Mercury, you must get up.'

The messenger shook his head. 'It is too late—'

He started to cough. Blood pooled in the corners of his mouth. 'Listen to me, Paelen,' he panted. 'You must join the fight. The Nirads must not extinguish the Flame.'

'Me? Fight?' Paelen repeated. He shook his head. 'I cannot. Look at me, Mercury. I have no real powers of my own. I am not big and strong like Hercules and I cannot fight like Apollo. I do not know how to use weapons and I am not fast like you. All I am is a thief. My only skill is to stretch my body to escape prisons and squeeze into tight spaces. And you know how

I hate doing that because it hurts too much. I am a coward – nothing more.'

Mercury reached for Paelen's hand and drew him closer. 'Listen to me, Paelen. I know you are still very young,' he gasped. 'And I know you are not as big as the rest of us or as strong. But you are clever and much braver than you think. It lies in you to make a difference.'

Again Paelen shook his head. 'You are asking too much of me! I am not the person you think I am. I am nothing.'

Mercury squeezed Paelen's hand as he struggled to speak. 'You are special, Paelen. This may be the only chance you will ever have to prove it. I know you have never considered yourself a true Olympian. But you are one – and you carry it within you to be great. This is the time to join your people and defend your home. Show me, Paelen,' Mercury coughed. 'Show all of us what you can do.'

'But I . . . I . . .' Paelen stammered.

'Please,' Mercury begged. 'Help us.'

The approaching battle cry of rampaging Nirads filled the air. It wouldn't be long before they arrived.

'A second wave of fighters is coming,' Mercury continued weakly. 'You must get away from here. Take my winged sandals. My helmet is lost, but you can still fly with the sandals. Take them and join the fight.'

'Your sandals?' Paelen cried. 'I cannot! They only work for you!'

Another choking cough came from the fallen messenger. His eyes started to glaze over. 'I am dying, Paelen,' Mercury said softly. 'I give them to you. You are their master now. They will obey your commands.'

With a final agonized cry, Mercury closed his eyes and became still.

Paelen couldn't believe the messenger was dead. Somehow, the invading Nirads had the power to kill the most powerful Olympians. If Mercury could die, so could everyone else.

He lay Mercury down gently on the ground and wrestled with himself as he thought of the messenger's final words. Part of him still wanted to steal the bridle from Pegasus and flee. But another part of him wondered if Mercury was right. Was there more to him than he realized? Did he really have the courage to join the fight? A thief was all he'd ever been. It was all he knew how to do. He did not have the powers of the other Olympians. If they were being defeated by the Nirads, what chance did he have?

Paelen finally decided fleeing was the only option.

Why should he sacrifice his own life if the war was already lost? If Pegasus hadn't already fallen in battle, this was the time to make his move to capture the stallion.

'I am sorry, Mercury,' he said sadly. 'But you were wrong. I am not the person you thought.'

Reaching down, he carefully removed the messenger's winged sandals and put them on his feet, hoping at least that Mercury had been right about them working for him.

Paelen heard roaring and grunting behind him. His eyes flew wide in terror as countless Nirad warriors approached. He'd never seen a Nirad up close before. They were massive. Their skin was grey marble and looked as hard as stone. Each of their four arms waved a weapon in the air and their eyes blazed with murderous hatred. These creatures had no intention of negotiating. No plans for taking prisoners. All Paelen could see in their bead-black eyes was the desire to kill. Seeing the invaders up close, he understood what everyone was up against. They didn't stand a chance. Olympus was doomed.

He quickly looked back down at the sandals.

'Fly, for Jupiter's sake, fly!' he shouted.

The tiny wings started flapping. He was lifted into

the air just as the first Nirad warriors arrived. Panic-stricken, Paelen yelled, 'Sandals, go! I do not care where. Just go!'

Mercury's sandals obeyed, and Paelen was carried away from the rampaging Nirads. He heard their angry roars at losing their prey.

With the immediate danger now well behind him, Paelen looked ahead. 'Stop!' he ordered.

The sandals obeyed his command and he hovered in mid-air. He looked in stunned disbelief at the devastation beneath him. He was sick to see that there wasn't one building left untouched, nor one statue unbroken. The Nirads were destroying everything.

'Go,' he finally said. 'Take me to the Temple of the Flame. I need to find Pegasus.'

As the sandals carried him towards the temple, the sounds of Jupiter's thunderbolts grew more intense and bright flashes lit the area. The battle was still raging, but it had now reached the base of the Temple of the Flame.

Paelen saw more fallen Olympians. Yet amongst the dead and dying, he saw no dead or wounded Nirads. Not one. It was as though the invaders couldn't be killed, even by the most powerful amongst them.

He glanced forward and saw smoke rising in the

distance. The Flame at the temple was still lit. But as he approached the heart of the battle, Paelen saw Apollo and Diana crouching back to back. They were surrounded by Nirads. Diana was using her bow, but every arrow she fired glanced off the grey invaders without causing any damage at all. Apollo was using his spear, but was having as little luck as his sister.

A Nirad warrior lunged forward and knocked Apollo's legs out from under him. More followed as Diana fought bravely to save her twin brother. But she was driven away quickly. As Paelen passed silently overhead, he heard her anguished cries filling the air as Apollo was killed by the invaders.

Pegasus. He had to find Pegasus.

The sandals drew him away from the horrible scene. Closer to the Temple of the Flame, he saw Jupiter fighting at its base. Roaring in rage, the leader of Olympus was shooting lightning bolts and thunder at the Nirads, to no effect. The invaders were steadily advancing up the tall marble steps.

Paelen finally saw Pegasus. The stallion was rearing on his hind legs and kicking out at the invaders. He was covered in blood from countless stab wounds as the Nirads used their vicious weapons to bring down the powerful stallion. A Nirad pounced and stabbed his spear deep into the flanks of the rearing stallion. Pegasus shrieked in pain and dropped back down to all fours, viciously kicking the Nirad with his golden hoof. But even as the wounded warrior crawled away, others moved in for the kill. They caught hold of the stallion's wings and were trying to tear them off.

Pegasus continued to fight but was quickly overpowered. As more and more Nirads attacked, the stallion was knocked to the ground. As he fell, the spear in his side broke and was driven deeper into his flanks.

Paelen watched in horror as Pegasus was swamped with Nirad warriors. There was no way the stallion would survive the attack.

Diana arrived. Shouting her battle cry, she attacked the Nirads tying to kill Pegasus. Stabbing at them with her brother's spear, her grief transformed to rage as she used all her strength against them.

One Nirad shoved past her and made for the stallion's head. But when its four hands made contact with the golden bridle, it howled in agony. Diana turned on the attacker and lunged forward with her brother's spear. Unlike all the other attempts to stop the Nirads, this time the spear worked and she managed to kill her first invader. With Diana's help, Pegasus got back on his feet. But that was one small victory in a losing battle.

'Paelen!'

Jupiter was surrounded by Nirad fighters but he was pointing at the temple. 'Quickly,' he shouted. 'Stop them!'

Paelen turned to the temple and saw other Nirads cutting through the defenders and advancing further up the marble steps.

'Stop them, Paelen!' Jupiter ordered again. 'They must not extinguish the Flame!'

Paelen knew the moment the Flame of Olympus went out, the war would be over and Olympus would fall. But if Jupiter himself couldn't stop the invaders, what could a thief possibly do?

In the time it took for him to decide whether or not to join the fight the battle was lost.

Nirad warriors tore down the entrance gates to the temple and tossed them down the steps. They poured into the temple, howling in rage. Moments later, there was the sickening sound of the plinth that held the Flame being knocked over. Guttural roars of triumph filled the air as the invaders went to work extinguishing the Flame.

Soon more and more Nirads abandoned the battleground and rushed up the steps to join in the destruction. The survivors of Olympus could do little more than watch in terror as their world ended.

Paelen saw Jupiter run over to Pegasus. Catching hold of the wounded stallion, Jupiter pointed in the air and shouted something. Pegasus snorted and nodded his head.

Moments later, the few survivors parted to give Pegasus room to spread his wings. With a shriek, the stallion launched himself into the air.

Paelen's heart leaped with excitement. This was his moment! Finally, an opportunity to seize the bridle and control the fleeing stallion.

'Go after Pegasus!' Paelen ordered his sandals. 'Get me to the stallion!'

3

Emily made her way back to her bedroom having finished collecting water. Without electricity, there would be no TV, no radio and no lights. With nothing more to do, she got into bed.

Emily knew she wouldn't sleep. Even if the storm hadn't been so noisy, she was on edge. She just wished she weren't alone. Her mother would have known what to do. But her mother was dead and nothing Emily could do would ever change that. She was alone. She started to regret not asking her Aunt Maureen to come over.

Outside the window there was another blinding flash of lightning and terrible explosion of thunder. Emily felt the whole building shake. But as she listened, she heard more than thunder. Directly above her head was the sound of something very big, very heavy hitting the roof.

Living in the top-floor apartment, the only thing

above them was the flat roof. Emily's family paid extra to have access to it, and her mother had planted a large flower and vegetable garden. But no one had been up there since her mother got sick and died. Emily worried that maybe a piece of the Empire's antenna might have just hit her building. Or maybe lightning had struck her mother's garden shed and knocked it over.

She considered calling her father to ask him what to do. Would lightning start a fire? Was her building about to burn down? The rain outside was coming down in heavy sheets, but would it put out a fire if it had started? As more and more questions and fears built up within her, Emily's heart practically stopped.

There were more sounds from above.

It was almost as though someone or something was kicking the roof.

Raising the flashlight, Emily sucked in her breath when the beam of light revealed a huge crack in the ceiling plaster. The overhead light was swinging on its cord. Small chips of paint and plaster were starting to fall.

Emily reached for her cell. But even before she used the speed dial, she closed it again. What was she going to tell her father? That something big had hit the roof and cracked her bedroom ceiling? Maybe he'd tell her to get out of the building. But that would mean going out in the dark hallway and finding her way to the stairwell. Then she'd have to walk down twenty flights of stairs, just to arrive on the street where it was pouring with rain.

'No, Em,' she told herself. 'There's nothing up there. It's just the garden shed fallen over and the door banging in the wind.'

Long before Emily could convince herself it was nothing serious, the thumping from above started again.

'This is crazy!' she said. Even as she spoke, she was climbing out of bed. 'You're not going up there . . .'

But it was as though her body and mind weren't speaking to each other. The more Emily's mind tried to stop herself, the more determined her body was to investigate the strange sounds coming from the roof.

Emily drew on her long raincoat, reached for the apartment keys and made for the door. As a quick afterthought, she grabbed the baseball bat they kept for security beside the door.

With only the single beam from the flashlight to show her the way, Emily climbed the stairs. She heard hushed sounds of footsteps and chattering voices as more of the building's occupants used the stairwell to get to their homes.

'This isn't smart, Em. There's lightning up there,' she warned herself. Once again, part of her wasn't listening.

She made it to the top of the access stairs and faced the locked door that led directly out to the roof. Clutching the bat in one hand and the flashlight in the other, Emily struggled to get the key in the lock. When she managed to turn it, the door opened a fraction. Suddenly the wind caught hold and wrenched the door from her hand. It flew open wildly and made a terrible crashing sound as it was nearly torn off its hinges.

'So much for being quiet,' she chastised herself.

Emily stepped into the blowing rain, and started passing the beam of light over the rooftop, searching for fire. It was almost a year since she'd been up there. The whole area was badly overgrown. Strange vines had taken hold, covering the once lovingly tended flower beds.

The vegetable patch was unrecognizable. In the dark, with the storm at its peak, this was no longer the garden Emily knew. Instead it was a dark and frightening place filled with mystery and danger.

Through the noise of the pounding rain, Emily

heard other sounds. It was the thumping again. Only this time, there was more. As she strained to listen above the terrible weather, she was sure she could hear whining, or the sound of someone or something crying out in pain.

Creeping forward, she passed the beam of light over the wild garden. To Emily's right was the large rose patch. This had been her mother's pride and joy. Every summer without fail, their apartment had been filled with the fragrance of the fresh cut flowers her mother had grown here. Now the rose bushes had run wild and were spilling out over the roof.

A sudden movement in the roses caught Emily's attention. Directing the light back, she thought she saw the glint of gold. She inched closer and kept the light trained on the bushes. There! The flash of gold again. Taking another nervous step, Emily held up the bat.

'Whoever you are, come out of there!'

As she took another tentative step, a blinding bolt of lightning cracked in the sky. The entire roof was bathed in light. And what Emily saw in the rose garden was impossible.

She stumbled backwards, lost her footing and fell hard to the ground.

'It's not real!' she told herself. Rising to her hands

and knees, she reached for the flashlight. 'You didn't see what you just saw. It's just the storm playing tricks on you. That's all!'

Shining the light once again in the direction of the rose bushes, her heart was pounding so badly she thought she might pass out. Climbing unsteadily to her feet, she crept forward.

'It's not real, Em, it's not real,' she repeated over and over again as she drew near. 'You didn't see anything!'

But when the light found its mark, she couldn't deny the truth.

It was very real.

A huge white horse was lying on its side in the middle of the rose garden. What had glinted in the beam of the flashlight was one of the horse's hooves. As Emily looked, she sucked in her breath. It was gold. Raising the flashlight, she received an even greater shock. A wing! Massive in size, it was covered in mud, leaves and rose petals, but unmistakable with its long white feathers.

'No!' Emily cried. 'This is impossible!'

More lightning lit the rooftop, confirming what Emily was trying so hard to deny.

A white horse with golden hooves and a vast white wing was lying on its side in the middle of her dead mother's rose garden.

Unable to move, barely breathing, Emily stared at the animal in disbelief.

As she watched, the wing on the horse's side stirred, followed by a terrible shriek of pain. The sound tore at Emily's heart. The animal was in agony. Racing forward and heedless of the sharp thorns that tore into her flesh, Emily entered the bushes and started to shove them away from the stricken horse.

She worked her way along the animal's side, towards its head. Lying flat on the ground, it was completely trapped within the rose bushes as the vicious thorns tore into its tender skin.

Emily cried out in her own pain as the thorns dug into her flesh as she tried to free the horse's head from the cruel bushes. It was awake, and looking at her with a huge dark eye.

'It's all right. I won't hurt you,' she soothed. 'I'll get you free in a moment. Then maybe you can stand up if you're not too hurt.'

When most of the horse's head was free, it tried to rise. It screamed in agony as the wing on its side moved.

'Wait, stop!' Emily reached out and stroked the horse's quivering neck. 'Don't move. Let me see what's wrong.'

Emily continued to stroke the strong, warm neck as she raised the flashlight and trailed the beam down along its body. She could see one wing resting on the side, but she couldn't see the other.

'I don't suppose you've only got the one wing?'

The animal raised its head and looked at her with imploring eyes that begged for help.

'No,' she sighed. 'I guess not.'

Emily soon freed the horse from the bushes. As she held up the flashlight, she glimpsed the upper edge of the other wing. Only it was at an odd angle, pinned beneath the weight of the horse's body.

'Your other wing is trapped beneath you,' she explained. 'But I guess you already know that.'

With the last of the bushes gone, she moved back to its head.

'I've done all I can, but we have to get you off that wing. If I go around to your back and push, will you try to get up?'

As if in answer to her question, the horse seemed to nod its head.

'You really are going crazy, Em,' she muttered. 'He's a horse. He can't understand you.'

She knelt down in the slippery mud and stroked the horse's side. 'OK, I'm sorry but this is probably going to hurt. When I start pushing, I want you to try to get up.'

Placing her hands firmly on its back, Emily leaned forward and started to push with all her strength. 'Now!' she grunted. 'Get up now!'

Emily could feel the horse's back muscles tensing beneath her hands as it struggled to rise.

'That's it!' Pushing and straining, Emily felt her knees starting to slip beneath her. 'Keep going, you can do it!'

Putting all her weight against the horse, Emily felt it move. But as it rolled forward, the trapped wing sprang free and hit her squarely in the face. Emily cried out as she was knocked backwards into the rose bushes. Lying in the centre of the patch, the vicious thorns tore large holes in her jeans and raincoat and pierced right through to her skin.

But the fresh pain from the thorns was quickly forgotten when lightning flashes revealed the horse now standing on its feet and facing her. Despite the filth from the mud and leaves that covered its body and matted its mane, and ignoring the countless cuts and gashes from the thorns, Emily was awestruck. She'd never seen anything so amazing in her whole life.

From the moment she'd discovered the horse on the

roof and seen its wing, a name had sprung to mind. A name long forgotten from an old book of myths her mother used to read to her. But worry for the animal had distracted her from those thoughts. Now it came flooding back. Stepping clear of the bushes, Emily approached. As she did, the stallion stepped up to her.

'It's really you, isn't it?' she whispered softly as she fearlessly stroked the soft muzzle. 'You're Pegasus, aren't you? I mean the really real Pegasus.'

The stallion seemed to pause for a moment. Then he nudged her hand, inviting another stroke. In that one rain-drenched instant, Emily felt her world changing.

For ever.

4

Paelen awoke, stiff and in a lot of pain. His back felt like it was on fire and every muscle in his body cried out in protest.

Around him he could hear the soft sound of voices. Keeping his eyes shut, he took a moment to remember what had happened to him. The last thing he recalled was finally catching up with Pegasus and reaching for the golden bridle. He remembered tearing it away from the stallion and feeling its weight in his hand. Then there had been a blinding flash . . .

After that, everything went blank.

Opening his eyes, Paelen discovered he was in bed in a very strange room. The walls were white with no decorations and it smelled very odd. Over to his right was another bed, but it was empty. Outside the large window, the storm was still raging. It shocked Paelen to see the flashes of lightning and hear the roaring thunder. The way the battle had been going, he thought it would all be over by now.

Paelen turned away from the window. He saw a strange assortment of devices with beeping sounds and blinking lights. Above him, he was alarmed to see clear bags of fluid dripping down tubes that actually *entered* his left arm.

'Doctor, he's awake,' said a woman from beside the bed.

Paelen focused his eyes on a man in a long white coat approaching the bed.

'Welcome back to the land of the living, young man. I'm Doctor Bernstein and you are in Belleview hospital. We thought we were going to lose you there for a bit. That was a rather nasty fall you took.'

Paelen said nothing as the man leaned forward and shone a bright light in his eyes. When he finished, he straightened again and whistled. 'I'll be darned if I know how you're doing it, but you are healing faster than anyone I've ever treated before. At this rate, those broken bones of yours will be knitted together in no time. As it is, that burn on your back is healing even as we watch.'

Switching off the light, he put it in his pocket. 'Now, can you tell me your name?'

As Paelen opened his mouth to speak, the lights

in the room flickered and dimmed.

'I hope the generators keep working,' said the woman as she looked up at the lights. 'I've heard the blackout hit the whole city. They're saying it's as bad as the one in seventy-seven.'

Paelen understood the words, but not their meaning. What was a 'blackout'? Seventy-seven what? What did it all mean?

'The generators are fine, Mary,' said Doctor Bernstein. He reached out to touch Paelen's arm reassuringly. 'The hospital has spent a fortune keeping the back-up generators serviced. So don't you worry about a thing, we have plenty of electricity and you are perfectly safe.'

Paelen was about to ask where he was when a new person entered the room. Dressed in dark clothing, the man drew up to the side of the bed.

'I'm Officer Jacobs from the Fourteenth Precinct,' said the man, holding up his police badge. 'I've been called in to take the details of your mystery patient. So, is this the young man who fell from the sky?'

The doctor and nurse nodded.

'I'm Doctor Bernstein,' the doctor said, offering his hand. 'This is Nurse Johnston. As for my patient, well,

I don't as yet know his name. But I was just about to ask.'

Officer Jacobs opened his notebook. 'Allow me.' He turned his attention to Paelen. 'So young man, can you give us your name?'

Inhaling deeply, Paelen raised his hand in a flourish and bowed as best he could in the bed. 'I am Paelen the Magnificent, at your service.'

'Paelen the Magnificent?' Doctor Bernstein repeated as his eyebrows rose. 'Paelen the Lucky, more like.' He turned to the police officer. 'This young man was found in the middle of 26th Street and Broadway. The paramedics think he was at a costume party, stood too close to a window and was struck by lightning. They think he might have fallen out. We've been treating lightning burns and electrocutions like his all night. Though I must admit, most of the others haven't been so lucky.'

'Were you hit by lightning?' Officer Jacobs asked Paelen.

Paelen thought back to the last thing he remembered and frowned. 'Perhaps, but I am uncertain.'

Officer Jacobs started to write. 'All right then, Paelen, can you give me your last name? Where do you come from? Where do you live so we can notify your family and tell them you are here?'

Paelen looked at both men, then at the strange room again. Suddenly his thief's instinct took over and told him not to say anything more about himself or where he came from. 'I – I do not remember.'

'Don't remember?' Dr. Bernstein repeated. 'Well, you did have a rather nasty knock on your head. Though I'm sure the memory loss is only temporary. Maybe this will help . . .' He crossed over to the small cupboard against the far wall. He pulled out a bag and poured out the contents on to the bed.

'When you were found, this was all you were wearing: this small tunic and this pair of winged sandals. You were clutching this horse's bridle. We had a nightmare of a time prying it out of your hands.'

'Those are mine,' Paelen protested as he tried to grab the items. 'I want them back!'

'Hey, that looks like real gold,' the police officer said as he reached for the bridle. Feeling its heavy weight, he frowned. 'Feels like real gold too.'

'You cannot have that!' Paelen cried as he snatched at the bridle. He winced when it pulled at his broken ribs. 'I told you it is mine.'

'Where did you get it?' Officer Jacobs demanded.

'Get it?' Paelen repeated. 'I, I,' he paused as he tried

to out-think these strange people. Finally a solution came to him. 'It was a gift.'

'A gift?' the officer repeated curiously. 'You're telling me that you can't remember your full name or where you came from, but you can remember that this was a gift?'

'Yes,' Paelen said confidently. 'That is correct. It was a gift.'

Officer Jacobs moved closer to the bed and frowned. 'Well, Paelen, shall I tell you what I think?' Not waiting for an answer he continued. 'I don't think this was a gift at all. In fact, I don't believe you fell out any window. I think you were pushed.' He held up the bridle. 'If this is real gold, which I think it is, then it's got to be worth a fortune. I'm sure someone of your age wouldn't be getting it as a gift. Tell me, how old are you? Sixteen? Seventeen maybe? So I'll ask you again, where did you get it?'

Paelen wasn't about to tell them how old he was or that he hadn't been pushed out any window. He especially couldn't tell them about the bridle or from whom he'd taken it. Instead he shrugged. 'I cannot remember.'

'That's a very convenient memory of yours,' suggested Officer Jacobs. 'You say this was a gift, but you won't say who gave it to you.'

He next turned his attention to the beautifully tooled winged sandals. Fine, colourful feathers adorned the tiny wings and beautiful cut diamonds, sapphires and rubies had been sewn into the soft leather.

'What can you tell me about these? They also look very valuable.' Officer Jacobs winked at the doctor before he chuckled, "Or do you want to tell us that Mercury, messenger of the Gods gave them to you?'

'That is correct,' Paelen simply answered.

'What's correct?' Officer Jacobs said, suddenly confused.

'They were a gift from Mercury.' Paelen dropped his eyes and felt his throat tighten. 'He gave them to me before he died.'

Officer Jacobs frowned and shook his head. 'What? Who died? Paelen, tell me, who gave you these sandals before they died?'

Paelen felt the conversation turning in the wrong direction. 'No one. I told you, they were a gift.'

'No, you just said someone died. I know it wasn't Mercury. So who was it? Where are they now?'

'I was wrong,' Paelen said defensively. 'Mercury did not die. The Nirads are not invading Olympus and there is no war. Everyone is fine and happy.'

'Nirads? Olympus?' Officer Jacobs repeated. 'What are you talking about?'

Paelen realized he'd said too much. 'I . . . I don't remember. My head hurts.'

He was grateful when Doctor Bernstein stepped forward. 'I think that's enough for now, Officer. This young man has obviously been through a terrible ordeal. It's best if we let him rest.'

The police officer kept his sharp eyes on Paelen, but finally nodded. 'All right, we'll leave it there for the moment.' He started to put the bridle, sandals and toga back in the hospital bag. 'But in the meantime, I think I'll hold on to these until we can figure out who they belong to.'

Paelen started to panic. He'd fought very hard to get that bridle from Pegasus and didn't want this man to take it from him. Throwing back the covers, he tried to climb from the bed but found the heavy casts on his legs stopping him. 'Please, those are mine. You cannot take them.'

'Paelen, calm down.' Doctor Bernstein gently pushed Paelen back against the pillows. 'You can't walk. Both your legs are broken, as are most of your ribs. You need rest. Officer Jacobs won't be taking your things far. He'll just keep them safe until we can figure out who they belong to.'

'But they belong to me!' Paelen insisted.

'Doctor?'

A nurse had entered the room. She was holding a patient chart in her shaking hands. The colour had drained from her face and she appeared to be very frightened as she studied Paelen. With a tremble in her voice, she said, 'The blood tests on your patient just came back.'

The nurse handed over the chart as though it were burning her hands. Without waiting for a response, her eyes shot to Paelen a final time before she raced out of the room.

Shocked by her odd behaviour, Doctor Bernstein opened the chart and read the test results. His expression changed as his eyes darted from the chart to Paelen and then back to the chart again.

'What is it?' Officer Jacobs asked.

Saying nothing, Doctor Bernstein shuffled through the papers and checked and re-checked the results. When he finished, he closed the chart and concentrated on Paelen.

'Who or should I say, *what* the hell are you?'

5

Emily was still on the roof with Pegasus.

Sometime during the seemingly endless night the storm ended just as abruptly as it had begun. The rain stopped and the skies cleared. With the city cast in total darkness from the power outage, for the first time in her life, Emily was able to see stars sparkling in the midnight sky over New York City. She peered up Broadway and listened to the eerie silence. There was some traffic on the wide road, but not much. Only the occasional sounds of a car horn or police siren shattered the overwhelming stillness.

Pegasus was standing close beside her as she looked down to the world below. Her hand was absently stroking the stallion's muscled neck.

'It looks so strange down there,' she said softly. 'It feels like we're the only ones left alive in the whole city.'

Looking at the stallion, Emily still couldn't believe

her eyes. Even touching him didn't seem to help. It was just so hard to accept that the real Pegasus was actually here in New York City, standing beside her on the roof of her apartment building.

But as the sun started to rise, she was finally able to see him clearly. The rain had washed most of the mud away, and returned his colour to white. Walking around his side, she saw his left wing was hanging at an odd angle. Without knowing anything about horses, or birds for that matter, she immediately knew the wing was badly broken.

Further down his back, she was shocked to discover a terrible burn she hadn't noticed before. She could see the singed hair and open, weeping wound.

'Were you struck by lightning?'

Pegasus turned his head back to her. As Emily looked into his dark, intelligent eyes, she felt perhaps he *could* understand her. But he gave no response.

'Well, it must have been the lightning, considering how bad it was last night.' She sighed before she continued, 'You poor thing, that must have really hurt.'

As the light increased, further inspection of the horse's body revealed that what Emily had first thought was simply mud from the rose patch covering his body, turned out to be blood. A lot of it. Working her way around the stallion, Emily quickly discovered that most of Pegasus's wounds were not caused by the lightning strike or thorn cuts from the rose bushes.

'You've been in a fight!' she cried as she inspected deep gashes cutting into the stallion's back and legs. 'With who? Who'd want to hurt you?'

Pegasus gave no answer. Instead, he opened his unbroken wing, inviting her to peer beneath. As Emily did, she gasped. Hidden under the fold of the wing was the exposed end of a broken spear. The other end went deep into Pegasus's rear flank.

'You've been stabbed!'

With trembling hands, Emily felt around the spear wound.

'It goes in so deep,' she said. 'I have to do something. Maybe call a vet.'

Pegasus whinnied and shook his head wildly. Emily didn't need to speak his language to know he didn't want her contacting anyone else.

'But you're hurt!' she insisted. 'And I don't know what to do to help you.'

Once again, Pegasus snorted, pawed the tarmac roof and shook his head. He then turned back to her and nuzzled her hand. Emily stroked his soft muzzle and rested her forehead against him. It had been an endless night and exhaustion was taking hold.

'You need help, Pegasus,' she said softly. 'More help than I can give you.'

To the east, the sun finally climbed over the top of a tall building. It shone golden light on the rooftop garden and felt wonderful on Emily's tired face. It also made her realize that anyone in a building taller than hers would now be able to see Pegasus on the roof.

'We've got to get you under cover,' she warned. 'If anyone sees you, they might call someone who'll take you away.'

Pegasus quickly shook his head, snorted and started pawing the tarmac roof with his sharp hoof again.

'Don't worry. I won't let that happen,' Emily promised. 'We'll just have to find somewhere to hide you until that wing heals.'

Her first thought had been to take Pegasus down to her apartment. Then her father could come and help figure things out. But that thought was quickly dismissed. Even though the freight elevator made it up to the roof, it wasn't working with the power off. The stairs were not an option either. If she were to hide Pegasus, it would have to be up here.

Then her eyes landed on her mother's large garden shed. 'That will have to do. I know it's probably not what you are used to, but for now, it's all we've got.'

With Pegasus patiently watching, Emily quickly emptied the shed of all the garden furniture and potting supplies. When she finished, she was surprised by how much room there was inside.

'Well, it's not fancy,' she said as brushed dirt off her hands and invited Pegasus in. 'But at least it will keep you hidden until we figure this out. Is that all right with you?'

Pegasus stepped forward and entered the shed.

With the immediate problem solved, Emily put her hands on her hips and looked at the stallion. 'Next, we should get those wounds of yours cleaned. We can't let them get infected. So if you stay here, I'll go down to my apartment and get some water and clean cloths.'

As she drew away, the stallion began to follow her. Emily shook her head and smiled. 'You have to stay here, Pegasus. You won't make it down the stairs and the elevator isn't working. I promise I'll be right back.'

Back in her apartment, Emily raced into the bathroom. She caught sight of her reflection in the mirror and received quite a shock. She was a mess. Rose leaves and petals were tangled in her hair and her face and arms were covered in dried mud and blood from the thorns. But most shocking of all was the huge black eye. As she prodded the tender area, she found the entire right side of her face was bruised and painfully swollen from where Pegasus's wing had struck her.

'Great,' she muttered to herself. 'What are you going to tell Dad about that?'

She decided to worry about that later. Instead she opened the medicine cabinet. It was still filled with all the medicated creams they'd used to treat her mother's sores when her illness had confined her to bed. Neither she nor her father had had the heart to throw them out. For once, she was grateful.

Grabbing all she could, Emily then went into the kitchen. There she gathered together clean dish towels, disinfectant soap and one of the large pots of collected water.

As she packed the items into bags, she noticed a pool of water on the tile floor in front of the refrigerator. Without power, the freezer section was starting to defrost. Pulling open the door, she saw two tubs of ice cream mixed in with the thawing bags of frozen vegetables. She suddenly felt very hungry. She hadn't eaten anything since lunch the previous day.

Emily reached for one of the tubs, grabbed a spoon and put it in her bag of supplies for the roof. She then thought to take some carrots, fresh green beans and a few apples for Pegasus.

She caught hold of the flashlight and headed back up to the roof.

The sun was steadily climbing higher in the sky. But as she stepped out on the roof, Emily still found the city was unnervingly quiet. It was Wednesday. Usually the garbage trucks were out early making all the noise they possibly could. But not today. With the blackout, Emily figured they would have the day off. She also assumed her school would be closed. Even if it wasn't, she wasn't going in. Pegasus needed her, school didn't.

'I'm back,' she called as she walked up to the garden shed. Part of her expected to find nothing there; as though everything that had happened the previous night had been some kind of strange dream. But as she approached, she heard the sound of hooves moving on the shed floorboards.

Pegasus poked his white head out and nickered softly to her.

'Told you I wouldn't be long,' Emily said as she started to unpack the bags. 'OK, I've got some water here, a bit of disinfectant soap and some medicated creams we used to treat my mom's bedsores. The package says it's good for burns too. So I thought it might help you.'

Pegasus peered into the bags as she unpacked them. Emily giggled as his long mane tickled her face. He soon found the tub of ice cream and pulled it out of the bag.

'Hey, that's for me,' Emily complained as she tried to reach for the tub. 'I've got some apples and vegetables for you.'

But the stallion ignored her. Putting the tub on the ground, Pegasus used his hoof to hold it still while his sharp teeth tore off the top. His long tongue started to lick the melting chocolate ice cream.

'I don't know if you should be eating that,' Emily warned. 'Chocolate isn't good for dogs, maybe it's the same for horses.'

Pegasus stopped and looked at Emily. The expression on his face gave her the impression that he didn't much care for being called a horse.

'Well, I'm sorry,' Emily said. 'I just don't want you to get sick. You've got enough problems already.'

Pegasus stared at her a moment longer before going back to the ice cream.

'Fine, suit yourself,' she said as she unfolded a deck

chair and sat down to eat the fruit and vegetables that Pegasus had refused.

As the morning passed, Emily did her best to clean and treat Pegasus's many wounds. While working on his neck, her cellphone went off.

'Hi Dad,' she said, reading his name on the screen.

'Hey Kiddo, you all right?'

Emily looked at the cuts on her arms, then over to Pegasus. 'Sure, everything's fine. You wouldn't believe what happened last night! There was this big crash on our roof—'

Before Emily could say more, Pegasus nudged her and pounded the floor with his hoof. He shook his head and snorted. Emily looked at him and knew he didn't want her to tell her dad about him.

'What happened?' her father repeated. 'Emily, did something happen?'

'Um, no Dad. It was just the garden shed. The wind blew it over. But there are no problems here at all apart from the power being out. What about you?'

Her father sighed. 'I've been held up a bit, so I'm going to be late getting home. I'm at Belleview Hospital at the moment, trying to do a report on this kid that fell out a window. Things have gone

48

from weird to really, really weird.'

Emily was looking at Pegasus. He was still staring at her intently, as though he was listening to her every word.

'Em, you still there?' her father called.

'Sure, Dad,' she answered quickly. 'Sorry. What's so weird about the kid?'

'I can't get into it right now. I'll tell you when I get home later. Should be sometime before dinner. Just take it easy today.'

'I will,' she promised.

After she hung up, Emily looked at the stallion. 'You didn't want me to tell my father about you, did you?'

Pegasus shook his head and snorted. Again, Emily had the strange feeling he knew exactly what she meant.

'I don't understand. My dad's a good man. He's a police officer and would help you. He'd never hurt you or turn you in.'

Pegasus shook his head and stomped his hoof.

'I sure wish you could tell me what's wrong.' Emily sighed. 'Well, if you don't want my dad to know, I'll do as you wish. But I need help. I can't get that spear out of you on my own and your wing needs to be set properly. I'm not strong enough to do it all alone.'

Pegasus moved his head closer to Emily and gently nuzzled her hand. She leaned against his thick neck as she tried to think.

Finally someone else came to mind. Someone from her school who would be strong enough to pull out the spear. Someone who was always sketching pictures of winged horses on his textbooks. The trouble was he was the meanest boy in Emily's class. He was probably the meanest boy in the whole school.

Joel DeSilva had only joined Emily's class a couple of months ago, but he'd already been in several fights. He never talked to anyone and didn't have any friends. Most of the kids in her class were terrified of him and left him alone. Joel DeSilva was the last person in the world Emily wanted to talk to. But he was the only person she could think of.

'Pegs, I think I know one boy you might let me ask,' Emily said. 'He's from my school. His name is Joel. He's a bit older than me, but really big and strong. And I know he already loves you because he's always drawing your picture on all his books. The teachers yell at him about it, but he doesn't care. He lives across the street from the school, so I could go ask him to come and help. Will you please let me do it?'

The stallion considered her words. He neighed softly.

'Thank you,' Emily said, patting him. 'If I leave now, I should be back very soon. With Joel's help, we can get that spear out of your side and set your wing.'

She pulled out her cellphone and stepped up to his side. 'I'm going to take your picture. It might be easier then to convince Joel that you're really here.' Making sure she got his wing in the shot, she took the stallion's picture.

'Perfect. OK, I'm going now. You've got extra water for drinking, and there are still some carrots and beans left if you get hungry. I really shouldn't be too long. But even if I am, please keep hidden in this shed. I don't want anyone to see you and take you away from me.'

Emily wondered if she should lock him in the shed. But then she thought better of it. If Pegasus were to get frightened, he might break down the door or even destroy the shed. Then there would be no place to hide him. Instead she left the door open and hoped the stallion would remain inside.

'I'll be back soon,' she called as she turned on the flashlight and entered the stairwell.

Emily was surprised by how many people there were on the stairs. Some, like her, had flashlights; others used lighters or candles. Everyone seemed in bright spirits. Neighbours who usually never spoke to each other laughed and chatted as they slowly descended or climbed the stairs.

It took ages getting down to the ground. But as Emily stepped into the lobby, she realized that going down was a heck of a lot easier than climbing back up was going to be. She only hoped she could get Joel to come back with her.

Once outside, Emily was struck again by the eerie silence of the city. There were people on the sidewalk, but very little traffic. All the shops and wholesalers were closed. It was like some strange holiday.

Emily ignored the stares of the people she passed along the way. She'd forgotten to comb her hair or even wash her face. She knew she looked even worse than Pegasus.

The journey seemed endless, but as she arrived at 21st Street and 2nd Avenue, she looked at the line of brownstones across from the school. Which one was Joel's?

She considered calling out his name in the hopes that someone would hear and tell her where he lived. But as she walked down the street, she saw a well-built boy sitting on the front stoop of one of the buildings. His wide shoulders were slumped and his head of wavy black hair was lowered. As she drew near, she was grateful to see it was Joel.

Then the nerves started.

Emily wasn't sure how she should approach him. His expression was as threatening as the storm from the previous night. She took a deep breath and climbed the few steps to the stoop.

'Hi Joel.'

Joel looked her up and down.

'I'm Emily Jacobs,' she pressed on. 'We both have the same home-room and math class.'

Her comment received only a blank stare.

'That was some storm last night, wasn't it?' she said with forced cheerfulness. 'I saw the lightning hit the Empire and blow the top right off. It did more damage than King Kong!'

Joel looked at her blankly. Finally he broke his silence. 'Go away.'

At that moment, seeing his angry, unwelcoming face, there was nothing on earth Emily would have rather done. But thoughts of the spear in Pegasus kept her feet locked on the spot.

'Look, Joel, I know we've never talked before, but I really need your help—'

His dark eyes flashed. 'Are you deaf or just plain stupid? I said go away!'

'I would love to, but I can't,' Emily said desperately. 'Something happened last night and you're the only person I can think of to help. Please, will you speak to me for a moment? Then if you still feel the same, I'll go.'

'What do you want?' Joel demanded. 'What's so important that you had to come here and bother me? Have you looked at yourself in the mirror lately? You're a mess.'

Emily's own temper flared. The pain from her swollen eye and many scratches told her exactly what she looked like. But she also knew that Pegasus was her only priority. He needed her more than her pride did.

'You really want to know what's so important?' she shot back. 'Why I would come here and try to talk to you when I know for sure you hate the whole world? Pegasus, that's why. He's what's so important!'

Joel's expression changed for the briefest of moments. In that instant, Emily saw a flicker of interest. But just as quickly, the veil of anger came crashing down again.

'What about him?' he challenged.

Emily advanced on the bully. 'I've seen the pictures you've sketched on your books. He's all you ever draw.'

'So?' Joel demanded.

Emily looked up to the sky, not knowing what to do.

Did she dare risk telling him her secret? Did she really have a choice?

'What if he were real?' she started. 'I mean, if he was, and he was hurt, would you want to help him?'

Anger flashed again in Joel's chocolate brown eyes. He stood quickly, looming over her. 'What kind of dumb question is that? Are you making fun of me because I like Pegasus? If you are, I swear I'll thump you!'

'No I'm not making fun of you!' Emily said, just as quick and just as angry. 'Joel, listen to me. Please . . .'

She reached into her pocket and fished out her cell. Opening it, she held up the photograph of the winged stallion.

'You may not believe me but last night Pegasus, the *real* Pegasus, wings and all, was struck by lightning and crashed on my roof. He's there right now and he's badly hurt. I've done all I can, but one of his wings is broken and I don't know how to set it. If you really care about him like I think you do, you'll come with me and help him!'

Emily's hands were shaking too much to allow Joel to see the photograph on the small screen. He reached out and took hold of the cell.

'He landed in my mother's rose garden. That's why

I'm such a mess. Then when I tried to help him stand up again, his broken wing hit me in the face and gave me this black eye.'

Suddenly the exhaustion of the long night caught hold of her and she sat down. 'Please,' she begged. 'He's in so much pain. I don't know what to do for him.'

Joel was still clutching the cell as he cautiously sat down beside her. 'Go on, I'm listening.'

'Pegasus is hurt. He's hurt really bad,' Emily explained, relieved at last that Joel was listening. 'He's also been in a terrible fight. He can't tell me why or with whom. But he's cut all over and there's a big spear that's still in him. I'm not strong enough to pull it out on my own. That's why I thought of you.'

'Why? Because I'm so big?' Joel challenged, suddenly growing angry and defensive again. 'Just a big dumb Italian?'

Emily shook her head. 'No, that's not it at all. Listen to me. Pegasus is hurt! I came here because I thought you cared and wouldn't want to see him captured.'

Joel hesitated. There was now an expression of doubt rising on his face. 'How do I know it's not a trick? Or some kind of stupid joke?'

Emily shook her head and stood again. 'Look at me,' she said wearily. 'Do I look like I'm joking? Does this black eye look like make-up? You think I gave myself all these cuts from the rose bushes just so I could come here to cause trouble for you? This isn't a trick, Joel, I swear on my mother's soul. Pegasus needs our help!'

Joel was silent for so long that Emily almost gave up.

Starting to descend the stairs again, Emily looked up at him. 'I can't leave him alone too long. It's a simple question. Are you coming or not?'

Joel looked from Emily up to the doors of the brownstone, then back at Emily again.

Finally he started to descend the stairs. 'All right, I'm coming.'

When he reached the pavement, he stood before her. 'But if this is a joke, I don't care if you *are* a girl. I swear I'll knock your head off!'

6

Little was said between Emily and Joel as they made their way back to her corner-apartment building. When they arrived, Joel stopped before the lobby doors.

'How high is it?' he said, looking up.

'Twenty storeys,' Emily said. 'I live on the top floor. Pegasus is on the roof above that.'

'What? Twenty storeys?' Joel complained. 'You expect me to climb twenty flights of stairs?'

'I told you, Pegasus is on the roof.'

When Joel hesitated, Emily sighed. 'Look, you've come all this way. Are you going to go back now just because you've got to climb a few stairs?'

'Twenty flights aren't a few stairs!' he complained. 'It's a marathon!'

Too tired to fight any more, Emily shook her head. 'Fine, Joel, go home. I guess I was wrong when I thought you liked Pegasus. Just do me a favour, will you? Keep your mouth shut. You may not believe he's here, but others might.'

Emily said nothing more and pulled out her flashlight. She entered the lobby and walked towards the stairwell. As she pulled open the heavy metal stairwell door, she heard footsteps behind her. Looking back, she saw Joel.

'It's still going to be twenty flights,' she warned.

Joel shrugged. 'I know. But I haven't got anything better to do.'

Climbing the first five flights was easy. Making it to ten was tiring. By the fifteenth floor, both Emily and Joel were out of breath and feeling nauseous. Taking a break, they both sat down on a stair.

'I didn't think it would be this hard,' Emily panted. 'I thought walking to school was enough exercise. But I'm really out of shape.'

'Me too,' Joel agreed between breaths. 'I used to live in Connecticut and played school football. But it's been too long.'

In the dim light from the flashlight, Emily looked at him. 'So you're from Connecticut?'

Joel shook his head. 'I'm from Rome. You know, Italy. But when I was a kid my father got a job at the United Nations. So we moved to the United States and found a house in Connecticut. My parents commuted into the city every day for work.'

Emily was surprised. Joel didn't have any trace of an accent. She'd have never guessed he was foreign. For as long as he'd been in her class, she'd never known anything about him. Just that he was a troublemaker. 'So then you moved into the city and now live in those brownstones?'

'Not exactly . . .' he started. He paused. Suddenly his mood changed. He stood up abruptly. 'I don't want to talk about it any more,' he said. 'Are we going up or what?'

Without waiting for her, he charged forward into the darkness of the stairwell.

The final five flights were climbed in silence. When they reached the top, Emily drew the keys to the roof door from her pocket and stepped up beside him.

'He knows you are coming, but I don't think he's too happy about it. So take it easy on him. You can get as mad at me as you like. But I don't want you yelling at him. You got it?'

'I didn't yell at you,' Joel challenged.

'Well, whatever you call it,' Emily responded as she inserted the key and turned the lock. 'I don't want you doing it to Pegasus. He's hurt and in pain. You're going to be nice to him or I swear I'll push you off the roof.'

Joel looked shocked by the sudden change in her. 'If he's really here, I promise I won't do anything wrong.'

'Oh, he's here all right.'

Emily shoved open the door and stepped out on to the tarmac roof. 'He's in that shed over there. 'You still here, Pegs?' she called out.

A soft nicker came from the shed. Joel's expression changed from doubt to absolute wonder.

'Remember,' Emily held up a warning finger, 'be nice or you'd better learn to fly real fast!'

She drew Joel towards the shed.

'Did you miss me?' she asked as Pegasus came forward to greet her. She stepped up to his head and started to stroke his smooth white face. A sharp intake of breath was all Emily heard from Joel. She turned back, and saw his disbelieving expression.

'Pegasus, I would like you to meet Joel.' She beckoned Joel forward. 'Joel, this is Pegasus.'

Joel entered the shed and stood before the stallion a full minute before he was able to move or speak. Finally he shook his head and raised a hand tentatively to reach out and stroke Pegasus's head.

'I can't believe it. Pegasus is real! And he's really here!' Joel's eyes were beaming.

Emily watched his thick armour of anger melting away.

'He sure is. But he's also very hurt.' She led him to the broken wing. 'This needs to be set, but I don't know how.'

She then directed him around to the other side. 'Pegs?' she said, speaking softly. 'Would you lift your good wing so I can show Joel the spear? He's going to help me get it out of you.'

Without hesitation, the stallion lifted his wing to reveal several centimetres of broken spear sticking out of his side. 'Oh my Lord,' Joel cried as he inspected it. 'Who did this to him?'

Emily shrugged. 'I don't know. All I do know is he needs our help before someone finds him and takes him away.'

As she spoke Emily started to frown. It seemed that a lot of the deeper cuts and scratches were much smaller than they had been earlier. Further inspection revealed that the lightning burn had also shrunk and was less angry. As for the thorn scratches, they were all gone.

'You're healing so fast,' Emily gasped. She looked at Joel. 'This morning, these cuts were much deeper. You see all these scratches on me? They were ten times worse on him. But all the thorn marks are gone.'

'I'm not surprised.' Joel continued to inspect the stallion's side. 'Pegasus is an Olympian. He's immortal. Of course he would heal quickly.'

'What's being Olympian got to do with it?' Emily asked. 'He's still a living being, just like you and me. And we sure don't heal this quickly!'

'Yes, he's a living being,' Joel explained. 'But he's also very different from us. If you'd asked me before, I wouldn't have thought he could be hurt at all.'

'If I'd asked you before, you'd have bitten my head off.'

Joel frowned and shot back, 'I would not!'

Emily dropped the subject before it started another argument. Joel had a very short fuse and was easily provoked. 'Well, Olympian or not, that spear has got to come out. I'm not even sure how to set his wing.'

Joel stroked the smooth white feathers of the stallion's good wing. 'In movies, all they ever do is pull the person's broken leg or arm to set it. Then they put a splint on it.'

'But this isn't an arm or leg. It's a wing,' said Emily. 'And aren't most wing bones hollow? We could do more damage if we pull it and set it wrong.'

Joel nodded. 'Maybe, but we can't leave him like this either.' Suddenly he had an idea. 'What if we take a really good look at his unbroken wing? We study it and learn how it works. Then if we look at the broken wing, we should be able to see the difference and know how it should be. After that, we could try to set it.'

'Good idea,' Emily agreed. 'But where do we start? With his wing or with the spear?'

It was Pegasus who answered that question. As though he'd been listening to every word, the stallion lifted his good wing again and then whinnied and pounded the shed floor.

Emily stroked his muzzle. 'You want us to pull out the spear first?'

In answer Pegasus nuzzled her hand.

Joel joined Emily at the stallion's head. 'Then I guess we start with the spear,' he said.

Emily and Joel went back down to her apartment to collect more supplies.

Joel looked around and whistled. 'You apartment is a whole lot nicer than the dump I live in. Is it just you and your folks?'

'My mother died of cancer three months ago. Now it's just me and my dad.' Emily felt the familiar lump start to form in the back of her throat. Taking a deep breath, she forced it back down before the tears began. 'What about your place? I always heard brownstones were great. Lots of room and you've actually got backyards.'

Joel shook his head. 'Not where I live. Our brownstone is small and falling apart. The plumbing doesn't work and the paint is peeling.'

Emily grabbed the last of the medicated creams and antiseptics from the medicine cabinet.

'Did your mother ever teach you how to sew?' Joel asked.

'Sew?' Emily repeated. 'Why?'

'Because once we pull that spear out of Pegasus, he's going to bleed. We'll need to sew the hole closed to stop the bleeding and start the healing.'

'You want me to sew Pegasus back together?'

'Do you have a better idea?' Joel asked.

'Yeah,' Emily said. 'Superglue. They sometimes use that stuff in micro-surgery instead of stitches. They actually used it on my mother for one of her surgeries. After they told my dad, he got a supply of it for emergencies.'

Joel frowned. 'Really? Glue?'

Emily nodded and walked back into the kitchen to collect the glue. It was tossed in the bag of supplies. Finally she pulled open the freezer and reached for the last tub of ice cream.

'I offered Pegasus vegetables earlier and all he wanted to eat was my ice cream. So maybe he'll want some more.'

'Pegasus likes ice cream?'

When Emily nodded, Joel looked embarrassed. 'Do you think I could have something to eat? I haven't had anything today and I'm starving.'

Emily stopped and looked at him as though seeing him for the first time. This Joel was nothing like the angry Joel from earlier. 'Sure, grab what you like. But let's take it upstairs.'

Back on the roof, they unpacked the supplies. Emily had been right, the moment Pegasus smelled the ice cream he went straight for the tub. When he finished it all, he stole the box of breakfast cereal from Joel.

'Hey,' Joel protested. 'That was mine! You've got your own food.'

'I don't think he likes anything healthy,' Emily said. 'Look, he hasn't touched the apples I left for him. Or the carrots either. All he wants is really sweet things.'

'Well, he could have left me a little,' Joel complained. 'All that sugar can't be good for him. It's not like you can get it on Olympus . . .' Suddenly Joel snapped his fingers. 'Of course, now I understand. It makes perfect sense.'

'What does?'

'Don't you see? Pegasus needs sweet foods. That's all he eats on Olympus!'

'How do you know?' Emily asked.

'Because I've read all about it.' Joel sounded more and more excited. 'The Roman myths are my favourite books! All the legends say that on Olympus, the Gods eat ambrosia and drink nectar. It's what keeps them immortal. That's why Pegasus wants it, to help him heal. Some say that ambrosia is very much like honey, so he wants sweet food. Do you have any honey in your kitchen?'

'Honey?' Emily repeated. 'Joel, you're crazy. Those are just legends. We can't base our treatment of Pegasus on some dusty old myths.'

Joel nodded, 'Oh yes, we can. Pegasus is real, right?'

Emily nodded.

'And Pegasus is from myth, also true?' When Emily nodded again, he continued, 'So if he exists, the others must too.'

'Wait,' Emily said, holding up her hand. 'You're saying that Zeus, and Hera, Poseidon and all the others are real?'

'Jupiter, Juno and Neptune,' Joel corrected. 'Zeus is the Greek name. Since I'm Italian, I prefer the Roman myths. The leader of Olympus is Jupiter.'

'Zeus or Jupiter,' Emily protested, 'it doesn't matter. But you can't really think all those myths are true?'

'Why not,' Joel said jumping to his feet. 'Look at him! Pegasus is standing right here, just as real as you or me. So if he's real, why not the others?'

Emily also stood. 'Because it they were, why haven't they come to get him? If Zeus—'

'Jupiter,' Joel corrected.

'All right,' Emily said, exasperated. 'If *Jupiter* is real, why doesn't he know Pegasus is hurt and come to help him?'

'I don't know,' Joel admitted. 'Maybe he can't. Or, maybe he doesn't know yet. But I do know that if we don't help Pegasus, Jupiter is going to be really angry with us when he does get here.'

'I don't care about Jupiter or any of the others,' Emily said as she started to unpack the medical supplies. 'All I care about is Pegasus. So let's get started.'

They cleaned the wounded area around the spear. Then Emily said to the stallion, 'I'm really sorry, but this is going to hurt.'

Standing beside Pegasus, towel at the ready, Emily

helped support the heavy wing. Beside her, Joel wrapped his hands around the broken end of the spear. He braced himself against the side of the stallion. Together they counted down. Three, two, one, go! Using all his weight and strength, Joel started to pull.

Pegasus did his best not to buck as the spear was drawn slowly from his side.

'Hurry, Joel,' Emily cried, trying to hold the stallion steady.

Pegasus's head was thrown back and was twisting in the air. His large, wild eyes revealed his agony and his front hooves ripped at the shed's floorboards. His screams tore at Emily's heart.

'Hurry, it's killing him!'

In one final, grunting heave, Joel drew the vicious barbed spear from the stallion's side. Blood flowed from the deep open wound.

'Put pressure on it!' Joel panted, trying to recover from the strain. 'We've got to stop that bleeding!'

Emily pulled down the towel from her shoulder and pressed it to the wound. Beneath her hands, she could feel Pegasus trembling.

'You're all right, Pegasus,' she soothed. 'You're going to be all right. The worst is over, the spear is gone.'

'We're not done yet,' Joel said grimly as he took over

applying pressure to the wound. 'Go get the glue, Emily. We've got to finish this.'

With Joel's help, Emily was able to squeeze the open edges of the wound together and use the glue to hold it closed. They covered it in clean bandages and taped it in place using silver duct tape.

'Well, it's not pretty, but it might just work.' Joel gently patted the stallion's side. He turned to Emily. 'That was a great idea about the glue. I would have never thought of that.'

Emily shrugged. 'I'm just glad it worked. I don't think I could have put stitches in him.'

'Me either,' Joel agreed. 'Now, we just have to sort out that wing, and he'll be well on his way to recovery.'

It was late in the afternoon when Emily and Joel finished setting Pegasus's wing. Despite Emily's concerns, it wasn't nearly as awful as removing the spear had been. Joel's idea of using the stallion's good wing as an example worked perfectly. Before long, they had pulled the broken bones into place as best they could and were applying a splint and holding it steady with bandages and duct tape.

When they finished, even before they could celebrate their success, Emily's phone started to ring.

'It's my dad. He doesn't know about you or Pegs, so try to keep quiet.'

When Joel nodded, Emily answered the phone, 'Hi Dad.'

'Em, where are you?' Her father asked, sounding worried. 'I'm home and you're not here.'

Emily checked her watch and was shocked to see the time. 'I'm on the roof,' she explained.

'What are you doing up there?'

Emily improvised. 'Well, remember I told you I heard sounds from up here? I wanted to see the storm damage from last night and I lost track of the time.'

'Stay there, I'll be right up.'

Emily felt a sudden rush of panic. 'No Dad, don't come up. I'm um, I'm working on a surprise for you and I don't want you to see it yet. I'll be right down.'

Before she gave her father the opportunity to say anything further, she hung up.

'My dad's home,' she explained. 'I've got to get down there so he doesn't come up. Will you stay with Pegs? I promise to be back as soon as Dad goes to bed. He's been working long shifts and will be tired. When he's asleep, I'll bring up some more food for all of us.'

'Don't forget the honey if you've got some,' Joel called after her. 'And anything else with sugar in it.

Pegasus will need it if he's to heal.'

'I won't,' Emily promised as she walked over to the roof entrance. Turning on her flashlight, she gave Joel a wave before entering the darkened stairwell.

On her way down, Emily tried to think of what she was going to tell her father. She worried what he would say when he saw her black eye. But whatever she said, she knew she couldn't tell him about Pegasus. She had given the stallion her word and wasn't about to break it. Even to him.

She opened the door of her apartment. 'Dad?'

'I'm in the kitchen,' her father called.

Inhaling deeply, Emily made her way to the kitchen. She saw her father standing at the refrigerator in his police uniform, his back to her. He looked almost funny as he pulled out multiple items and tried to hold them all in his arms.

'What a mess,' he said without turning to her. 'Everything is defrosting. We'd better eat a lot of this before it goes bad.'

He turned around, saw her face and dropped everything in his arms. Bottles of pickles and vegetables went rolling around the kitchen floor.

'What happened to you? Em, your eye is black!'

'I know,' Emily said, trying to sound casual. 'I

tripped when I was on the roof and fell into the rose bushes. Somehow I managed to hit myself in the eye. Actually,' she corrected, 'I think I *kneed* myself in the eye.'

As her father inspected her face, he whistled in appreciation. 'Good grief! I haven't seen a shiner like that in ages. It must hurt like the devil!'

'Kinda,' Emily admitted. 'But not as bad as the thorn scratches.' She pushed up her sleeves to reveal the deep gashes on her arms. 'I guess the roses won the first round.'

'Looks like they won the whole fight,' her father agreed. 'We have to get those cleaned up.'

Emily remembered that she and Joel had taken all the medicated creams and bandages up to the roof for Pegasus. 'It's OK, Dad,' she said quickly. 'I already put some stuff on it. Really, I'm fine.'

'All right,' he said reluctantly. 'But look, I don't want you going back up there alone. By the looks of things, it's become dangerous.'

'But Dad,' Emily protested. 'I want to do something special for you. I . . . I'm fixing the garden! You know how much Mom loved her garden, we all did. After so long, it's gone completely wild. Please let me do this. It's really helping me deal with things.'

Emily hated herself for using her mother's painful death as an excuse to continue to go up to the roof. But she couldn't allow her father to forbid her, not while Pegasus was still up there and in desperate need of help.

'Please Dad, I really need to do this.'

Finally he sighed. 'Well, at least wait for me to help you. After the blackout, I'm owed a few days' leave. Why don't we make it our special project?'

Emily knew this was the best she could hope for with her father.

'That would be great. But if I promise not to do anything heavy, can I at least go up there to try to clean up a bit before we get to the real work?'

'Agreed,' he said. 'But only if you promise to be careful and keep away from the edge.'

'I will.' Emily quickly changed the subject before her father could change his mind. 'So what are they saying about the blackout?'

'Well, it's not good,' he said as he went back to work in the refrigerator. 'The power company has put its entire staff on it, but it looks like we'll have no electricity for at least two days, maybe three.' He paused and looked at her again. 'You know what that means, don't you?'

Emily nodded. 'It means you have to go back to work, doesn't it?'

'I was going to tell you that it means no school for a few days.' Then he reluctantly added, 'But yes, I've got to go back to work. I'm due back in at midnight. It was only because of you being home alone that I was able to steal a few hours away.'

Emily lifted the jug of milk out of her dad's arms. 'Then you shouldn't waste this time here. Go sit down and I'll see what I can make us for dinner. Then I think you should try to get some sleep.'

When her father smiled, it made his dimples appear. 'Hey, who's the parent here?' he demanded, laughing.

'I am,' Emily teased as she started to use as many thawing items as she could to prepare their supper.

'Fair enough,' he admitted. 'This has been one strange twenty-four hours.' He sighed heavily as he sat down at the kitchen table. 'There is looting going on all over the city because of the power outage and security systems going down. Uptown, people are getting hysterical. Some even went into their local police stations claiming to have seen these huge, grey, four-armed creatures coming out of the sewers. Insisting they were some kind of demons and this was the end of the world.'

'Wow,' Emily said as she pulled out a frying pan and set it on the gas stove. 'That is strange.'

'But that wasn't the worst of it,' her father said. 'Remember I called you from Belleview? I was there to draw up a report on this mystery kid that had been brought in. Seems he was hit by lightning and fell out a window.'

'Ouch! That had to hurt,' Emily said as she started to scramble some eggs. 'Was he killed?'

'Nope,' her father answered. 'The doctor said he should have been. Not only did he not die, he's healing faster than anything they've ever seen before. His bones are knitting together in record time and the burn on his back is shrinking by the minute.'

Emily stopped scrambling her dad's eggs. 'He's healing really quickly?' she said. 'Who is he?'

Her father shrugged. 'I'm not really sure. He said his name was,' – he paused and stood up, then bowed at the waist and raised his hand in a flourish – 'Paelen the Magnificent, at your service.'

Emily couldn't help laughing as her father repeated the sweeping, formal gesture. 'Where's he from?'

'I haven't got a clue,' said her dad, sitting down again. 'He claims he doesn't remember much, but after being a cop so long, I know a lie when I hear one.' He paused as if reaching for something just beyond his grasp. 'It's . . . it's really strange, Em. There is something seriously wrong with that kid, but I just can't put my finger on it.'

'Like what?'

'A few things, really,' her father answered. 'The strange way he speaks. Real formal, you know? Then there's the way he was found, wearing only a bloodstained tunic and winged sandals studded with jewels. He'd obviously been struck by lightning, but somehow he survived that as well as the fall. When the paramedics arrived, they found him clutching this beautiful golden bridle. Between the jewelled sandals and the horse bridle, it all had to be worth a fortune. But he refused to tell me where they came from or how he got them.'

Emily felt her pulse quicken. Paelen the Magnificent? Healing quickly? Wearing a tunic and sandals, and clutching a golden horse bridle? She knew it had something to do with Pegasus. She just didn't know what.

The eggs were quickly forgotten as Emily took a seat at the table beside her father.

'So is he still at the hospital?'

'No,' he answered darkly. 'And that's another story all its own. When the staff saw his blood test results, they nearly had a fit. Things kind of went downhill from there.'

Emily's ears were ringing. Everything her father said was shouting Olympus. Somehow, there was another Olympian in New York! She had to tell Joel as soon as she could.

'What do you mean? What happened?' Emily finally asked.

'It seems one of the nurses called the CRU when she saw the results. Not long after that, several of their agents arrived at the hospital to collect him. But when I challenged them on it, they called my captain. I was immediately ordered back to the station and told to forget everything. As always, it's all very Government hush, hush. I have no idea where they took him or what they plan to do with him. But from what we know of the CRU, I sure wouldn't want to be in that kid's shoes. Or winged sandals either, for that matter.'

7

Paelen was sitting up in bed in a secure hospital unit. Men in white coats were hooking up a lot of strange wires to him. Several were taped to his chest, while others were secured to his face and head. When he tried to rip them off, two men in white overalls rushed forward and caught hold of his hands to restrain him. But when Paelen proved too strong for them, more men arrived. They wrestled his hands down until he was finally handcuffed to the sides of the bed.

'Where am I?' Paelen demanded as he struggled against the steel cuffs clamped on his wrists. 'What is this place? Why have you put me in chains?'

'We ask the questions,' said one of the men in overalls. 'Not you. So just lie still for a moment while we finish hooking you up.'

'I do not understand,' Paelen said as he looked at the frightening array of machines being drawn up to the side of the bed. 'What is hooking me up?

What more are you doing to me?'

'Just relax,' said a doctor. 'We're not going to hurt you. This equipment will tell us a little bit more about you. It will record your heart rate and brain impulses. It will show me if you are very different from us.'

'Of course I am different from you,' Paelen said indignantly. 'You are human and I, Olympian!'

The men in overalls raised their eyebrows at each other.

'Olympian, huh?' one of them said. 'And I suppose you're the great Zeus himself?'

'If I were,' Paelen asked, 'would I receive better treatment?'

The man shrugged. 'Maybe.'

'Then I am he. Zeus,' Paelen said quickly. 'And as such, I demand you release me.'

'Sorry Zeusie old boy, no can do,' the man said once he was certain Paelen's steel handcuffs were secure. 'There are a lot of folks around here very interested in speaking to you. So just lie still and be patient. They'll be with you soon.'

Seeing that his pleas were hopeless, Paelen lay back and became quiet. He couldn't believe what was happening to him. All he had ever wanted was to get hold of Pegasus and be free. Free of Olympus and Jupiter with all his rules. Free of the Nirads and the war.

He never wanted to visit this world or meet any of its people. He'd heard countless stories about it when he was growing up. Of the strange people who lived here and how they worshipped the Olympians. But he'd never been curious about them or tempted to visit. They were just human. What could they possibly offer someone like him? But in following Pegasus here, he'd been struck by one of Jupiter's lightning bolts and was now trapped.

It was bad enough waking in that strange place they called Belleview Hospital. But things had quickly gone from bad to worse when more men arrived to take him away. He had tried to fight them off, but his wounds were too great. Now here he was on this little island, enduring more horrors.

Paelen was helpless to stop them from stealing more of his precious blood. They'd cut off samples of his hair and shone their bright lights in his eyes until he could no longer see. He'd been studied like youngsters in Olympus study insects they find on the steps of Jupiter's palace. Poked and prodded and put in a strange device they called the MRI.

When they'd tired of that torture, Paelen had been brought to this room. It had no windows and was without any obvious means of escape except through a single door.

Paelen could smell the earth pressing in behind the white walls. He knew that wherever he was, it was in some kind of strange labyrinth deep beneath the ground.

He wondered if these same people had captured Pegasus. Was the great stallion somewhere in this place with him? Part of Paelen wanted to ask. But another part of him thought better of it. These were not good people. If Pegasus hadn't been captured, he wasn't about to alert them to his presence. He owed the stallion that much.

Watching the men as they buzzed around him like bees, Paelen tried to figure out how best to escape. That had always been one of his talents in Olympus. No matter where Jupiter locked him up, he always managed to get away.

But with those heavy white things they called casts on his legs and his obvious broken bones and deep burns, this wasn't the time to make his move. Instead he would tolerate his captors. Play with them, taunt them, and do his best to learn all their weaknesses.

Only when he was recovered and strong again, would he make his move. He would leave this place of pain and despair. And finally, he would capture Pegasus.

8

Emily picked at her food, unable to eat. The story her father had just told was spinning around in her head. She was convinced that Paelen had something to do with Pegasus. But with the stallion unable to speak, and Paelen now spirited away by the CRU, Emily had no idea how they were connected.

Not long after supper, Emily's father went to bed for a few hours of rest before his next shift. The moment he shut his bedroom door, Emily dashed back into the kitchen to gather together food and drinks to take up to Joel and Pegasus.

'You're not going to believe this.' Emily arrived breathlessly back on the roof. 'There's another Olympian in New York! His name is Paelen and—'

The moment Emily said the name, Pegasus started to shriek and tear furiously at the shed's floorboards.

'Pegasus, what is it?' Emily ran over and stroked the stallion's quivering muzzle. 'Do you know Paelen?'

Pegasus snorted angrily, rose on his hind legs and came down brutally on the floorboards. His sharp hooves cut into the wood, tearing up huge splinters.

'Please, stop,' Emily cried. 'You've got to calm down. My father's asleep in the apartment below us. If he hears you, he'll come up and find you!'

Pegasus stopped tearing at the boards, but shook his head, still snorting and whinnying. Emily looked desperately over to Joel.

'What do you think is wrong with him?'

'Easy boy, calm down,' Joel soothed. He turned to Emily. 'Seems that Pegasus doesn't like Paelen, whoever he is.'

'Is that it?' she asked the stallion. 'Don't you like Paelen?'

Pegasus became still and strangely silent. He looked Emily straight in the eye. In that moment, Emily felt that tight connection to him. Somehow she knew that Paelen was someone who had hurt Pegasus and caused a lot of trouble for him. As she stared into his large dark eyes, strange images suddenly flooded her mind. She saw Pegasus in the dark storm-filled sky with lightning flashing all around him. She felt his determination, his fear – and his urgent need to get somewhere, knowing it was a matter of life and death. Then she saw a boy in the sky beside the stallion. The boy was older than Joel, but not nearly as big. He was flying beside Pegasus and reaching across to the stallion. Then she saw him snatching Pegasus's golden bridle away. Suddenly there was a bright, blinding flash of lightning and terrible, searing pain—

'Emily,' Joel repeated. 'Emily, what's wrong?'

Breaking the connection, Emily blinked and staggered on her feet. 'Joel?' she said in a soft and distant voice.

'Are you all right?'

'I'm, I'm fine, I think,' Emily's head started to clear. She concentrated on Joel, now looking anxiously at her. 'I just saw the strangest thing,' she said.

'What?'

Emily looked back to the stallion. 'Pegasus, what I just saw? It was true, wasn't it? Paelen took the bridle from you. It was because of him you were hit by lightning.'

Pegasus snorted and butted Emily gently. *Yes.*

'Please tell me,' Joel pressed. 'What did you see?'

'I don't know how to explain it,' she said. 'But it was kind of like watching television, only much more intense. When Paelen got the golden bridle off Pegasus, it attracted lightning and they were both hit.'

'So now we've got to find this Paelen and get it back,' Joel suggested.

'That's going to be impossible,' Emily said. Stroking Pegasus, she explained about the conversation with her father and how Paelen had been taken by the secret government agency, the CRU.

'I've never heard of the crew,' Joel said, bewildered. 'And my dad worked for the United Nations.'

'Not crew,' Emily corrected. 'C-R-U. Central Research Unit. They just pronounce it like the word "crew". Not a lot of people know about them. These guys deal with weird science stuff and anything to do with aliens. My dad says, when the CRU come to get you, you're never seen or heard from again. He's had to deal with them a couple of times in his career, and each time, he was threatened and ordered to stay quiet or there'd be trouble. If the CRU ever learned about Pegasus, they would take him away and we'd never see him again.'

'If they're as bad as you say,' Joel said, 'we'd probably disappear too, just because we've seen him.'

'Exactly,' Emily said, 'which is why we have to be extra careful until Pegasus's wing heals. He's got to get safely away to finish whatever it is he came here for.'

'Did he show you what that was?'

86

'No,' Emily said. 'All I saw was Paelen stealing the bridle and then both of them getting hit by lightning. But it felt like life and death kind of stuff.' She turned back to the stallion, 'Isn't it Pegasus?'

The stallion nodded and pounded the floorboards.

'So if we can't go after Paelen to get the bridle, what do we do?' Joel asked.

Emily shrugged. 'I guess we just keep Pegasus safe and warm until he heals.'

Joel nodded. 'And to do that, he needs plenty of good food and care. Did you find any honey?'

Emily started to go through the bags she'd carried up from her kitchen. 'I've got some honey, corn syrup, brown sugar and white sugar and more sweet cereal. But I still can't believe a horse should be eating all this stuff.'

Pegasus protested loudly.

'Sorry Pegs,' she said. She looked at Joel with a half-smile. 'He really hates being called a horse, doesn't he?'

'Wouldn't you, if you were him?' said Joel.

As Emily poured half the box of sweet cereal into a huge plastic bowl, Joel opened the can of corn syrup and poured it on top. He added several spoonfuls of brown sugar.

'Yuck!' Emily said as the stallion started to eat

hungrily. 'How can you do that, Pegs? After this, I don't think I'll ever eat that cereal again.'

After Pegasus was fed, Joel sat down to eat the sandwiches Emily had prepared for him.

'What time do you need to get home?' she asked. Checking her watch, it was just past six in the evening. The sun was still up, but had already crossed the city and would soon start to set.

'I'm not going back,' Joel said casually after taking a long drink of milk right from the carton.

'Not going back?' Emily said in alarm. 'Won't your parents worry?'

Joel looked away. 'My parents are dead. I'm living in a foster home. The people there hardly ever notice me, so probably not.' He tried to sound indifferent but Emily could hear the quiver in his tone fighting through the bravado. She wasn't sure what to say, she had no clue about Joel's past.

'I didn't know. Joel, I'm so sorr—'

'It's OK,' he said almost too quickly. 'It's not like I've told anyone.' He looked down, avoiding her gaze, and began to speak slowly. 'Three years ago I was living with my family in Connecticut. We were going away for the weekend when a drunk driver lost control of his car and crashed into us. My parents and little brother were killed instantly. I was hurt too, but somehow I survived. Though every day since it happened, I wish I hadn't.'

'Oh, Joel,' Emily said in a hushed voice. 'It must have been terrible.'

Joel said nothing for a long time. Finally he looked at her. 'I've been in foster-care ever since. But I hate it.'

Emily was too stunned to speak. She could never have imagined this. She knew what it was to suffer the unending grief of losing one parent, but she couldn't imagine what it would be like to lose your entire family.

'Isn't there anyone in Italy you could go live with?'

'No,' Joel said sharply. 'No one wanted me. So I'm stuck here.' He lifted his chin in defiance. 'But not for much longer. I'm planning to run away. I'll find someplace where no one will be able to tell me where to go, what to do or anything ever again. I'll finally be free!'

Joel stood up quickly and crossed to Pegasus. Emily watched the tension in his shoulders fade as he stroked the stallion's face. 'I'm going to stay here tonight,' he said, his back to Emily. 'I don't like leaving Pegasus alone.'

Emily stood and put her hands on her hips. He may

have had a tough life, but there was no need to insult her. 'Gee, thanks, Joel, for the vote of confidence,' she said suddenly riled. 'But for your information, in case you hadn't noticed, I'm here. So he's not alone.'

'You know what I mean,' Joel said. 'You've got to get back down to your apartment before your father goes to work tonight. I can stay here so Pegasus doesn't get frightened.'

Emily was about to say something more, but the look in his eyes stopped her.

He was nothing like the angry person she met this morning on his front stoop. In his eyes she suddenly saw – need. Joel needed to stay with Pegasus.

'All right,' she said. 'You can stay. There are some extra blankets and pillows I can bring up. But just so you know, I'm planning to stay up here too. Once my father goes to work, we can bring everything up. It'll kind of be like camping.'

'Without the marshmallows,' Joel added.

'I think we might have some of those,' Emily said. 'But if I know Pegasus, he'll have them off me before I even open the bag!'

9

After the doctors finished hooking Paelen up to the equipment, they went over to their computers to check out the readings.

Paelen watched them curiously, but said nothing. Instead he concentrated on his surroundings. On the wall behind him, high above the bed, was a small ventilation grill. He could feel fresh air blowing gently down on him. He could also hear sounds coming from other rooms floating through the same grill. That meant that there was a system of tunnels up there which he could easily slip through. Tunnels were his speciality. There wasn't one tunnel in all Olympus he couldn't slip through, or find his way out of; including the great labyrinth of the Minotaur. Paelen knew that once he was free of the casts on his legs, he would be able to find his way to the surface.

Of course, there was also the issue of the handcuffs. But he'd seen the men in the overalls had keys to the locks. If he worked it out properly, he could easily get the keys away from them. Failing that, Paelen could always use his talent for stretching out his body; though he preferred not to.

As his mind worked on the problem, Paelen heard the same strange series of beeping sounds he'd heard before. Soon after the door to the room opened and two men entered.

One was middle-aged with salt-and-pepper hair. He was wearing a dark suit and had a grim expression on his face. The other man was much younger, with light blond hair cut short. Also wearing a dark suit, he looked equally unpleasant.

With their backs to Paelen, they started to whisper with the doctors. Paelen couldn't help but smile. They had no idea that he could clearly hear them discussing the test results and what had been learned so far. Just like they didn't know he could hear the other voices through the grill above him.

Once again, Paelen was reminded of how different he was to these humans. And even though the meaning of some of their words eluded him, he understood enough. They were discussing how extraordinary his brain patterns were. How he had superior muscle strength and density. How his bones were flexible and nothing like human bones, which partially explained how he survived the fall. They'd also found several organs they couldn't identify. When asked, one of the doctors suggested that Paelen was no more than seventeen years old.

That comment nearly had Paelen in fits of laughter. He had to bite his own tongue to keep from laughing out loud. If they knew the truth of his age, he was certain they would never believe him. But then again, maybe they would. That could only make things much worse for him.

Finally the two new men sat down in chairs beside Paelen's bed. The older man pulled out a small black device from his pocket and flicked a switch. He held it up to his lips and started speaking.

'CRU report, C.49.21- J. First interview. Date: June 2nd. Time: nineteen hundred hours. Subject is male. His approximate age is seventeen. Medical tests reveal multiple injuries consistent with a lightning strike and fall from a great height.

'Further tests reveal profound physical anomalies. The subject's organs are not where they should be. We've identified several other organs whose function is as yet undetermined. These warrant further investigation. Subject has multiple broken bones which are healing at a remarkable rate. Blood work has revealed an unknown cross-type with unfamiliar properties. Subject is physically strong despite his small size and youthful outward appearance . . .'

Paelen watched the man speaking into the device. It sounded like he was describing some kind of monster and not him. The more he listened, the more he started to understand the degree of trouble he was in.

Finally the man finished and turned his attention to Paelen. 'State your name for the record,' he demanded, holding the device towards Paelen.

At first Paelen remained silent. But when the man repeated the question, he thought this would be a good time to start his own investigation. Breaking his silence, he replied. 'Subject.'

'That is not your name,' the man said.

'Perhaps not,' Paelen agreed. 'However, it is the name you have given me. One name is as good as any other, is it not?'

'I didn't call you Subject.'

'Yes you did.'

'I don't think so,' the older man said.

'But you did,' Paelen insisted, 'Just now. You were speaking into that little black box and said, "Subject has multiple broken bones which are healing at a remarkable rate." Then you said, "Subject is strong despite his small size and youthful outward appearance".' So if it pleases you to call me Subject, then that shall be my name. I am Subject.'

'I don't want to call you Subject,' the man said, becoming irritated. 'I just want to know how we address you before we start with our other questions.'

Paelen noticed this man was easily flustered. He was worse than Mercury. And Mercury was always the easiest of the Olympians to upset. Lines of frustration and anger already showed on his face. He lips were pressed tightly together and his brows were knitted in a deep frown.

Paelen decided to push the man a little further to test him. 'You seem confused,' he said. 'If this happens so easily over the simple issue of my name, I am certain you would be far too challenged to understand the answers to any questions you might pose.'

The man shook his head in growing frustration. 'I am not confused,' he said angrily. 'And I know your name isn't Subject. Subject isn't a name. It is what you are.'

'And yet you still insist on calling me it.' Paelen lay back against the pillows, enjoying the game. 'I do not understand you. You are obviously a man of questionable intelligence. Please leave.'

The man's face turned bright red. He took several deep breaths to calm himself. 'Perhaps we'd better start again,' he said. 'Very simply, what is your name?'

'You may call me Jupiter.'

'What? Did you say Jupiter?'

'Are you hard of hearing as well as ignorant?' Paelen asked. He turned his attention to the younger man. 'I believe it is time you took him away. He is obviously unwell and should be restrained.'

The older man stood up in a fury. 'Why, you arrogant little—'

'Calm down, Agent J.' The younger man grasped the older man's arm. 'Sit down, and let me try.'

Paelen carefully studied the relationship between the two. The older man was obviously in command. However, he seemed to accept advice from the younger one, as he calmed somewhat.

The younger man directed his attention to Paelen. 'In the hospital, you told the doctor your name was Paelen the Magnificent. Which is it? Jupiter or Paelen?'

'If you insist,' Paelen said, 'I am Paelen the Magnificent. Now, release me.'

'Or what?' the older man challenged.

'Or I shall bring the wrath of Olympus down upon you.'

'The wrath of *Olympus*?' he cried

'Must you always repeat everything I say?' Paelen asked. 'It is really quite distracting.'

The older man's hand shot out and gripped Paelen's wrist. 'I have had enough of your games, young man. They stop right now. We're not letting you go. Not now, not ever. Now, you will tell us who you are, where you came from, and why you are here.'

The grip on Paelen's wrist was tight, but certainly not enough to hurt him. Yet he could see that this was the man's intention. 'I will answer your questions only after you have answered some of mine,' he said. 'I demand to know where I am. Who are you? And why you are holding me?'

'We ask the questions here, not you,' the older man said as he tightened his grip further.

'Then we have nothing further to discuss,' Paelen answered, turning away from their prying eyes. 'You may tell the others to bring ambrosia to me now.'

'We will do no such thing,' the younger man said. 'Look kid, this isn't funny. If you make my colleague much angrier, he'll break your wrist.'

Paelen grew serious and sat up, ignoring the pain from his broken ribs. He looked at both men, then concentrated on the older one. 'If you think you can hurt me with this baby grip of yours, you are sadly mistaken. I have faced down the wrath of the Minotaur and a Hydra. I have fought the Nirads and won. I am certainly not frightened of a human like you, or the empty threats you make.'

'I assure you, my threats are not empty,' the older man warned. 'So don't make me do something you'll regret. Just tell us who you are and where you came from.'

Paelen didn't like these men one bit. 'If you insist, I am Mercury,' he finally answered. 'I came to your world for a visit but was wounded during a storm. When I recover, I shall return to Olympus.'

'Still with the Greek myths?' Agent J said darkly.

'Mercury is from the Roman myths,' the younger man corrected. 'Hermes is the Greek.'

Paelen watched the older man flash the younger one a withering look. 'Whatever!'

He turned back to Paelen. 'That isn't an answer. Tell me what I want to know.'

'But I told you,' Paelen insisted. 'I am Mercury. You have my sandals. Surely you have seen their wings.

Who else but the Messenger of Olympus would use such things?'

Agent J took in a deep breath and held it. When he let it out again, he squared his shoulders and sat back. 'If you continue to refuse to answer, I promise you, we can make things very uncomfortable for you.'

'Things already are uncomfortable for me,' Paelen said. 'But I am still telling you the truth. That you refuse to believe me is not my fault.'

Agent J looked at the younger man. 'We're not getting anywhere with him.' He checked his watch, then spoke into the black device. 'Time: nineteen hundred, twenty. End of interview.'

Angrily, he shut off his device and looked at Paelen. 'Whether we call you Mercury, Jupiter, Paelen or Subject, it couldn't matter less. What does matter is that you belong to me. Soon you will answer all my questions. Even if I have to rip the truth from your lips one word at a time.'

Paelen saw the threat rise in his eyes. This man meant every word he said.

The men walked over to the small grey device beside the door. Paelen paid particular attention as the older man pressed several buttons. It made the same strange beeps he'd heard right before they entered the room.

'A sound lock,' Paelen muttered softly to himself as he watched them pull open the door and leave the room. 'If Jupiter could not build a prison to hold me, what makes you think you can?'

10

An hour before midnight, Emily's father was preparing for work.

'You sure you're going to be all right on your own?' he asked.

Emily nodded and handed over his packed meal. 'I'm really tired from working in the garden today. I bet I'll be asleep the moment my head hits the pillow.'

'All right,' he said as he kissed the top of her head. 'Just don't be too nervous with the power out. You've got the flashlight and plenty of extra batteries. I'd prefer you not to use candles if you don't mind.'

'I understand,' Emily said. 'What time are you going to be home tomorrow?'

Her father sighed. 'Late, I'm afraid. It's another double shift. I won't be home until supper tomorrow night. But you've still got plenty of food and there's lots of water left. You shouldn't have to go out anywhere. Now remember, if you need me—'

'I know, I'll call.' Emily smiled and gently started to shove her father towards the front door. 'Go to work, Dad. The city needs you.'

'I hope you need me too,' he said as he put on his cap.

'I'll always need you,' Emily assured him as she rose on tiptoes to kiss his cheek. 'Please be careful and come home safe.'

'I will,' he promised as he turned on his police flashlight and entered the dark hall. Turning back to her a final time, he said, 'Lock the door after me and keep the bat handy.'

'Will you please go?' Emily said, laughing.

After he had gone, Emily waited awhile before heading for the stairs. Stepping out on the open roof, she was once again struck by the beautiful star-studded night sky. 'Wow!' she said. 'I've never seen so many stars!'

'It's amazing, isn't it?' Joel agreed, moving away from Pegasus. 'You don't even need your flashlight.'

After sunset, Pegasus could leave the garden shed to freely wander the roof without the fear of being seen by curious neighbours. Emily saw the stallion standing before her father's strawberry plants. He was busily eating all the ripe berries he could find.

'He hasn't stopped eating since the sun went down,' Joel said. 'If it's growing and sweet, he's eating it. I'm afraid he's ruined what was left of the tomato patch.'

'Tomatoes?' Emily repeated. 'We didn't plant tomatoes this year. With my mother so sick, we didn't come up here at all.'

'They must have grown back from last year,' Joel suggested. 'There's lots of stuff growing. But all Pegasus wanted from them were the tomatoes.'

Emily approached Pegasus as he stood before the strawberries. 'Hi boy,' she said as she stroked his folded wing.

Pegasus reached out and dropped a single ripe strawberry in Emily's hand.

'Thanks Pegs!' Emily said in shock. She ate the berry and savoured the sweet flavour.

'I can't believe you just ate that,' Joel said in horror. 'It's been in his mouth.'

'So?'

'So, it's disgusting. It's got to be full of germs.'

'Don't be silly,' Emily said. 'I bet we've got loads more germs than him.' She turned her attention to Pegasus. 'So, how are you feeling tonight?'

'He's getting better,' Joel answered. 'He's even been stretching out his wing to test it. I don't think it'll be too long before he's ready to go.'

Emily suddenly felt a deep pang of sorrow. Pegasus couldn't be with her for ever, she knew that. But after the recent loss of her mother, losing him as well seemed too much to bear.

As if the stallion knew what she was thinking, he offered her a second strawberry. The simple gesture brought tears to her eyes.

'Thank you, Pegasus,' she said softly.

'Hey, are you crying?' Joel asked. 'What's wrong?'

'Nothing,' Emily said, furiously wiping tears away. 'I'm overtired. I didn't sleep last night and we've been on the go ever since. I just need a bit of rest.'

'Didn't you say we were going to camp out up here tonight?' When Emily nodded, Joel beamed. 'Well, let's go back down to your apartment and get the blankets. Then we can get some sleep.'

Emily nodded and sniffed back the last of her silent tears. 'I promised Pegasus marshmallows. So I'll grab them too.'

Soon, Emily and Joel were back on the roof with two sleeping bags, several blankets and two pillows.

One of the blankets was draped over Pegasus to keep the stallion warm. But as Emily and Joel settled down on two long lounge chairs, they were surprised when the stallion lowered himself to the ground and rested between them.

'Why do you think he's here?' Joel asked as he lay back in the lounge chair, staring at the stars.

'I don't know,' Emily said as she lay on her side and stroked Pegasus's neck. 'I know it's really important, but I can't see why.'

'Maybe it has to do with that other Olympian, Paelen.'

'From what I saw, Pegasus was already on his way here when Paelen stole his bridle. I think he was more of a nuisance than anything else.'

They settled into a comfortable silence. The evening was cool but not cold, and the stars above and silence of the city made them feel like they really were out camping.

'Joel,' Emily said tentatively, 'what's it like living in a foster home?'

She heard him take a deep breath and instantly regretted asking him.

'Why do you want to know?' he challenged, his voice growing hard.

'Please don't get angry again,' she said. 'It was just a question.'

'I'm not angry,' Joel fired back. 'I just don't like talking about it.'

'I'm sorry, I shouldn't have asked,' Emily said quickly. She turned over and pulled the covers up. 'Let's just forget it and go to sleep.'

Joel remained silent for a long time. She could hear his heavy breathing, but had no idea what he was thinking.

'Emily, I'm sorry,' he said at last. 'I shouldn't take it out on you. But you don't understand. After my parents died, I lost everything I've ever known. Everyone I ever cared about. I've been alone ever since.'

Emily turned back over to face him, but did not speak.

He inhaled deeply again. 'Things didn't work out too good with my first foster family. We were always fighting. So they sent me to this new one. But I really hate it. There are loads of other kids and my foster parents are always yelling. I have to share a bedroom with four other boys. They are always stealing my stuff.'

'Can't you ask to go somewhere else?' Emily asked.

'I've tried talking to my social workers, but they always say no. They say I should be grateful to have a place to live. They don't care what it's like there.'

'No wonder you want to run away,' Emily said thoughtfully, 'I would too.'

'And I will. Right after we get Pegasus healed.' Joel reached out to stroke the stallion. 'Maybe he'll take me away with him when he goes.' He paused and his voice became dreamy. 'Pegasus and me. Now that would be a dream come true.'

11

Long before dawn, the skies opened up and awoke Emily and Joel with shockingly cold rain. In the time it took them to find the flashlight and guide Pegasus back into the garden shed, they were both soaked to the skin and shivering.

Huddled together in the shed, they looked out at the heavy rain beating down on the roof.

'At least there's no lightning,' Emily said through chattering teeth.

'That would be all we need,' Joel agreed. When he saw how cold Emily was, he moved closer. 'I don't think we should stay up here much longer. We're both soaking wet and freezing.'

'But I don't want to leave Pegasus alone.'

'Me either,' Joel said. 'But we won't do him much good if we both get pneumonia.'

Emily reached out and stroked the stallion's neck. His skin was warm to the touch. He wasn't shivering at all.

'You're right. I'm really freezing.' Emily stepped closer to Pegasus, 'We'll be back soon, Pegs,' she promised.

Then she and Joel dashed across the roof and towards the stairwell door.

Back in the apartment, Emily borrowed some of her father's clothes for Joel, while she went into her own room to change. When she returned to the living room, she found Joel sound asleep on the sofa.

Pulling down a throw blanket, she covered her new friend. After a moment's hesitation, she went into her bedroom and sank into bed. Within a minute she had drifted off.

The rain continued all the next day. Despite it being early summer, with the rain, the temperature dropped, keeping Emily and Joel from spending the entire day on the roof with Pegasus. Instead, they split their time between the roof and gathering food for the stallion in the kitchen.

'We're now all out of sugar,' Emily said. 'And corn syrup, cereal and honey.'

'I've never seen such a big appetite,' Joel agreed. 'That horse doesn't stop eating!'

'Don't let him hear you calling him a horse,' Emily laughed. 'He hates that.'

'He does, doesn't he,' Joel chuckled.

Joel crossed to one of the apartment's many windows. 'The rain is letting up a bit,' he said. 'And I can see down on the street a couple of the wholesalers are opening.'

'With no power?' Emily asked as she joined him.

'Looks like it,' Joel said. 'Where is your nearest grocery store?'

'There's a big one a few blocks away,' said Emily. 'Dad and I usually go there on Saturday.'

'I'll go there,' Joel said. 'We've drained your kitchen and Pegasus needs more food. Besides, your dad is bound to notice everything missing.'

'How are you going to manage?' Emily said. 'Joel, there's no power. No elevator. If the store is open, you'll be carrying heavy bags up twenty flights of stairs. Remember how we felt the first time we did it?'

'I know, but I have to try.'

'Then I'll come with you,' Emily said. 'That way we can carry more.'

Joel shook his head. 'Thanks for the offer, but I don't think you should. You know how upset Pegasus gets when you leave him. You need to be on the roof with him. I promise I won't be long.'

Emily really wanted to help, but she knew Joel was right. As Pegasus healed, he was becoming more and more agitated. It was becoming difficult to keep him in the shed.

'You're right,' she finally agreed. She went into her father's room to open the secret drawer where they kept hidden cash. 'Dad keeps this here in case of emergencies,' she said. 'It should be enough to get everything we need.'

Joel accepted the money and the offer of her father's raincoat. Taking the flashlight and some heavy-duty shopping bags Emily gave him, he guided her up to the roof. Then, as he headed back down the stairs, he smiled over his shoulder at her.

'Don't take any test flights without me!'

Emily smiled back and promised not to. She shut the stairwell door and headed over to the shed.

'He's gone to get you lots of sweet things,' she explained as she adjusted the blanket over the stallion's wings. 'I just hope the store is open.'

As Emily stroked the stallion's neck, she felt Pegasus starting to quiver. But not from the cold rain. His blanket was clean and dry and his skin was warm to touch. Yet, he seemed to be growing even more anxious as his hooves pounded the floorboards.

'What is it, Pegs?' she asked. 'What's wrong? Are you in pain?'

Worried for the stallion, Emily checked on his broken wing. She could actually feel the broken bones had somehow knitted back together. 'Well, it's not your wing. What about the spear wound?' Crossing to the other side, Emily lifted Pegasus's good wing and pulled the duct tape away from his flank. She was shocked to see that the wound was completely healed.

'Wow!' she cried. 'It's gone. How are you doing that? Is it all the sugar?'

Pegasus pawed the ground. His eyes were bright and alert. But there was something in them that worried her.

They watched the rain together. It was coming down heavily again and she worried about Joel. Emily lost all track of time until she heard Joel calling her name from the stairwell.

'Are you all right?' she raced over to him.

'I will be once I throw up,' he panted, leaning heavily against the stairwell door frame.

Emily reached for the bags in his hands and was shocked by the weight. 'How much did you buy?'

'As much as I could. It's crazy out there. People are shopping like it's the end of the world! I had to fight an old lady for the last two bottles of honey. Don't even ask me what it was like on the cereal aisle.'

In the shed, Pegasus started to neigh.

'Someone's hungry again,' Joel said, tired. He pulled out a box of colourful kids' cereal and tore it open. He held it out for Pegasus to eat.

'He's more than hungry,' Emily said. 'Something is really bothering him.'

'Do you have any idea what it is?' Joel asked.

Emily shook her head. 'Whatever it is, I have a feeling it isn't good.'

After making sure Pegasus had enough to eat, they went back down to the apartment and unpacked the rest of the food.

'My dad is due home shortly,' Emily said. 'I don't think it's a good idea for you to meet him just yet.'

'Why?' Joel asked, looking hurt. 'Don't you want him to meet me?'

'Joel, my dad is a cop,' Emily pointed out. 'It's his nature to be suspicious. If he finds out you're in care, he'll want to contact your foster parents and they may want to take you away. Pegasus needs both of us.'

'So what are you suggesting?' Joel asked.

Emily sighed. 'I really hate to lie to him. But I think you should stay here, but keep hidden.'

'Where?' he said, looking around at the apartment. 'This place isn't that big.'

'I guess you could stay in my room.'

'Where will you stay?'

'In my room too,' Emily said. 'There's plenty of space on the floor. Besides, we'll be spending most of our time with Pegs. It's only for when my dad is around. And with the blackout, he's working double shifts.'

'I could always stay up on the roof with Pegasus,' Joel suggested.

Emily shook her head. 'It's still raining. You can't sleep outside, you'll freeze to death.'

'But what if your dad catches me?'

'You're going to have to be careful so he doesn't,' said Emily. 'That's all.'

Joel shrugged. 'That's easier said than done.'

The moment Emily's father returned from work, Joel dashed into Emily's bedroom. Despite his concerns, Joel kept hidden and actually slept well on the floor beside Emily's bed. By the time he rose the next morning, Emily was already up and her father had left for work again.

'Sleep all right?' she asked as she handed him a glass of orange juice.

'Great,' he said. 'I think that's probably the best night's sleep I've had in a very long time.'

When they arrived back on the roof, Pegasus was in a state. He was out of the shed, snorting and pawing angrily at the ground. His sharp hooves had cut deep trenches in the tarmac. Emily realized if they didn't stop him soon, he might make it all the way through to the apartment.

'What is it, Pegs?' Emily cried, racing over to the stallion. 'What's wrong?'

'Emily, look,' Joel said, pointing at the stallion's food. 'He hasn't touched a thing. I wonder if all the sugar is starting to make him sick.'

'I don't know.' Emily stroked the stallion's neck. She could feel every nerve in his body tensing. 'But he doesn't look sick. Look at his eyes, Joel, Pegasus is frightened.'

'Of what?'

Emily shrugged. 'Whatever it is, if it's got him frightened, it's got to be bad.'

All morning Emily and Joel remained with Pegasus. Instead of calming, the stallion grew more agitated.

He pawed the tarmac and succeeded in tearing a hole in the roof. Emily could now see down into her father's bedroom.

'How are we going to explain that?' she cried. 'Pegs, please – you have to calm down!'

Yet no matter what they tried, there was nothing they could do to calm the stallion.

As the afternoon wore on, they heard loud, warning voices calling from the tall building across the street.

'Oh no!' Emily looked desperately over to the people standing before their open windows. They were pointing and shouting at the roof. 'Joel, they've seen Pegasus!'

Joel stared at the groups of people gathering in the various windows. He could see more than curiosity on their faces. He saw fear.

'They look scared too,' he said. 'Emily, look at them. They're not pointing at Pegasus. They're pointing at the side of your building.'

As they listened, they heard the voices of the people across the street telling them to get off the roof and run.

'What do they mean, run?' Emily asked, as she stepped closer to the edge.

Suddenly Pegasus went mad. He stood on his hind legs and started to scream. As his wings flew open, he hit Emily and knocked her several feet away from the edge. Pegasus reared over her. He was shrieking in rage and kicking out his front legs.

'Emily, get back!' Joel cried. 'He's gone crazy!'

As Joel tried to drag Emily away, Pegasus lunged forward. Pushing past Joel, he charged the edge of the roof just as a monstrous-looking creature crested the top.

12

'Joel, look!' Emily screamed and pointed. Joel turned.

Several four-armed creatures were climbing over the top edge of the roof. They were pale grey, with mottled skin like marble. Pegasus kicked the first one in the head and sent him tumbling down the side of the building. But as he went for a second creature, a third made it to the top. Letting out a ferocious roar, it lunged at the stallion.

'No!' Emily howled.

Joel raced to the stairwell where Emily had left the baseball bat. Catching hold of it, he ran back over to the attacking creature.

'Get off him!' he howled. 'Leave him alone!'

Joel swung the bat. Then he swung it again. But every time it made contact with the creature's back, it had no effect. The only thing that seemed to slow it down was when Pegasus kicked it with a golden hoof.

More murderous marble-skinned creatures crawled

over the top edge. All focused on Pegasus. All determined to kill the stallion.

Emily's instincts took over. She ran to where she had left the contents of the garden shed and picked up a large pitchfork. Raising it in the air, she launched herself at the nearest monster trying to kill Pegasus.

But as they fought, one of them focused on her. Leaving the stallion, it started to stalk Emily.

'Joel!' Emily cried. She struck out at the creature. As it drew near, its foul stench was almost overwhelming. Emily could see its eyes were jet black with no whites or colour at all. Its teeth were large sharp points and it was drooling as it made ferocious, guttural sounds.

The horror attacking her was wearing rags tied loosely around its waist. But its upper half was bare. She could see the thick muscles rippling as it flexed its four arms that ended in filthy hands and fingers with long sharp claws.

Emily tried to defend herself. But wherever the three points of the pitchfork hit, nothing happened. They simply slipped off the creature's bare skin as if it were made of steel.

'Go for its eyes!' Joel shouted, running at the creature with Emily. Raising his bat, he used all his strength to hit it on the back of the head.

The blow only stunned it for an instant. But it was enough. Emily lunged forward and jammed the points of the pitchfork into its black eyes. Howling in rage, the creature fell to the ground and raised two hands to its face. Black liquid oozed between its fingers and dripped on to the tarmac. Where it hit the roof, the tar started to melt and smoke.

'Get down the stairs!' Joel cried as he raised his bat over the writhing monster.

'I'm not leaving Pegs!'

Emily ran forward to attack more of the creatures going after Pegasus. The stallion was still rearing on his back legs, kicking out at five attacking monsters. They had learned the damage Pegasus could inflict with his golden hooves and were staying out of his kicking range. Instead, they lunged forward and dipped back, trying to get at the stallion's exposed underside.

'Fly away, Pegs!' Emily cried. 'Get out of here!'

Instead of leaving, Pegasus shrieked in rage and crashed back down to all fours. He lowered his head and charged through the group of monsters, straight at Emily. Before she could react, he caught her by the shirt and hoisted her off the ground effortlessly. Lifting her easily over his head and wings, in one fluid motion he deposited her squarely on his back.

Next, he ran at Joel. As with Emily, he caught hold of Joel's shirt. But instead of tossing him on to his back, Pegasus held Joel firmly in his teeth and ran full speed for the edge of the building. Emily saw what Pegasus was planning and reached forward to catch hold of the stallion's thick white mane. An instant later, Pegasus launched himself into the air and was spreading his huge white wings.

Terrified but unable to stop herself, Emily looked down. They were over the edge and soaring twenty storeys above 29th Street.

'Emily, behind you!' Joel shrieked dangling in Pegasus's mouth.

Emily turned. She screamed. A creature had leaped off the building to follow them. But it had misjudged the distance and was barely holding on to the stallion's back legs. Pegasus kicked out, trying to dislodge it. But it was holding fast. Its sharp claws dug into the stallion's hind end and slowly started to climb up on to Pegasus's back. Emily could see the fury and blood lust raging in its bead black eyes. It wanted to kill. More than that – it wanted to kill *her*.

She let go of Pegasus's mane with one hand and slid further down the stallion's back. Emily started to kick at the creature.

'Be careful!' Joel warned struggling to turn back to her.

She knew her only chance was to go for its eyes. But every time she kicked at it, it moved out of her reach.

Emily repositioned herself to kick again as a grotesque hand sprang forward and caught hold of her left leg. She had never known such pain as the vice-like grip tightened on her calf. The sharp claws cut through her jeans and tore right through her skin to the muscle and bone. Crying in agony, she felt the creature draw her back towards it.

'NO!' she howled.

Suddenly Pegasus veered in the sky. They were heading straight for the side of a building. In the instant before they struck, Pegasus maneuvered his wings and turned so the creature and his entire back end smashed into a large window.

The window exploded with the impact. Shards of jagged glass cut into the back end of the winged stallion. Soon Pegasus's blood flowed, making his back too slippery for the creature to cling to. As it recovered from the brutal impact with the window, it started to lose its grip. The monster released Emily's leg and struggled to remain on the stallion.

Seizing the moment, Emily reached back and started

to pry the creature's fingers away from the stallion's flank. Raking its claws down the Pegasus's legs, it came away from the stallion and fell down to the ground twenty storeys below.

'Emily, are you all right?' Joel called.

Emily didn't want to tell her friend about her leg. 'I'm fine. But Pegasus is bleeding!' She shouted over the wind at Joel. 'We have to land.'

'Not here,' Joel cried. 'Look!'

In all the fear and excitement, Emily hadn't had time to think, let alone notice that Pegasus had lost a lot of height and changed direction. They were now flying up 5th Avenue, only eight or nine storeys high. Despite the blackout, there were thousands of tourists out on the famous street, most of them pointing up at the winged stallion soaring in the sky above them.

'Higher, Pegs, you've got to fly higher!' Emily cried.

Clinging to his mane, Emily could feel Pegasus trying to force more height out of his wings. But it wasn't working. They were steadily losing height.

'The park,' Joel cried. 'We can hide in Central Park!'

Emily was in too much pain, and far too frightened for Pegasus to have truly felt the terror of actually flying on the stallion's back. Let alone on a broken wing that had barely had the chance to heal. Now she clung to his mane, praying that they would make it to the safety of Central Park.

'Come on,' Emily coaxed. She could see the rise of trees in the distance. 'Just a little bit further and we can stop!'

As Pegasus struggled to stay in the air, Emily could see they were now only a few storeys off the ground. She looked over to his broken wing and could see a spread of red growing on the white feathers where the break had been. The bones were coming apart.

Glancing forward again, they reached 59th Street. Central Park was on her left.

'Go into the park, Pegasus. We can hide in the trees!'

Pegasus veered over the park. But the strain was too much for his broken wing. As they soared over the open sheep meadow, his wing finally gave out. The bones snapped completely. They started to fall out of the sky.

13

Emily awoke in terrible pain. Her back ached, her shoulder was badly bruised and her leg was on fire.

She heard voices and felt something wet on her face. When she opened her eyes, she saw a large pink tongue licking her cheek. She moaned weakly.

'Don't move,' a man's voice said. 'I'm just finishing with the bandages.'

Focusing her eyes, Emily saw a young man in soldier's fatigues working with Joel on her leg. Joel was holding her ankle in the air while the soldier started to wrap pieces of cloth around the bleeding wounds. Her jeans had been cut off at the knee. She could see the deep gouges in her skin and heavy bruising from the monster's brutal grip. Behind them, a young woman was tearing up a tablecloth and handing the pieces to the soldier.

Pegasus was resting on the ground beside her. A large plaid picnic blanket was covering his wings. He licked her face again.

'I'm all right, Pegs,' she said softly as she lifted her hand to stroke his muzzle.

'What happened?' she asked weakly, wincing in pain as the first knot was tied on her leg.

'We crashed,' said Joel. 'Carrying us both was too much for Pegasus. His wing gave out and we came down on the edge of the meadow. Lucky for us it wasn't crowded.'

'Just us,' the soldier said. 'And I'm glad. If the park had been as crowded as normal, you'd have had a riot on your hands.' He leaned forward and offered his hand to Emily. 'I'm Eric and this is my girlfriend Carol. I've been serving as a medic in Iraq and thought I'd seen a lot of strange things. But I couldn't believe it when I saw you in the sky.'

'I still can't,' Carol agreed nervously. 'And I'm standing right here looking at you. Part of my mind says it's real, the other part says you are hallucinations.'

'We're real, all right,' Joel said. 'And we're in big trouble.'

Eric finished tying the last knot. 'Well, that will do for the moment. But we have to get you to the hospital as soon as possible. Those cuts go right to the bone. You've got some serious muscle damage there. And by the looks of things, you need antibiotics to stop the infection.'

'We can't go to the hospital.' Emily struggled to sit up. The pain from her leg was making her feel sick. 'We have to stay with Pegasus.'

Eric sat back on his heels and stared over to the stallion. 'A horse with wings,' he said, shaking his head. 'How amazing is that? Pegasus really exists.'

'Yes he does,' Joel said. 'And so do the creatures that tried to kill us. If Pegasus hadn't flown off the roof, we'd all be dead now.'

Joel explained to Eric and Carol the events of the past few days. To their credit, they listened without interrupting. But the more they listened, the more frightened Carol grew.

'Whatever they are,' Joel finished, 'those things are still out there. Nothing seems to stop them. I watched the one that fell off Pegasus. When he hit the ground, he got up again and tried to follow us.'

This was news to Emily. 'But he fell twenty storeys! How could he get up?'

Joel shrugged. 'I don't know. I also don't know how they are tracking Pegasus, but they are. They all seemed to know he was on the roof with us.'

'I can hardly believe any of this,' Eric said. 'Pegasus

in New York City? Vicious four-armed monsters?'

'It's true, I swear it!' Emily said. 'And they want to kill Pegs.'

'I'm not saying I *don't* believe it,' Eric said. 'I'm looking at Pegasus right now and I saw the damage that thing did to your leg. But where did they come from?'

Emily recalled a comment her father had made. 'The sewers!' she cried. 'My dad is a cop. He said they'd been getting stories from uptown of people claiming four-armed demons were coming out of the sewers. They were being dismissed as crazies. I bet that was them!'

Eric shook his head. 'If those creatures are loose in New York, we have to call the military.'

'We can't!' Emily said at once. 'The CRU have already captured another Olympian. If they find out about Pegasus, they'll take him away as well.'

'What are the CRU?' Carol asked.

Eric shivered and took Carol's hand. 'You don't want to know,' he said. 'They're a real nasty Government bunch. Trust me, you don't want them on your trail.'

'It's already too late,' Joel added. 'Half the city saw us flying up 5th Avenue. If they didn't already know about us, they do now.'

'Then we've got to get moving,' Emily said. She

tried to stand up, but the pain from her leg drove her down again.

'You're not going anywhere but the hospital with that leg,' Eric said.

'I told you, I can't go to the hospital,' Emily insisted. She tried to stand again, but fell. Finally she looked over to Joel. 'Please, leave me here and take Pegasus. Hide him in the trees. But don't let the CRU or those creatures get him.'

Pegasus snorted and shook his head.

Emily turned to the stallion. 'You're the one they'll be after, not me,' she said. 'We can't let them get you. You've got to go with Joel.'

'He can understand us?' Eric asked, looking even more astonished.

Emily nodded. 'Please Pegasus,' she begged, 'go with Joel.'

Once again, the stallion snorted and stubbornly shook his head.

'Then we all go,' Joel said, making a decision. 'But we've got to get out of the open and under cover, right now.'

As everyone stood, Pegasus climbed to his feet. When Joel lifted Emily in his arms, the stallion nudged him.

'It's all right, Pegasus,' Joel assured him. 'She's coming with us.'

Pegasus nudged him again.

'I've got her,' Joel insisted.

But Pegasus nudged him a third time. 'What do you want?' Joel turned to the stallion.

'He wants to carry me,' Emily said as she looked at the way Pegasus was staring at her.

'How can he?' Joel said. 'His wing is broken again and his back end is a mess because of that monster and the glass. He might buck and throw you off.'

Emily saw the promise of protection in Pegasus's eyes. 'No he won't. Please put me on his back.'

Joel grunted and carried Emily over to Pegasus, muttering to himself, 'I can't believe I'm being ordered around by a horse!'

This time, Pegasus let the insult slide. He stood quietly while Joel settled Emily on the blanket on his back. Joel then led the group under the cover of the park's dense trees.

'Eric?' Emily asked. 'If you are a medic, do you think you could set a broken wing?'

'You mean his?' Eric indicated Pegasus. 'Maybe. But would he let me?'

Emily patted the stallion's strong neck. 'Would you,

Pegasus? That wing needs to be set again. Eric's better at it than Joel and me.'

When Pegasus didn't snort or protest, they took that as permission. Emily was taken off his back and stood unsteadily at the stallion's head while Eric and Joel got to work setting the wing. Tree branches were used as splints and Carol tore up the remaining piece of tablecloth to secure everything in place.

When they finished, Eric put his hands on his hips. 'I have been trained to do a lot of strange things. But I don't think the army could ever prepare anyone for that!'

'Thank you,' Emily said. 'I know Pegs appreciates it.'

'We all do,' Joel added. 'Now all we need is a lot of sugar.'

Emily saw Eric's confusion and explained, 'Sugar and sweet foods seems to help him heal really quickly. Joel thinks it's because sugar is close to ambrosia which they eat on Olympus.'

'We've got some chocolate cake with us,' Carol offered as she held up the picnic hamper. 'Do you think he'd like that?'

Emily nodded. 'He liked chocolate ice cream. I bet he'd like the cake as well.'

When Carol pulled the large cake from the hamper,

Pegasus immediately smelled the sugar and stepped forward. She barely had time to peel back the cover before the stallion was hungrily munching the cake.

'That's a start,' Joel said. 'But he's going to need a lot more than that. This stallion can eat!'

'Well,' Eric said. 'My mother has friends that live around here. There are no shops near the park, everyone orders their food delivered. But we did see a few shops open on 3rd Avenue. I'll see what I can find.'

'I'll come with you,' Carol offered quickly. She turned back to Joel and Emily. 'You stay here, we'll be right back.'

As they started to walk away, Joel stepped closer to Emily. 'Should we trust them? Eric is in the army. What if he calls someone the moment they leave the park?'

'I don't know,' Emily said. 'But what choice do we have?'

'I have an idea,' said Joel.

He ran over to Eric and Carol. Emily heard him offering to go with Eric to help carry back heavy items and ask Carol to stay to keep Emily and Pegasus company. Even from a distance, Emily could see that Carol's eyes were wide and frightened.

'But what if those creatures find us?' Carol said. 'Or the CRU come?'

'They were down on 29th Street,' Joel assured her. 'I'm sure they couldn't move that fast.'

'Joel's right,' Eric agreed. 'We won't be long. Please stay while Joel and I try to find more food.' He looked over at Emily. 'If you think that leg hurts now, wait a bit. By tonight you'll be screaming. I'll try to get you some disinfectant, bandages and something strong for the pain.'

Carol reluctantly agreed to stay behind, but her expression suggested she wasn't the least bit happy about it. Joel lifted Emily on to the stallion's back, and they all walked deeper into the trees.

'Try to keep hidden,' Joel warned, 'we'll be as fast as we can.' He stood back and looked at Emily on Pegasus. 'You know,' he said, 'with that blanket covering his wings and you sitting there, he almost looks like an ordinary horse.'

'Except for the fact that he appears whiter than white,' Eric added. 'Have you noticed how he almost seems to glow?'

'I thought it was just my eyes,' Joel said. 'But you're right. He is very bright. We may have to do something about that.'

'Like what?' Emily asked. 'Cover him with mud?'

'I'm not sure,' Joel said. 'Let me think about it.'

When Joel and Eric left, little was said between Emily and Carol. Emily realized Carol was terrified. She wasn't sure if it was just the creatures that had her frightened, or if it was spending time alone with Pegasus. Carol's startled eyes were darting everywhere; she jumped at the tiniest of sounds. The scurrying of squirrels in the trees nearly had her in tears. Emily actually welcomed the ringing of her cellphone. When she flipped it open, she saw her father's name on the screen.

'Dad, I'm so glad it's you—'

'Emily!' he cut in urgently. 'Thank God! Don't talk. Just listen. Don't say where you are, the CRU are probably listening to us. I know what's happened! I know about the apartment and the winged horse and your ride up 5th! Em, they're coming for you. Wherever you are, you've got to get moving and keep moving.'

'Dad, I . . .' Emily started as her heart pounded in her chest. 'There are four-armed monsters in the city!'

'I know! Bullets can't stop them. They're making their way uptown right now. Listen to me, Em. Remember Robin. Think of him and I'll be there!'

'What? Dad, I don't understand,' Emily said in terror.

'There's no time. I'm sorry sweetheart, but you must

destroy your phone. They'll be tracking it. Destroy it now. I love you, Emily! Remember Robin!'

The call was disconnected. Emily's hands were shaking as she closed her cell. She quickly opened the back and pulled out the battery pack. Then she threw everything on the ground. 'Step on it Pegs,' she said. 'You've got to destroy it!'

Pegasus stomped down on the phone with a sharp hoof. By the time he'd finished, there was nothing left but a lot of little unrecognizable pieces.

'Emily, what's happening?' Carol was approaching panic.

This time, Emily shared her fear. 'The creatures are coming for us.' She looked back into the direction Joel and Eric went. 'I hope they hurry. My dad said the CRU are hunting us as well.'

14

Paelen was unsure how long he had been in this strange and terrible place. Without windows, there was no keeping track of time. But each passing day was becoming worse than the one before.

He was taken to another lab. This time they didn't draw any more of his precious blood or put him in machines to study him. They didn't shine more lights in his eyes, or take samples of him to test. Instead the older man called Agent J ordered him strapped to an uncomfortable metal chair. The chair was facing a large white screen that seemed to shimmer like satin.

'Watch,' Agent J ordered.

The lights in the room went down as the screen lit up. The full-colour image was almost like the colourful mosaics scattered around Olympus. But not quite. As he studied the strange pictures, Paelen saw the tall buildings he'd first seen when he arrived in this strange world on the night of the storm.

'Do you recognize anything?' Agent J asked.

'It is your world,' Paelen responded. He looked at Agent J curiously, trying to figure out what new torture this was going to be.

'Yes it is. We call it New York City.'

'New York City,' Paelen repeated. 'That is very nice. Thank you for showing it to me. May I leave now?'

'No you may not,' Agent J shot back. 'Just sit there and keep watching.'

Paelen turned back to the screen. He saw different images of the city. Some were taken from the air, others from the ground. Next he was shown a collection of various people he didn't know. As he watched the changing images, he became aware of everyone in the room studying him.

'Do you know what those are?' Agent J asked when the image changed again.

Paelen looked at the picture of countless pigeons in a park. 'Birds,' he answered. 'We have them in Olympus. It infuriates Jupiter when they mess on his statue.'

'I'm sure it must,' Agent J said sarcastically. 'And this?'

Paelen saw the image of a dog. Then another image showing the same dog walking with its owner. 'Olympus has dogs too,' he answered. 'We also have Cerberus. He

137

has three heads and is particularly vicious. Do you have them here?'

'No,' Agent J answered. 'But recently, we've discovered that we do have these.'

Paelen's eyes flew wide as the picture of the dog was replaced by the image of several four-armed creatures charging through the streets of the city.

'Nirads!' he uttered.

'What did you call them?' Agent J demanded, moving closer.

'Nirads,' Paelen repeated. He was in shock and unable to draw his eyes away from the sight of the rampaging invaders.

'Who are they? Did they come on your starship?'

Paelen ignored the question and looked at Agent J fearfully. 'Are they really here in this world?'

'Yes,' Agent J answered, 'and they are wreaking havoc with the city. We've counted at least twenty, but there are reports of even more being seen. They appear to be practically unstoppable. We've only managed to capture a couple of the creatures. But they are ferociously strong and can't be sedated. We've got them stored at another high security facility. Now tell me. What are they? Can you control them?'

'Control them? Me?' Paelen cried. He shook his

head. 'No one can control the Nirads. They are feral creatures with killer instincts. They are indestructible! Please, you must let me go. They have followed me from Olympus. I must get away. They will kill me if they find me here.' Paelen struggled in the chair, desperate to flee. 'They will kill all of you as well.'

'What are they?' Agent J demanded.

'They are the destroyers of Olympus!' Paelen cried.

'Enough!' Agent J howled. 'We are in the middle of the worst security crisis this country has ever known and you are still talking about Olympus!' He leaned down until his face was just inches from Paelen's. 'Olympus doesn't exist! It's a myth! It was created by weak minds in a time of need. Now tell me. Where are you from? Where is your starship?'

'I do not understand what you want from me,' Paelen cried. 'I tell you I am from Olympus. But you claim it is just a myth. Why do you keep insisting I am from the stars?'

'Because aliens exist, Olympians don't,' Agent J snapped.

Paelen regained control of himself. 'Of course Olympus exists,' he challenged indignantly. 'It is where I am from. And I resent you calling it a myth. We are not myths! As for the Nirads, all I know of them is they have destroyed my home. Olympus is in ruins. Now they have followed me here, but I do not know why.'

Agent J straightened up again and turned furiously to the screen. 'All right, you say they are after you? If that is true, why have they left you untouched and are pursuing *them*?'

On the screen, Paelen saw the picture of Pegasus soaring through the canyons of buildings. The image was not as clear as the Nirads. But Paelen could see two young humans were with the stallion. Pegasus appeared to have fresh wounds on his hind quarters. And even though the image was unclear, Paelen knew Pegasus well enough to see the terror on his face.

'Why were they attacking that horse and those two kids?' Agent J demanded.

Paelen almost shouted, '*Pegasus is not a horse!*' but he bit back the comment. He realized he'd already made a terrible mistake by telling them as much as he had. Shock at seeing the Nirads in this world had made him drop his guard. He would not make that mistake again. 'I do not know.'

'You're lying!' Agent J shot at him. 'I saw your face. You recognized them. Those kids, are they friends of yours? Are you from the same planet? What about that winged horse? How is it possible for him to fly?'

'He flies because he has wings,' Paelen said sarcastically. 'I would have thought even you could figure that out for yourself. Now, I have answered your questions. I do not know who they are. Please release me before the Nirads arrive.'

Paelen's gaze followed Agent J as he walked over to a man in a white coat.

'Give it to him,' he heard him say. 'He's not telling us what we need to know.'

Moments later, the man in the white coat injected something into Paelen's arm. As the drug took effect, Paelen started to feel what it must have been like to be Medusa. His head was full of writhing angry snakes; his veins were coursing with fire. He could no longer see clearly.

When Paelen felt at his worst, Agent J repeated all the same questions he'd asked moments before. Where did they come from? Who were the Nirads? Who were the kids on the flying horse? And why did the creatures want to kill everyone?

Despite the sensation of snakes squirming in his head, Paelen still had complete control over his thoughts. He wouldn't answer their questions. He especially wouldn't betray Pegasus. So as always, Paelen did what he did best. He lied. He told Agent J the most outrageous story he could think of.

This time, he claimed he was Hercules, son of Jupiter and hero of Olympus. Paelen went into long details of his achievements as Hercules. Telling one amazing story after another and claiming all the glory for himself.

The more he talked, the angrier Agent J became.

Driven to fury, the older man started to slap Paelen violently across the face. But instead of hurting, the blows helped to clear away the snakes and fire raging through him. Paelen silently took Agent J's blows. As before, human strength was nothing compared to the pounding the real Hercules had once given Paelen for stealing from him.

As others crowded forward to pull Agent J off, Paelen slipped a hand into one of the orderly's pockets and retrieved the keys to the handcuffs. With the keys clenched tightly in his fist, Paelen pretended to pass out.

He heard Agent J's heavy panting as the older man was pulled away.

'We're done for the day,' the agent spat. 'Take him away before I kill him!'

Paelen remained perfectly still with his eyes closed. Two orderlies lifted him on to a stretcher and transported him back to his room. They transferred him to the bed and handcuffed him to the side bars.

'Stupid idiot kid,' Paelen heard one mutter. 'If he keeps pressing Agent J like that, the man will have him sliced and diced and poured into Mason jars.'

'Better him than us,' the other orderly said. 'Where do *you* think he comes from?'

'Don't know, don't care.'

'What do you think they'll do to him?'

'I guess they'll wait till they catch all the other freaks out there. Then they'll question the lot of them until they spill their guts. Then when there's nothing left to say, they'll do what they always do. Ice the lot of them.'

'Shame,' the second orderly said. 'I kinda like this kid. He's got a real fire in his belly. He's the first one I ever saw get the better of Agent J. Let's face it, the man needs an attitude adjustment. This kid's just the one to do it.'

'That's if he lives long enough.'

When they'd finished securing him, Paelen heard both men cross to the door.

'Well, that's my shift over, I'm outta here,' one of them said. 'Want to join me and the boys for a beer later?'

Paelen heard the beeping of the sound lock. When

the door closed after the men, he remained still for a moment more. Finally he opened his eyes and looked around. He was alone.

He still couldn't believe there were Nirads in this world. Agent J had been right about one thing. The Nirads were after Pegasus, not him. As he tried to slow his racing heart, Paelen recalled the last thing he'd seen on Olympus. How the Nirads were specifically going after Pegasus. If Diana hadn't come forward, they surely would have killed him.

But why did the Nirads want Pegasus dead? And why were there two humans with him?

Paelen realized the answers were not to be found in this strange and horrible place. He needed to get out.

He recalled Mercury's last dying words, begging him to join the struggle for Olympus. Much to his own shame, Paelen had turned his back on his people and fled the fight. But now, the fight had followed him here. He could not turn his back again. He would escape from these humans and find Pegasus.

Then he would finally join the battle.

15

Emily felt terror building up inside her as she sat waiting for the others on Pegasus's back. It seemed like hours since Joel and Eric left. But finally, there was movement in the trees around them and Emily heard Joel call out her name.

'Over here,' Emily called back. 'Hurry.'

Moments later, Joel and Eric reappeared. 'We've got big trouble,' Eric said as he put down the shopping bags and hugged his girlfriend. 'All military leave has just been cancelled. I've been ordered to meet up with my unit not too far from here. It seems there is an emergency in the city.'

'The emergency's us,' Emily said. 'My dad called. The police know about Pegasus and our flight up 5th Avenue. They know about the creatures too. He said the CRU are after us.'

Eric nodded. 'And they're calling us in to help find you. I'm so sorry, but I've got to go.'

'You're not going to tell them where we are, are you?' Emily asked fearfully.

'Of course not!' Eric answered. 'I'll do everything I can to lead them away from you. But it's not just you they're after. There are those creatures out there as well. Those I will try to stop.'

'You can't,' Emily said. 'My dad said bullets won't even stop them.'

'Yeah,' Joel added. 'When I hit one on the head with a baseball bat, it only stopped him for a moment. Even the fall from Pegasus didn't slow it down.'

'That being the case, the city has more to worry about than Pegasus,' Eric said. He took Carol's hand. 'We've got to go. I want you out of the city as soon as possible.'

Carol smiled weakly. She turned to Emily and shrugged. 'I'm so sorry you kids are in trouble. But I just don't have the stomach for this.'

'I understand,' Emily said softly. If she had a choice, she'd love to run away too. But she couldn't. Pegasus still needed her.

Eric jotted down two names and telephone numbers on a piece of paper he pulled out of his pocket. 'Memorize these if you can,' he said, handing the numbers to Emily. 'They are to my brother in Brooklyn and my parents in New Jersey. Call either of them if you really get stuck. My dad is ex-military. You tell them I told you to call and they'll help you. I wish I could do more. But all hell is breaking loose in the city and I've got to go.'

As he and Carol started to move away, Eric called back: 'You've got bandages and antiseptic in the bags. Get that leg cleaned up as soon as you can. And remember, memorize those phone numbers. You might need them.'

'I will,' Emily promised softly. 'Thank you so much for everything.'

'Good luck, kids, and God bless,' Eric said with a wave as he and Carol slipped away through the trees.

When they had gone, Emily started to shake.

'What are we going to do, Joel? The CRU are after us.'

Joel shrugged. 'I really don't know. But we can't do anything until it gets darker.' He started going through the bags of shopping. 'If we have any luck at all, the CRU and military will concentrate on finding the creatures before they come after us. In the meantime, let's get Pegasus fed and that leg of yours cleaned up.'

* * *

As the sun started to set, Emily and Joel cleaned and treated the deep cuts on the stallion's hind end. They had already cleaned and bandaged Emily's leg. The painkillers were working and she was feeling much better.

'At least we now know who stabbed Pegasus with the spear,' Emily said as she gently rubbed antiseptic cream into a deep wound on the stallion's hind leg.

'The real question is why?' Joel asked.

Emily gave Pegasus a soft kiss on the muzzle, then sat down on the ground and reached for an apple. But before the fruit reached her lips, her eyes flew open wide.

'Robin!' she cried.

'What?' Joel said, running to her side. 'What's wrong?'

'The last thing my dad said to me was to remember Robin!' Emily caught hold of Joel's hands and climbed to her feet painfully. 'I didn't understand what he meant. He was talking in code in case the CRU were listening. But now I remember!'

'Remember what? Emily, what are you talking about?'

As she spoke, Emily started to pack their supplies into Eric and Carol's picnic basket. 'When I was really young, my mom and dad used to bring me up to the park. We'd go to this really hidden area at the upper end. Dad would pretend to be the Sheriff of Nottingham. Mom would be Maid Marion and I'd be Robin Hood! Every Sunday we'd come and play sword fights.'

'I still don't understand,' Joel said helplessly.

'Before he hung up, my dad said "remember Robin". He said he'd be there. Don't you see, Joel? Dad told me to take you and Pegasus to where we used to play Robin Hood. It's really private. No one will find us there. We could hide for a bit and plan our next move.'

'Then what are we waiting for?' Joel cried. 'Let's get you on Pegasus and get moving!'

Remaining in the safe cover of trees, they travelled north. The sun finally set, and they walked for much of the way in complete darkness. As they travelled, they heard the sound of multiple helicopters arriving in the sky over Central Park. Peering up through the trees, they saw the bright searchlights shining down to the ground.

'They're looking for us,' Joel said darkly.

Emily looked down at Pegasus and saw that in the dark, he appeared even whiter than before. He no longer looked like an ordinary horse. There was no mistaking that he was different. If the beam of a searchlight were to touch him, there would be no escape.

'Joel, wait, we've got to stop. Please help me down.'

'We can't. We're meeting your dad at the play area—' Joel stopped when he saw Emily struggling to get down off Pegasus. 'What is it?' he said, helping her. 'What's wrong?'

'Pegs, you are just so brilliant white! We've got to do something about your colour,' Emily turned to Joel. 'He wasn't like this when I first found him on the roof. Even last night he wasn't this white. But look at him now! It's like he's becoming brighter by the minute.'

'You're right. He's really starting to glow.'

Joel put the picnic hamper down on the ground and started to dig through their supplies. 'While we were out shopping, I had an idea. We bought all we could.'

'What did you get?' Emily asked.

Joel held up a package, but in the dark, Emily couldn't see what it was.

'What is that?'

'Hair dye,' Joel explained. 'We got ten packages. But there was one little problem: they aren't all the same colour. We got dark brown and black.' He paused and added, 'They're not the same brands either. Do you think that could cause a problem?'

Emily shrugged. 'I don't know. I used to help my mom colour her hair, but she always used the same kind. I don't even know if this will work on a horse.'

Once again, Pegasus complained at the 'H' word.

'I'm sorry, Pegs.' Emily reached out to stroke his face. 'But you know what I mean. This is meant for people. I just hope it doesn't hurt you.'

'We've got to try,' Joel said. 'He's shining like a star. It won't take long for the CRU to find us if he stays like that. It's not so bad in daylight, but now he's glowing like a beacon.'

The decision was made to use the hair dye before they went much further. They picked their way through the trees until they came to one of Central Park's many ponds. The major work would be done under the cover of the trees, and they would only risk exposing themselves once it was time to rinse Pegasus off.

'If you work with his head and mane, I'll start with his tail and back end. We can meet in the middle,' Joel suggested. 'It's too dark to read the instructions. Do you know what to do?'

Emily explained to Joel how her mother used to mix the chemicals together before applying it to her hair. They both put on the latex gloves that came with the packages and started to work.

'I'm so sorry, Pegs,' Emily apologized as she applied the dark, smelly liquid to his beautiful white face, 'but this is to help hide you. We are going to try to make you look like a regular dark horse. That way, if anyone sees you, they'll never know the truth.'

Covering the entire stallion seemed to take ages and used all of the dye that they had. They were careful not to get any on the feathers of his wings. When they finished applying the last of it, Emily pulled off her latex gloves.

'Now we wait,' she said as she sat down tiredly. Her leg was really starting to hurt. 'It used to take my mother thirty minutes to set the colour.'

'How about we give him thirty-five,' Joel said, setting his digital watch and sitting beside her.

As they waited, they listened to the sounds of the helicopters endlessly searching the park. More than once, a helicopter passed directly over their heads, but the cover of trees kept them from being seen.

'Time's up,' Joel finally said, helping Emily up.

'Let's get you rinsed off, Pegs,' Emily said as she put on a fresh pair of gloves.

Leaving the protection of the trees, they looked up to check the position of the helicopters. The military were concentrating their efforts at the lower end of the park. Pegasus entered the dark water of the pond. Emily started to follow him in.

'Emily, stop,' Joel held up a warning hand.

'But I can help,' she protested.

'Yeah, and your leg can get really infected by this filthy water,' Joel argued. 'Stay on the shore and keep watch. Let me know if anyone is coming.'

Emily resented being told what do to. She could do as much as he could. But deep down, she knew Joel was right. Her leg was throbbing badly. There was something seriously wrong with it. Adding dirty water would only make things worse.

'All right,' she agreed. 'But be as quick as you can.'

Standing on the edge, Emily nervously watched the searching helicopters overhead as Joel led Pegasus into deeper water. The stallion submerged himself and Joel rubbed him down quickly.

'Hurry,' Emily cried as two of the helicopters started to veer away from the others and move towards them. 'They're coming this way!'

They were moving faster than expected. There was no way Joel and Pegasus would have time to get out of the water before the helicopters were upon them.

'Get down!' Joel cried as he and the stallion ducked beneath the surface.

Emily barely had time to dash into the trees before the bright searchlight shone on the spot where she'd just been standing. With the blood pounding in her veins and wounded leg, she followed the progress of the helicopters as they continued north over the park.

'All clear!' she called as she limped back to the water's edge.

Joel and Pegasus both raised their heads above the surface cautiously. With renewed urgency, Joel finished rinsing off the stallion.

Pegasus emerged from the water looking as dark as the night, though his wings were still brilliant white. As Emily covered the wings with a blanket, a new voice startled them.

'What have you done to him?'

A tall woman stormed forward. She was dressed in filthy rags, but had an elegance and authority when she walked. She carried a long spear that had a sharp point that glowed bright gold. Her eyes were electric blue and blazed in the dark.

'How dare you touch him!' she challenged, shoving Emily aside and going straight up to Pegasus. 'And what is this horror you have done to him?'

She turned her attention to Pegasus. 'How could you let these foolish children touch you like this?'

'Excuse me,' Joel said. 'But he belongs to us.'

'Pegasus belongs to no one,' the woman spat furiously. She turned back to the stallion and her voice softened. 'Look at you, my old friend. You look like a plough horse.'

As the woman continued to inspect Pegasus, the stallion nickered with excitement. She laid her forehead against him and dropped her voice. 'Pegasus, we have fallen,' she said sadly. 'Father is in chains. Apollo is dead and Olympus lies in ruins. The Nirads have defeated us.'

'Nirads?' Emily asked cautiously.

The woman looked down to Emily's wounded leg. 'I can smell them on you too,' she said. 'You have fought the Nirads? You are lucky to be alive.'

'Is that what those four-armed creatures are called?' Joel asked. 'Nirads?'

The woman nodded. 'They murdered my brother. Killed countless others and conquered Olympus.'

'You said they killed Apollo. Was he your brother?' Joel asked breathlessly. 'Are . . . are you *Diana*?'

'That is one of my names,' the tall woman

answered. She studied Joel for a moment. 'And you are a Roman.'

The sound of the helicopters cut short further conversation.

'Please, Diana,' Joel entreated. 'I know you are a great warrior, but trust us – you can't stay here. Those flying machines up there will capture you. We have to hide.'

'Hide?' Diana repeated in confusion. 'I do not hide from a battle.'

'You do now,' Emily said as she moved closer to Pegasus. 'Come on, Pegs. We've got to go before they see you.'

Pegasus let out a soft neigh to Diana but followed Emily away from the pond.

'Pegs?' Diana repeated as she trailed behind them. 'Did I just hear you call him Pegs?'

When they were safely hidden in the trees, Emily turned to her. 'He doesn't seem to mind. I think it's a cute name for him.'

Diana was incredulous. 'Cute? Child, do you have any idea of whom you are speaking? This is Pegasus, the great stallion of Olympus. To make him suffer such indignities is beyond tolerance.'

'Of course I know who Pegasus is,' Emily shot back

as reached out and stroked the stallion's dark muzzle. 'But he's also a friend of mine.'

'Emily, stop,' Joel warned fearfully. 'You don't understand who you're talking to. Please, show some respect!'

'Respect?' Emily repeated. 'Where's her respect for me?' She turned back to Diana. 'If Pegs doesn't mind me calling him that, then why should you?'

'You insolent little nothing!' Diana cried. She stepped forward and raised her hand to strike Emily. 'You have yet to learn your place—'

Pegasus quickly placed himself between Diana and Emily. He looked at Diana and let out a series of strange sounds. The expression on her face softened. The tall woman looked at Emily several times before dropping her head.

'I am sorry. My behaviour is unforgivable. Pegasus has just explained to me what you have done for him and how you have helped him. Please forgive me. I have witnessed my father's defeat, my brother's murder and my home destroyed. I am not myself.'

Emily frowned. Diana could understand Pegasus? She looked at the woman with envy and more than a touch of jealousy. She secretly wished she were an Olympian too. Then she and Pegasus could actually communicate.

'I understand,' Emily finally said. 'I'm so sorry for your losses.'

'Is Olympus really destroyed?' Joel asked, timidly coming forward. 'How? You're Gods. Who could defeat you?'

'The Nirads,' said Diana sadly. 'Soon they will destroy your world too, unless we stop them.'

'Destroy our world?' Emily said in shock. 'Why? What do they want?'

'We do not know,' Diana said. 'Until now, we had never encountered the Nirads before. We know nothing about them or where they come from. They have made no demands on us and taken nothing from our ruins. All they desire is destruction. And unless we find a way to stop them, all will be lost.'

'How can we stop them?' Emily asked. 'Nothing seems to hurt them. Even falling twenty storeys doesn't slow them down.'

'There is one thing we have discovered,' Diana said. 'In the course of battle, right before Pegasus fled to this world, I bested a Nirad. But it was only after the creature had touched Pegasus's golden bridle. He was poisoned by it. We believe he died as a result of touching the bridle and not my spear.'

'You need his bridle?' Emily asked, trying to make sense of everything she was hearing.

Diana nodded. 'This is why I have come here. I need it to forge new weapons to use against the Nirads. I see you have taken it off Pegasus to colour him. May I have it?'

'It's not here,' Emily said. 'Another Olympian called Paelen stole it from Pegasus right before they were both hit by lightning. He's got the bridle. But now the CRU have taken him.'

'Paelen?' Diana's face darkened. 'That foul little thief! Even he would not keep the bridle if he knew what it could do for our people.' She looked back to Emily. 'What are the CRU who have captured him? Where do I find them?'

'You can't,' Joel warned. 'They are too dangerous.'

'I have fought the best armies of Greece and the Romans. I do not fear these people.'

'You should,' Emily advised. 'They're really dangerous.'

Joel looked at Diana. 'How long has it been since you were last here?'

Diana paused and considered. 'Many ages. Your people did not have devices like those in the sky. You travelled on horseback and fought with swords.'

'Then this isn't the same world you knew,' said Joel. 'We've changed.'

'Yes,' Emily agreed. 'These days, people don't even believe in you.'

'That's right,' Joel said. 'And we have new weapons that can hurt you. Look at Pegasus. He broke his wing, and even though it's healing, he needs time. If he can be hurt, so can you.'

'It is not your world or those noisy flying vehicles that can wound us,' Diana said, suddenly sounding very defeated. 'The death of the Flame of Olympus has weakened us.'

'What's the Flame of Olympus?' Emily asked curiously.

Diana looked over at Emily and sighed heavily. 'The Flame is the source of all our power and strength. It has burned in Olympus since the beginning. But recently, its strength has diminished. As it became weaker, we did also. The Nirads used this weakness to launch an attack on us. If the Flame had been at its full strength, we would have fought them off easily. As it is, the Nirads reached the Temple of the Flame and extinguished it completely. We all believed we would perish without it. But we haven't.'

'But you've lost your powers?' Joel guessed.

Diana nodded. 'My father hoped to use the gold from the bridle to defeat the Nirads and relight the Flame,' she said. 'Moments before he was captured, he used the last of his powers to send me here to collect the bridle and help Pegasus on his quest.'

'What *is* his quest?' Emily asked. 'He can't tell us.'

Diana looked at Pegasus. 'Why did Father send you here?'

Both Emily and Joel stood in silence as Pegasus started to nicker softly. It continued for several minutes.

'I never knew any of this,' Diana said in a whisper. 'None of us did. Only my Father, Vesta and Pegasus knew.'

'Knew what?' Emily asked impatiently.

'Please get off your wounded leg and sit down,' Diana said as she helped Emily settle under a tree. Joel, still a little starstruck, sat beside her.

'Pegasus is on a precious quest,' she started. 'He says it is doomed to failure without your help. That the survival of Olympus and your world rests entirely with you.'

Emily was suddenly unsure she wanted to hear this.

'Long before I was born, at the end of the Great War between the Olympians and the Titans, a Flame emerged in the heart of Olympus,' Diana continued. 'It was Vesta's duty to ensure the new Flame was kept alive and strong. For its power was our power. Its life was our life. A wondrous temple was built around the Flame and it has burned brightly in Olympus ever since.'

'Vesta?' Joel said suddenly. 'The Goddess of the Hearth? She used Vestal Virgins to keep the flame alive at a temple in ancient Rome.'

Diana nodded. 'That was the symbolic Flame of Olympus. Those virgins were the servants of Vesta. The real Flame has always been in Olympus. But right from the beginning, my father worried that if this Flame were ever extinguished, we would lose our powers. So he sent Vesta to Earth with the heart of the Flame and commanded her to hide it in a human child. A girl child. This secret Daughter of Vesta would carry the heart of the Flame within her, without ever knowing it.'

'But that was long ago,' Emily said, frowning. 'She's got to be dead by now.'

'She is,' said Diana. 'But Vesta made certain that upon her death, the heart of the Flame would pass to another baby girl being born. It would go from generation to generation, across all the waters of the Earth.'

'So out there right now,' Joel said, working it out,

'there is another Daughter of Vesta carrying the heart of the Flame of Olympus.'

'That's crazy,' Emily said. 'How can a flame have a heart?'

'Emily—' Joel warned.

'No Joel, this is getting too much,' said Emily, cutting him off. 'First Pegasus is real and crashes on my roof. Now Diana, also an Olympian, is here and telling us that a flame has a heart and that it goes from girl to girl. I can believe a lot of stuff, but this is just too crazy. How can you accept it so easily?'

'Because I've read the books!' Joel shot back. 'I do more than fight, you know. I read. *The Iliad* and *The Odyssey* are my favourites. They tell some of the stories of the Gods!'

'Stories, that's right,' Emily challenged. 'This is real life and a flame can't have a heart!'

'Emily, I know these books,' said Diana. 'My father had them in his palace before the Nirads attacked. They are not lies, just retelling of certain events. Believe me. The Flame of Olympus has a living heart. And my father sent Pegasus here to find the girl who possesses it. He is charged with bringing her back to Olympus to reignite our Flame.'

'Wow,' Emily said softly, struggling to take it all in.

'But after so many generations, how will he know who she is if she doesn't even know about herself?'

Diana smiled. 'Pegasus alone can see the flame burning within her. She will draw him to her. He won't be able to resist her, for she is the source of his strength.'

Joel nodded his head in understanding. 'So, Pegasus came to Earth to get this girl. But he got hurt and crashed on Emily's roof instead.'

'That is correct,' Diana said. 'With his wing broken, he has been unable to fly to her.'

'Where is she?' Emily asked. 'Is she even in America?'

Pegasus neighed softly.

'Pegasus says the daughter of this generation is here in this country,' Diana translated. 'That she is not far away. But he says something is very wrong with her because the flame has grown weak within her. This is why it became so weak in Olympus, and enabled the Nirads to attack and defeat us.'

'Maybe she's sick,' Emily suggested.

'Perhaps,' Diana agreed. 'But whoever she is, she has a great destiny to fulfil. But a tragic one. For hers must be the greatest sacrifice of all.'

'What do you mean?' Joel asked.

'When the Daughter of Vesta is taken back to Olympus, she must willingly sacrifice herself to the Flame,' she said. 'It will consume her. But in offering herself, Olympus will be reborn and all our powers restored.'

'She's got to die?' Emily asked in a whisper.

Diana nodded. 'She must be willing to sacrifice herself in order for the Flame to be reborn,' she said. 'She cannot be forced.'

'But what can we do?' Joel asked.

Diana dropped her head. 'Pegasus needs you to talk to the girl when we find her. You are from this world. You can better explain it than I. You must make this child understand that her sacrifice will not only save Olympus, but this world too.'

'The Daughter of Vesta is a child?' Emily asked. 'And you want us to tell her she's got to die to save everyone?'

'No way,' Joel said, shaking his head. 'I know you guys have your own special Olympian ways. But this is too much. You can't expect us to tell a kid she's got to kill herself.'

'I do not know how old she is. Nor does Pegasus,' Diana explained. 'He only knows that she is near. She may be an old woman nearing her natural death or a young child just starting her life. But whoever, or whatever she is, ultimately, it must be her decision. None of us can force her to sacrifice herself.'

'So,' Emily said slowly, 'we're going to knock on someone's door and ask them to commit suicide in order to save the world.' She felt light-headed with shock. 'What would you do if it were you, Joel?'

'I'd tell us to get lost and call the police.'

'Me too,' Emily agreed.

'Then all is lost and our worlds will perish.' Diana said flatly. 'The Nirads have enslaved the survivors of Olympus and destroyed our home. You have already seen them here in this world. They know of Pegasus's mission, and will send more to kill him before he finds the Daughter of Vesta. I am here to help him any way I can.'

'So will we,' Emily said finally. She looked at Joel. 'We haven't got a choice. If there are more Nirads on the way, we've got to do all we can to stop them.'

'Wait a minute,' Joel said as an idea came to him. 'What if we got the bridle back? Maybe we can make weapons to destroy the Nirads. Then when we take the Daughter of Vesta to Olympus, Jupiter will have time to figure out another way to relight the flame without her having to die.'

Emily looked at Diana. 'Do you think it's possible?'

'I do not know,' she said. 'It might work.'

'I'm willing to try,' Joel said. 'It's better than telling some poor girl she's got to kill herself.'

'I agree,' Emily said excitedly.

Joel led the group forward. 'Come on, let's get moving.'

16

Paelen opened his fingers. The key he had taken from the orderly's pocket was still resting in the palm of his hand. He manipulated the key into the lock on the handcuff. With one hand free, it was little effort to open the second cuff.

Paelen knew his body was mostly healed. The burn on his back was gone and his broken ribs no longer hurt. They had left the casts on his legs. He suspected they had done that to keep him from escaping. But as he stretched out his feet and flexed his calf muscles, he felt the plaster on the two casts crack. He felt no pain from the bones in his legs.

Paelen sat up, threw back the covers and started to break away the casts from both his legs. Before long, his legs were free. He tested his muscles. They were a bit stiff from lack of use, but apart from that, the bones had healed.

With both legs free, Paelen climbed quietly from

his bed. He pressed his ear to the metal door and heard activity in the hall. There were still a lot of people out there.

He recalled the orderlies making plans for the evening. They were going home for the night. As Paelen stood by the door listening, he heard the guards outside change. Two men were leaving. They were reporting the events of the day to the one man who would remain outside the door for the rest of the night. Paelen would wait a while longer before he made his move. He always did his best work late at night.

Paelen waited. Somehow he would always feel when it was time to move, rather than plan anything specific. As he lay back, he recalled everything he had seen of the facility so far. He knew they were deep underground. There were multiple halls, countless doors and several levels. So far, he had been taken to three different laboratories for testing. They were all two levels below this one.

Each time they took him from his room, Paelen had been careful to memorize where they went. He had been taken past a set of doors with a symbol of stairs above it. More than once, he'd seen people enter or exit at that point. That would be his escape route after he had found the lab containing Pegasus's bridle and Mercury's sandals.

Paelen now concentrated on the air vent above his bed. The sounds of people in the rooms connected by the tunnels faded slowly. Moment by moment, the facility was shutting down for the night.

When more time had passed, Paelen felt that strange tingle that told him it was time to move. He walked quietly back to the door. He heard nothing from the outside except the faint sound of paper being shuffled and a soft breath being taken. The guard was still out there. But he was alone.

As he looked at the key pad that controlled the sound lock, Paelen counted twelve buttons. To open the door, the men always pressed four. But which four? From his angle on the bed, he had never been able to see exactly which buttons. This left only two options. To start pressing buttons until he heard the sound combination he needed, or simply use his strength to force open the door.

Neither option was particularly appealing. As pressing buttons always made sounds on both sides, any attempt he made would be heard by the guard. However, there was an equal chance of the guard hearing him force the door.

Finally Paelen chose the first option, but with a slight change. Even though the tingle in his senses told him to go, he held back. Waiting . . . waiting . . .

He eventually heard movement outside his door. The guard was saying something about leaving his post for a toilet break. A moment later, another voice gave the authorization. Immediately the guard left his desk, leaving Paelen's door unattended.

Paelen looked at the buttons on the key pad. Starting with the number one, he closed his eyes and pressed the button. He listened to the distinct sound it made. It was not one he'd heard before.

One by one, Paelen pressed the twelve buttons, familiarizing himself with their sounds. When he hit the last one and heard its unique tone, he smiled. He confidently reached up and pressed the correct sequence of four buttons to open the door. A faint click immediately followed. Paelen pulled the door handle. It gave without any resistance.

Paelen saw no one. He dashed down the hall in the direction of the stairs, entered the stairwell and descended two levels to where all the laboratories were located.

Remaining in the stairwell, Paelen lowered himself to the floor. All of his senses were alert to any sounds.

There were two people in the laboratory corridor. Paelen heard their voices drawing near, and then passing the doors and fading in the opposite direction.

When they had gone, he entered the hall quietly.

A series of doors lined the long corridor. Paelen recognized the first laboratory he'd been taken to. He shivered when he recalled what they'd done to him in there.

Further along the wide, white corridor, Paelen approached a big metal box against a wall. Even before he drew near, he could smell a sweet fragrance that made his mouth water and stomach grumble. It was almost like ambrosia, but not quite.

Paelen had asked countless times for ambrosia to be brought to him. Instead he was given food that he couldn't eat. The only thing he'd managed to get any nutrition from was what the doctors had called dessert. But it was never enough.

Feeling half starved, Paelen approached the glass front of the vending machine. Behind it he could see stacks of brightly coloured items. They all smelled of that same sweet, delicious fragrance. His need for food quickly outweighed his need to get the bridle and sandals. At the side of the machine, he found a lock where a small round key should be inserted. Paelen used all his strength to tear at the lock.

He pried open the front glass door of the machine and reached for the first item. Tearing off the paper, he hungrily bit into the soft candy bar. He nearly cried out in joy as the sweet chocolate went down his throat. It was only then he realized just how hungry he had been.

As he tore open another candy bar and shoved it all in his mouth, he quickly checked the hall. He was exposed and vulnerable. But he had to eat.

Pulling up the bottom of his hospital gown, Paelen made a small pouch. This he filled with as many candy bars and chocolates he could carry. But he was also careful to leave enough in the machine so that anyone who came by would not see that he'd been there.

When he had taken as much as he dared, Paelen closed the glass front of the vending machine and ran back to the stairwell. He crept to the back of the stairs and tucked himself under the base. It wasn't the best hiding place in the world, but it was better than nothing.

Paelen started to eat. As he tore open each package, he discovered new flavours and delights. Until this moment, there'd been nothing about this world he liked. But as he stuffed his face with candy and chocolate from the vending machine, he realized there was at least one good thing about this world – sugar.

When the last of the candy was gone, Paelen sat back and sighed with contentment. It was the first time he'd felt satisfied since he arrived. Already he could feel his strength increasing as the sugar went to work on his body, healing the last of his wounds.

Soon, Paelen was ready to move again. Creeping out from his hiding place, he felt refreshed, alive and alert. Every sense was working properly. He was himself again.

He could hear the sound of people moving around on the levels above him. But on this level, he was alone. As he moved further along the corridor, Paelen suddenly smelled something he hadn't smelled since Olympus. It was the awful scent of rot and filth. It was the scent of – Nirads!

The odour grew worse as he continued down the hall. The stench was coming from behind a locked door. He pressed his ear to the door, but heard nothing. The smell told him there was a Nirad in there, but something was wrong. It didn't smell like other Nirads. This one smelled dead.

Paelen pressed the same code from his door into the sound lock, but nothing happened. He pushed hard against the door. If there was a dead Nirad in there, he needed to know how it had died, and if there was some way of defeating the awful creatures. Perhaps with that information, he could save Olympus.

With the sugar coursing through his body, Paelen felt almost as strong as he did when he was home. No human door could withstand his Olympian might. With a grunting shove, the lock and hinges gave way and the door burst open.

Paelen found himself in another laboratory. But this was nothing like the labs he'd been in before. This room smelled of death and decay. There were similar machines in it. But there was also something else. Something awful.

In the centre of the room, Paelen saw a large metal table. There was a big round light hanging above it, shining its brightness down on the table's occupant. The table had metal sides that folded up several centimetres, to keep the blood and fluids from spilling on to the floor.

Lying on the table was a dead Nirad.

Paelen could see the four arms lying limply at the sides of the creature. The stench rising from the table was so awful he had to plug his nose to keep from losing the precious food he'd just eaten. But the sight of the dead Nirad was almost enough to make him sick anyway.

The doctors of this place had clearly been cutting the Nirad open to see what was on the inside. He didn't want to look. Instead, his eyes were drawn to a deep scar burned on the folded-back skin of the Nirad's open chest.

Closer inspection revealed several other similar scars along its exposed body. There was a big one on the Nirad's bloated face. When Paelen crept closer, he immediately recognized the shape of the scars. They were caused by Pegasus's hooves.

Suddenly all the pieces of the puzzle came together. Back in Olympus, it was Pegasus and Diana who had killed the first Nirad. This Nirad here was also dead because of an encounter with the stallion. Pegasus was the only Olympian capable of killing them and they knew it. The Nirads needed Pegasus dead before they could complete the destruction of Olympus and all the other worlds. So they had followed him to this world to kill him.

Paelen had to warn the stallion. Pegasus had to be protected. He was the Olympians' only weapon against the ferocious Nirads.

'Was that a friend of yours?'

Paelen jumped. Turning quickly, he saw Agent J standing there, flanked by several security guards.

'You must let me go,' Paelen said desperately. 'Pegasus is in terrible danger. The Nirads are here to kill him.'

'Pegasus?' Agent J asked.

'Yes, Pegasus,' Paelen insisted. 'We must help him! He is the only one who can defeat the Nirads. I must go to him.'

'You aren't going anywhere,' Agent J said. 'You didn't think you could get away from us that easily, did you? We have been following you on the corridor cameras from the moment you left your room.'

'Cameras?' Paelen repeated. 'I do not understand.'

'Yes, cameras.' Agent J theatrically waved his hands in the air. 'It is like great serpent's eyes that show us what you are doing,' he said. 'You were never alone. We were watching you the whole time. I must say, that was a neat little trick with the vending machine. I'm surprised you weren't sick from eating all that chocolate.'

'I told you before, I need ambrosia,' Paelen insisted. 'You would not provide it. That food was the closest I could find. Now please, I need to help Pegasus.'

Paelen started to move, but several security guards stepped forward to block his path. 'I do not wish to fight you, but I will. I must go.'

'I told you, you aren't going anywhere,' Agent J said. Then he looked at his men. 'Take him down.'

Paelen charged forward as the guards surrounded him. It was little effort for him to fight them off. He tossed them around the laboratory like they were rag dolls. When all the guards were down, Paelen shoved Agent J aside and made it to the corridor. He ran in the direction of the stairwell.

'He's running, he's running. Lock down the facility. Repeat, subject is running. Lock it down!' Agent J cried.

Loud alarms burst to life throughout the building. Paelen looked back and saw the men running towards him.

Paelen concentrated on getting to the stairs. But as he entered the stairwell, he heard the sounds of many feet charging down the stairs in his direction.

'Stop!' they ordered. 'Stop or we'll open fire!'

Paelen felt the sharp stinging of bees. He looked down at his chest and saw darts sticking into him. He pulled several out and threw them back at the men who shot him. When they struck home, the men fell to the ground unconscious. Paelen realized the darts were intended to make him go to sleep.

He continued up the stairs, using the darts against the men coming for him. But as each man fell, more replaced them. Soon the stairwell was filled with men chasing after him from below as well as above.

'Stop!' they shouted.

But Paelen couldn't stop. He needed to get to Pegasus, to warn the stallion. Charging forward, he started to fight with the guards. But even though he was much stronger than all of them, their numbers were too great. He was quickly overwhelmed.

A sudden brutal blow came from behind and he was struck in the back of the head. Paelen turned to see the man pulling back his weapon to hit him again. It wasn't necessary. As Paelen's world started to go dark, more men pounced on him and drove him down to the floor.

17

It seemed to take half the night to work their way to where Emily used to play with her family in Central Park. Emily was back on Pegasus and trying to lead the group. But without a flashlight, and still no city lights to guide them, the way was dark and treacherous. The constant sound of the helicopters was a reminder of the danger they were in.

'You sure you know where you're going?' Joel asked.

'Not really,' Emily admitted. 'It's been years since I've been up this high in the park. But it shouldn't be much further.'

As they picked their way through the trees, Pegasus suddenly stopped. His dark ears sprang forward and he pawed the ground. Diana also stopped. She held up her hand and listened.

'There is someone moving ahead,' she said softly as she raised her brother's spear and prepared to fight.

'Em?' a voice called softly. 'Is that you?'

'Dad!' Emily responded. 'Dad, we're here!' Weak with relief, she reached forward and patted Pegasus's neck. 'It's all right, Pegs,' she said. 'It's my dad.'

Forgetting her wounded leg, Emily slid off the stallion's back. But when her feet hit the ground, her leg gave out and she fell. Her father was at her side in an instant, taking her in his arms.

'Oh, Em, I've been so worried about you!'

Emily put her arms around him and immediately felt better. 'Dad, I'm so sorry I didn't tell you what was happening.'

'What *is* happening?' he asked. 'Em, the city's in an uproar!' He looked at her bandaged leg. 'And what happened to you?'

'Do you remember the night of the big storm?' Emily asked. 'Not long after the Empire's top blew up, Pegasus was hit by lightning. He crashed down on our roof. That's how I got my black eye. When I went to help him, his wing accidentally hit me.'

'Pegasus?' her father repeated. 'That winged horse I heard about was the actual Pegasus from the Greek myths?'

'Roman,' Joel corrected, stepping out of the shadows. 'And they aren't myths, they're all real. I'm Joel, sir. A friend of Emily's from school.'

Emily's father shook Joel's hand. Joel indicated Diana. 'Officer Jacobs, I'd like to introduce you to another Olympian. This is Diana.'

'Diana? The Great Hunter?' Emily's father asked as he studied the tall woman.

Diana nodded formally. 'Officer Jacobs. It is an honour to meet the father of Emily.'

'Call me Steve,' her father said a little helplessly. He looked back to Emily. 'I don't understand any of this,' he said. 'What's happening here? How and why are there Olympians in New York?'

Emily and Joel tried to explain as best as they could, right up to the point of being in the park.

'It's hard to accept any of this.' Steve stared at Pegasus and shook his head. 'I'd heard it was a white stallion you were riding today. What happened to him?'

'He was white,' Emily said. 'Too white. As he got better, Pegasus was starting to glow. So we dyed him black to try to hide him from the CRU.'

Emily kissed the stallion softly on the muzzle. 'Pegs, this is my dad,' she said. 'Dad? I'd like you to meet Pegasus.'

Emily's father cautiously stroked Pegasus's muzzle. He lifted the edge of the blanket to see the glowing white feathers of his wings resting on the dark body.

'I'm seeing you, but I can't believe you're here.' He patted Pegasus's strong neck. 'Even touching you doesn't seem to help.'

'He's real, Dad,' Emily said. 'And he's broken his wing again. But now there are these awful creatures after him.'

'Nirads,' Diana corrected.

'I – I still don't understand.' Steve shook his head. 'How can any of this be real? What can it all mean?'

'It means that the war in my world has sprung forward into yours,' said Diana. 'And unless we get the golden bridle back, neither world will survive.'

Emily explained to her father about the golden bridle – how it killed Nirads – and about the history of the Flame and how Pegasus had to find the Daughter of Vesta to relight it.

Steve combed his fingers through his hair and cursed. 'I held that bridle in my hands a few days ago. If only I'd kept it!' He looked at Diana. 'Why don't you make more golden weapons?'

'Minerva made the bridle for Pegasus,' Diana explained. 'But we do not know how she created it or what other metals she used. She was one of the first captured by the Nirads. Vulcan tried forging other Olympian gold.' She showed everyone the golden tip of her spear. 'It can wound the Nirads, but only the special gold from the bridle can kill them. We must get it back if we are to defeat them.'

'That won't be easy. I met the kid who stole it from Pegasus. The same night he arrived, the CRU were informed. They took him and everything with him away. I don't even know where they are holding him. They keep their locations quiet.'

Pegasus neighed behind Diana.

'Pegasus says our main concern is the Daughter of Vesta,' said Diana. 'We must get her back to Olympus.'

'But we've got to wait for his wing to heal first,' Emily pointed out, 'which means we need somewhere safe to hide until then.'

'Well, we can't stay here,' Steve said. 'You've seen the helicopters. By dawn, this entire park will be crawling with CRU agents and the military. We're going to have to keep moving and try to stay one step ahead.'

'How do we hide a large horse in the middle of New York City?' Joel asked. 'No offence, Pegasus, but you know what I mean.'

The stallion remained silent as he rested his head on Emily's shoulder. She suddenly had a thought.

'I know! We hide him in plain sight!' Emily looked over to her father. 'Dad, you know how they've been trying to shut down the carriage rides in the park because of that campaign for better treatment of the horses?'

'Yes,' he said. He looked at Diana and explained. 'Several groups aren't happy about the treatment of the horses in the city, and I agree with them, it's awful. Finally the number of carriages is dropping.'

'Exactly,' Emily said excitedly. 'So there are extra carriages at the stables . . .'

'I get it!' Joel said. 'You want to steal a carriage and attach Pegasus to it. We'll keep his wings covered. Then we'll simply walk right out of the city and find the Daughter of Vesta!'

'Great idea,' Steve said. 'Let's do it!'

Getting out of Central Park with Pegasus proved more difficult than they expected. It was well past midnight and there was still a lot of traffic on the roads. What disturbed them the most was the sheer number of police cars, running with their sirens off but lights flashing, followed by countless army vehicles travelling throughout the city.

They waited until almost two in the morning before they made their move. They exited the park on 104th Street. The closest livery was on 50th.

'We've got to walk Pegasus over fifty blocks downtown?' Joel moaned.

'Unless that wing of his is strong enough to fly, he's got to stay on the ground like the rest of us,' said Steve. 'We'll head over to one of the quieter avenues and make our way downtown.'

As the long night progressed, Emily felt her leg begin to swell. But she kept it to herself. She brushed aside the feeling of nausea and concentrated on getting to the stables. Above them, helicopters broadened their search patterns so the group kept close to the shelter of the buildings.

'Wouldn't they be after the Nirads first?' Joel asked.

'I'd imagine so,' Steve answered. 'I'm sure they think Pegasus is still in the park.'

'I hope you are both correct,' Diana said as she looked up. 'I do not like those flying machines one bit.'

Suddenly all around them the city burst into brilliant light as the blackout finally ended and the power came back on. Soon the air was filled with the horrendous noise of shrieking alarms as endless security systems came online again. Street lights started to work and 10th Avenue was lit up like a carnival.

'It couldn't have waited just a few more minutes?'

Joel complained. 'Just a few more stupid minutes! Is that really asking so much?'

'All right,' Steve said tersely. 'We didn't expect this. But we've only got a few more blocks to go. Let's speed up.'

They had travelled no more than a block when they heard the sound of police sirens drawing near. They ducked into a large doorway just as several police cars raced past.

'They didn't even slow down to look at us,' Emily commented.

More police cars rushed by.

'Something big is up,' Joel said. 'I have a bad feeling about this.'

'Nirads are in the area,' Diana warned as she sniffed the air. 'I can smell them.'

Beneath her, Emily could feel Pegasus quivering. 'Pegs can smell them too.'

'I can't,' Joel added. 'Where are they?'

Diana sniffed again and pointed along 58th Street towards 5th Avenue. 'Down there.'

'That's the entrance to the park!' Emily said. 'The Nirads have made it to Central Park?' She looked down to Pegasus. 'Pegs, how are the Nirads tracking you?'

'They have tasted his blood,' Diana answered. 'They

are using it to follow his trail. We can not lose them. The only thing in our favour is they cannot run very fast.'

'If the Nirads are only a few blocks away from us,' Joel added, 'they don't have to run fast to catch us.'

'Come on,' Steve said. 'Let's get that carriage and get the hell out of this city!'

When they reached 50th Street, Emily's father led the group to a tall grey roller door. Posted above the door was a sign: *O'Brian's Livery*.

'This is it?' Joel asked. 'What a dump!'

'How do we get in?' Emily asked.

'We break in,' her father replied.

Emily studied her father in his police uniform and realized how difficult this must be for him, being an officer of the law.

'This isn't going to be easy.' He inspected the pad lock. 'I can't use my gun. It'll make too much noise.'

'There's another entrance here,' Joel suggested as he stood before a normal-sized door beside the bigger one.

'True, but we won't get Pegasus or a carriage through that. We need to open this big one here.'

'Let me try,' Diana said. She reached across and

easily tore both the lock and the hasp away from the door.

Everyone looked at her in shock.

'I may have lost my powers,' Diana said, 'but not my strength.'

Steve hoisted the large roller door up on its rails. 'That will come in very handy!'

Emily ducked as Pegasus stepped under the door. Steve pulled it closed again once everyone was through. As they looked around, the overwhelming smell of horses and filthy, soiled straw filled their nostrils. Up ahead, multiple carriages stood in a long row.

Above them on the upper floors, they could hear the sound of horses' whinnying.

'They know we are here,' Diana said as she listened to the calls of the horses. 'They are suffering.'

'So will we be if we don't grab a carriage and get out of here,' Joel warned.

'You choose a carriage, I must see to the horses.' Diana started to climb a tall ramp to reach the upper floors.

'Diana, wait! We don't have time for this!' Joel cried.

'There is always time for animals,' Diana called back as she disappeared up the ramp.

Beneath her, Emily could feel Pegasus reacting to the distress calls from the horses. She looked around at the filthy walls and chipping paint. 'Dad, this place is disgusting,' she said.

'I know, honey. I would love to see all of the stables in the city shut down. But until then, we've got to get moving.'

Emily wanted to help her father and Joel look around. But she was feeling too ill. She knew now that something was seriously wrong with her leg. Sensing her pain, Pegasus turned back to check on her.

Emily could see the question resting in his eyes. 'I'm not feeling very well, Pegs,' she admitted quietly. 'But I can't tell them yet. We've got to get out of the city and find the Daughter of Vesta first.'

She looked into his beautiful face and felt a rising twinge of jealousy. Somewhere out there was another girl who was calling to him. This stranger held the stallion's heart, not Emily. Despite all the danger they were in, Emily found herself resenting the unknown girl and the place she would hold in Pegasus's life.

'We've got something,' Joel called from the back of the building. 'Emily, bring Pegasus here.'

Suddenly shouts and screams came from above. Emily barely had time to catch hold of Pegasus's mane before the stallion had dashed down the hall and up the ramp. At the first level, Pegasus kept moving. He was starting to race up the second ramp towards Diana when an unconscious man tumbled down from above.

'Diana!' Emily called, as a second man was also thrown forward and tumbled down the ramp.

'I am here.'

Pegasus leaped over the second man and made it to the next level. He ran down the narrow hall between the tiny stalls, skidding to a stop a short distance from Diana. She was standing before the open door of a stall. Her head was down. Emily could see tears shining on her cheeks.

'What's wrong?' Emily asked. She looked into the stall and saw a chestnut mare lying on the floor. It wasn't moving.

'She is dead,' Diana said softly. 'They worked her to death. But those men didn't care. I heard them cursing her. She lived a life of misery in this wretched place and they were complaining about what it would cost them to replace her.'

When Emily's father arrived, Diana charged forward and seized him by the collar and hoisted him in the air. 'What kind of world has this become where you treat your animals like this?'

'Diana, please, put him down!' Emily shouted. 'Put him down! He didn't do anything!'

'Perhaps not. But he lives in a world that allows this to happen.' Diana lowered Steve to the ground. 'It is unforgivable.'

Both Joel and Steve looked at the dead horse.

'I know it's terrible,' Steve said. 'I'm ashamed of what we've become and how we treat our animals. But some of us are trying to change things. To make them better.'

'Then you are failing in your attempt!' Diana spat. She pointed at the dead horse. 'I have been away far too long. When this is over and my world is restored, I will return. This will not be allowed to happen again. Such places as this will know my wrath.'

She looked at Joel. 'You said you knew of me from your books?' she said. 'Then you know I feel about animals. I will not tolerate this kind of abuse.' She crossed to another stall and started to open the door. 'These horses must be set free. This is no life for them.'

'I agree with you completely,' Steve said. He stepped over to Diana and put his hand over hers. 'But we don't have time to help them all. Diana, listen to me. We don't have long before those two guys wake up or someone else notices we're here. We may have already tripped some alarms. Who do you think will be interested to hear of a break-in at a livery stable? A LIVERY STABLE, Diana. The CRU, that's who. And who will they think of?' Without waiting for an answer, he pointed at Pegasus. 'They'll think of him. We must get out of here as quickly as possible.'

Pegasus stomped his foot and started to whinny. Diana paused. Finally she calmed as she walked over to the stallion and patted his neck.

'Of course, my dear friend, you are correct.'

She looked at the others. 'We must get the carriage and go. I will come back to free these horses later.'

Emily looked at the other sad horses in their tiny stalls anxiously waiting for Diana to open their doors. Her heart went out to them. When this was over, she promised she would join Diana in freeing them all.

On the way down the ramp, Emily saw one of the unconscious men starting to stir. It wouldn't be long before he woke up.

When they made it back down to the main floor, Joel led the way towards the back of the building.

'We found this in their storage area,' Joel explained as he pointed at a broken-down white carriage. It was resting on its side. The top canopy was torn, but its wheels and frame looked sturdy enough. 'They won't notice it missing as quickly as they would one of the better ones.'

'I also found us these.' Steve held up two sets of overalls. 'I can't exactly go out dressed like this.' He indicated his police uniform. 'And Diana? You certainly can't go out in those rags.'

Diana nodded. Without a word, she took the overalls and went to another area to change.

18

Emily stood wearily by Pegasus's head as her father, Diana and Joel did their best to hook the stallion up to the carriage. As they fought and argued how best to get the harnesses on him, Emily realized just how different the stallion was to horses. His entire frame was much bigger and none of the harnesses came close to fitting. The huge set of wings didn't help.

In the end, they had to piece together several parts of multiple harnesses to get the stallion roughly hooked up to the carriage. Pegasus refused to allow the leather straps to go over the top of his wings, which would bind them down to his body. He insisted that they remain unrestricted. In order to achieve this, they had to try to attach everything under his massive wings, and hoped that the blanket would cover them enough not to look too suspicious in daylight.

'Forgive me for doing this to you, my old friend,' Diana said softly. 'You deserve better.'

Emily looked at Pegasus, dyed a poor mottled dark brown and black, as he stood tethered to the tatty old white carriage. He was covered in harnesses that didn't fit and wearing a full heavy bridle that rested uncomfortably on his face. He looked nothing like the majestic winged stallion that had crashed on her roof a few nights ago. Emily felt terrible for having to do this to him.

'I'm sorry too, Pegs,' she mumbled, leaning heavily against him. 'We just have to get out of the city and then we can take it all off you again.'

Pegasus let out a soft nicker and licked Emily's face. His tongue lingered on her cheek for a moment. He neighed to Diana.

'Fever?' Diana looked at Emily. She raised her hand to Emily's forehead and frowned. 'You do have a fever.'

'What?' Steve also felt Emily's forehead and face. 'Em, you're burning up!'

Emily knew Pegasus had done it for her. But his timing couldn't have been worse. 'I don't feel very well,' she finally admitted. 'I think it's my leg.'

'Let me see it,' her father insisted.

Emily was helped up into the carriage. Her father started to undo the bandages covering her wounded leg. 'My God,' he cried when he saw the raging infection caused by the Nirad's claws. 'Why didn't you say something?'

'I couldn't. We've got to worry about keeping Pegasus safe from the CRU and the Nirads. He's got to find the Daughter of Vesta and get her back to Olympus to relight the Flame.'

'Emily is correct,' Diana said. 'Relighting the Flame of Olympus is the only hope for both our worlds.'

'We have to get her to a hospital!' Steve insisted. 'Look at her. She isn't well!'

Pegasus started to whinny and pound the floor.

'Pegasus does not agree with you,' Diana said. 'He knows very well she is ill. But the Nirads have tasted her blood also. They can track her. If you were to take her somewhere for care, I assure you, the Nirads will follow. She must stay with us so we can protect her.'

Joel held up the picnic hamper. 'We've got more medicated cream and fresh bandages in here,' he assured Steve. 'We can clean up her leg and get it wrapped again. Then when we find the Daughter of Vesta and Pegasus takes her back to Olympus, we'll get Emily to the hospital.'

'Dad, it's the only way,' Emily added weakly. 'Keeping Pegasus safe is much more important than me. If he fails his quest, the Nirads will destroy our world. Then whether I'm sick or not won't matter.'

Steve sighed. He reluctantly lifted Emily out of the carriage and carried her over to a slop sink to thoroughly clean her wounds. He applied the last of the medicated cream and bandaged her leg again.

'That won't last long,' he said as he finished.

'It won't have to,' Emily said. 'Just long enough for us to get Pegs out of the city—'

Suddenly Pegasus started to shriek.

'Nirads!' Diana cried as she sniffed the air. 'They are coming.'

'From where?' Steve asked.

'That way!' Diana picked up her spear and pointed at the tall grey metal roller door.

'That's the only way out. We're trapped!' Joel cried.

From above they heard the sound of the horses reacting to the approach of the Nirads. They were shrieking in their stalls and pounding wildly against the doors.

'I've got an idea!' Steve cried. 'Joel, Diana, come with me. Em, you stay here with Pegasus. If they break down the door, make a run for it. You've got to get away.'

'What are you going to do?' Emily cried.

'We're going to release the horses.'

19

Pegasus was pawing the ground and snorting angrily as the sickening growling sounds of the Nirads approached the large grey metal door.

'What's going on here?'

Emily saw the two men Diana had attacked come stumbling down the ramp. Their faces were bruised and bloodied and they were limping from their encounter with the enraged Olympian.

'You attacked us!' shouted one of the men. 'Who are you?' His eyes fell on Pegasus, harnessed to the old white carriage. 'Where did that horse come from? He's not one of ours.'

'But that carriage is!' said the other man angrily.

'Please listen to me,' Emily pointed at the roller door. 'There are four-armed creatures out there that are after us. They'll kill you if they see you. They don't know you're here. Just hide until we're gone!'

The men went pale as they heard the awful sounds

coming from outside the stable.

'Four-armed what?' one of them said weakly.

'Creatures, monsters, demons,' Emily said. 'Whatever you want to call them. We're going to free the horses to distract them so we can get away. Please listen to me, you have to hide!'

From above came more sounds of shrieking horses, kicking at their doors. They were becoming frantic in their stalls.

'You aren't freeing my horses,' one of the men shouted. They both turned and started back up the ramp. 'Just stay where you are. We're calling the cops!'

Everyone heard the sound of pounding on the floors above, then the rush of hooves racing down the ramp. Both men jumped aside as the first of the horses arrived. They wildly charged the carriage, panic in their eyes.

Emily was certain they would stampede and knock it over. But Pegasus opened both his wings just in time and reared up on his hind legs. Still in the carriage, Emily was lifted high in the air. The stallion let out a shrieking whinny that stopped the terrified horses in their tracks.

'What the heck is going on here!' One of the men cried as his eyes went wide at the sight of the stallion's huge white wings. He looked back at Emily. 'Who are you?'

'What are you?' demanded the other.

The Nirads began to pound at the grey door. Their snarling, growling roars promised a terrible death to everyone if they managed to get in.

'Dad!' Emily screamed up the ramp as the carriage crashed down again. 'They're here!'

'We're coming!' Joel called down as more horses arrived from above. Emily could see the flared nostrils and wild terror in their eyes as the frightened animals gathered around Pegasus. The stallion was back down on all fours, but his wings were quivering and he was shaking his head with rage.

Steve, Joel and Diana reappeared, pushing through the horses on the ramp to make it to the carriage. When Diana saw the two men, she charged forward furiously.

'You deserve the fate awaiting you behind that door for what you have done to these horses. Do not expect any help from me. You are at the mercy of the Nirads!'

'Diana, we don't have time,' Steve warned. 'Get upstairs and hide,' he advised the terrified men. 'The Nirads want us, not you. Keep hidden and you might just survive!'

Without waiting to be told twice, the men pushed through the panicked horses and dashed up the ramp.

'We're still calling the cops!'

'Go ahead,' Steve called. 'I *am* a cop!'

'Dad,' Emily shouted, pointing at the roller door. 'They're trying to tear the door down.'

The heavy metal was starting to buckle under the brutal impact of the Nirads' fists.

'That door isn't going to hold for long.' Steve raced to Pegasus and snatched up the blanket from where it lay on the ground. 'The moment the door goes, the horses should charge forward. With luck they'll cut a way through the Nirads for us. Pegasus, it will be up to you to get us away from here as quickly as possible.'

Pegasus snorted and shook his head. His sharp hooves pounded the concrete beneath him as his wild eyes watched the roller door starting to give.

Steve leaped into the carriage and snatched up the reins. Joel and Diana vaulted in behind him.

'Hold on tight everyone,' Steve warned as he took the driver's seat. He snatched up the reins. 'This is going to be bumpy.'

More dents were forming in the heavy metal of the grey roller door. It started to give at the top. The long sharp claws of multiple Nirad fingers appeared and ripped at it.

The door finally tore free of its rails and gave way. It crashed backward on to the street, trapping two Nirads beneath it.

Pegasus shrieked. The horses panicked. Wild with terror, they started to stampede. They raced over the collapsed door and crushed the Nirads beneath. Without concern for their fallen warriors, other Nirads sprang forward and tried to force their way past the charging horses.

'Pegasus, go!' Steve shouted. 'Go now!'

Emily felt the carriage jerk forward as Pegasus started to run. Several Nirads fought to climb over the terrified horses and charge towards them. One of them leaped in the air, passed over the top of the panicking horses and landed on the side of the carriage. While two arms clung to the carriage, the other two reached for Emily and started to pull at her hair. Emily screamed clawing at the heavy muscled arms as the Nirad drew her closer.

Joel reacted instantly. He went for the Nirad's eyes. But the Nirad fought back. It released one of its arms holding on to the carriage and swung at Joel, knocking him back with a brutal blow just as Diana raised her spear and lunged forward.

When the golden tip struck the Nirad's exposed chest, it released Emily and howled in agony, then fell away from the carriage.

'Hang on!' Emily's father cried as they approached the collapsed door.

Pegasus charged up the metal door. The carriage immediately followed. With the two Nirads still trapped beneath it, the broken door worked as a ramp. The carriage sailed off the end and flew several metres into the air.

Everyone screamed.

The carriage crashed down to the ground. Although the occupants were tossed down to the floor, somehow the carriage remained upright. Without pausing, Pegasus sprang forward at full speed along 50th Street.

Emily struggled to climb back up in the seat. She peered back to the livery stable and gasped. More Nirads were charging forward, raising their four arms in threat and howling with rage at losing them. They ignored the panicked horses as they concentrated on chasing the carriage.

'Go, Pegs, go!' Emily screamed.

Emily was only able to count to twelve before she lost track of how many Nirads were following them.

With the two still under the door, that made at least fourteen Nirads in New York City, all hunting them.

'Emily, are you all right?' Diana anxiously checked Emily for fresh cuts. 'Did they wound you?'

Emily shook her head and gingerly prodded her painful scalp. 'No, I'm fine. But I think I'm going to have a bald patch where that thing ripped out my hair.'

'That's nothing,' Joel complained, clutching his side. 'I think I've got broken ribs! Those Nirads really pack a punch.'

'They bested Hercules,' Diana explained. 'It is no surprise that they should defeat you.'

After several more blocks, Pegasus slowed to a trot. A few blocks later and he stopped completely. Everyone climbed shakily out of the carriage.

Emily limped up to Pegasus and stroked his muzzle. 'Are you all right, Pegs?'

The stallion's eyes were wide and bright with fear as his nostrils remained flared. He gently nuzzled her neck.

'That was too close,' Joel said as Steve inspected the carriage for damage. 'This thing was ready to break before the attack. One more flight like that and it won't last another minute.'

'We were lucky back there,' Steve said grimly as he tested the large wheels. 'But we've got to keep ahead of the Nirads. Those four arms are lethal.'

'They are,' Diana said. 'And with their three eyes, they have full directional vision.'

'Three eyes?' Joel asked. 'Really? Where's the third one?'

'In the back of their head, under all that filthy hair,' Diana explained. 'From what we have learned, they do not see well out of it. But it is enough that you can never take them by surprise.'

'How can we ever beat them?' Emily asked. The fever flared, making her feel even more weak and tired. 'They're too strong.'

'We need that bridle,' Diana uttered. 'With it we can defeat them.'

'Plus the Flame,' Joel added. 'Once Pegasus gets the Daughter of Vesta back to Olympus to relight the Flame, you should have your powers back. Right?'

Diana nodded. 'That is correct. But we must keep away from the Nirads until Pegasus is ready to fly again. He is our only way home.'

Emily was leaning heavily against Pegasus for support. Her father felt her face.

'You're getting worse,' he said worriedly. 'Come

on. Let's get you back into the carriage. You need some sleep.'

Emily didn't resist when her father lifted her into the carriage. A second blanket had been stored under the seat. He pulled it out and draped it over her. 'Settle down and rest,' he advised. 'I'm going to try to find us somewhere to hide for the night. Then when the city starts to wake again, we can blend in with the other carriages and start to make our way off Manhattan.'

As her father climbed back up into the driver's seat, Diana settled in beside her. She put her arm around Emily protectively and drew her closer. 'Sleep, child,' she said softly. 'We will be going home soon.'

When Emily awoke, the sun was up and the sounds of the city had returned to their normal noisy pitch. But there still seemed to be more police sirens than usual, and the frightening sounds of the helicopters could still be heard overhead.

Diana was still beside her. But her father and Joel were gone.

'Where are we?' Emily asked groggily as she looked around.

They appeared to be on a building site hidden amongst several large cement mixers. A large scaffold was built above them, blocking them from the view of the helicopters that still flew very low over the city.

'Your father knew of this place and brought us here,' Diana explained. 'He said we should be safe for a while. He said it was in a place called Downtown. Though I am not certain what that means.'

Emily felt relieved. 'That means we're well away from the stables,' she said.

Pegasus was still tethered to the carriage. He nickered softly and tried to look back at her.

'Morning, Pegs,' Emily said softly.

'Sleeping Beauty wakes,' her father called.

Steve and Joel were approaching through a hole in the tall fence surrounding the building site. They both carried several bags of food. At their approach, Pegasus whinnied.

'He smells the sugar,' Joel said. He looked at Diana. 'I bet you'll need some too. We've got lots for you both.'

'And I've got more stuff for your leg,' Emily's father told her as he put the bags down on the ground. He reached for her forehead. 'The fever's down a bit, but not a lot. How are you feeling?'

'Not too bad,' Emily lied. The truth was she felt awful. Her head was pounding, her body ached and her leg was throbbing painfully to each beat of her heart. 'I'm fine for today. I just hope we can get out of New York before the Nirads find us again.'

'We will,' her father said. 'Now, we've got fresh bagels and cream cheese for us. Diana, you and Pegasus can have the cereal.'

'Guess what?' Joel added, reaching into one of the bags. 'We made the front page of all the papers!' He handed several newspapers to Emily. 'Look at the headlines. *FLYING HORSE EXPOSED AS A HOAX!* Can you believe it? Half a million people saw us soaring up 5th Avenue and they are calling it a big hoax!'

Emily looked at the grainy images of their panicked escape flight. The pictures looked like they had been taken from a camera phone and blown up too large to clearly see any details. She could see Pegasus and his huge white wings. But she couldn't see her or Joel's faces.

She quickly scanned the article. 'A movie stunt? Do they really expect the people who saw us to believe it was a stunt to promote a new movie? And look, they don't even mention the Nirads! How dumb do they think people are?'

'They don't think they're dumb at all.' Steve pulled more items from the bags. 'But you can bet the CRU ordered the papers to print that. I'm sure if anyone tried to challenge the story, they can expect a visit from a not so friendly CRU agent to set them straight. This is probably the best thing that could have happened for us. The public won't be adding to the search. Especially now that Pegasus is . . .' Her father paused and tried to think of the best possible words. Finally he said, 'Now that he's not white any more.'

In the bright daylight, Emily could see that their midnight dye job on Pegasus was awful. The stallion's head and part of his neck and mane were black. But further down his front legs, a sharp, distinct line changed to brown. Then a bit further down his back, the colour changed to medium brown. At the end of the blanket, his exposed rump and tail were black again. He looked as strange now as he had when he was glowing white.

'Let's eat and then get moving again.' Steve pulled out the rest of the food. 'We've got a lot to do today and not a lot of time to do it.'

As expected, Pegasus was starving. The stallion hungrily went through three large boxes of sweet, sugary cereal and several bags of brown sugar and honey before he started to slow down.

Diana was much the same. Emily watched in

amazement as she ate handfuls of the cereal from the box and washed it down with honey straight from the bottle.

'This is delightful,' Diana said with a mouth full of food. 'What do you call it?'

'Some like to call it breakfast,' Steve chuckled. 'But most of us call it garbage. There's enough sugar in that cereal to keep a kid hyperactive all day.'

'But it's as close to ambrosia as we could get,' Joel added.

'It is very good,' Diana agreed. 'Different from ambrosia or nectar, but it will do nicely.'

After the cereal, Diana and Pegasus finished off two boxes of honey-glazed doughnuts.

Emily watched Diana wolfing down the food and thought she was going to be sick. Her father had brought a bagel for her, but she couldn't eat it. She caught him watching her, but was grateful when he didn't nag her to eat.

'Your world has changed a great deal since I was last here,' Diana said as she reached for the last doughnut. 'It is not all bad after all.'

'Well, we do have our good points,' Steve said as he began cleaning Emily's wounds and changing the bandages. Though he didn't press Emily to eat her bagel, he made sure she took the painkillers. When he finished bandaging her leg, he sat back and shook his head. 'We've got to get that looked at soon. It's getting worse.'

Emily didn't need her father to tell her that. She already knew it. And she suspected that Pegasus knew as well. The stallion kept looking back to check on her, whinnying softly.

'Well, it's almost seven,' said Steve, checking his watch. 'We'd better start making a move. The contractors will be back to work any minute. I don't want them to find us here and see what we've done to their fence.'

'Isn't it too early for the other carriages to be out?' Emily asked.

'We don't have much choice,' said her father. 'If we take our time heading uptown, maybe no one will notice.'

As the food was packed away and the stallion's wings thoroughly covered, Emily's father sat in the driver's seat again. 'You ready to go, Pegasus?' Pegasus whinnied and started to move. 'We've got to make it to the 59th Street Bridge.'

'59th Street?' Diana repeated. 'Excuse me, Steve, but is that not where the CRU are concentrating their efforts to find us? You wish to go there?'

'We don't have much choice,' he explained. 'The bridge is the closest above-ground route off Manhattan,' said Steve. He took up the reins. 'We can't take the tunnels or the ferries. Besides, with the Nirads rampaging through the city, I'm sure the CRU and military have their hands full. Hopefully, we can stay under their radar.'

He looked at the stallion. 'All right, Pegasus, let's get going,' he said. 'But nice and easy. We don't want to draw too much attention to ourselves.'

Pegasus nickered once and started to move.

20

Paelen was once again handcuffed to the bed. This time, there were cuffs on his ankles as well as his wrists.

The blow to the head had only stunned him for a few moments. But when he awoke and begged the men to help Pegasus, his pleas were ignored.

Agent J stood beside his bed, glaring at him. 'I would suggest you reconsider speaking to us,' he said. 'I am authorized to use full force to get what I need from you. You have until dawn to decide. You will either tell me the truth, or I will use methods infinitely more unpleasant than you have ever known. The choice is yours.'

But Paelen already knew what he planned to do. He had no intentions of cooperating. His only thoughts now were to get to Pegasus and warn him.

When Agent J and his men had gone, Paelen concentrated on the problem at hand. Getting the cuffs off wouldn't be difficult. The big problem was getting out of the facility. Agent J had claimed they had serpents' eyes watching him. The fact that they caught him on the lower level proved Agent J's words to be true. But was there anything watching him in here?

Paelen strained his eyes carefully studying every wall and every area of his room, searching for anything that might look like a serpent's eye. He saw nothing out of the ordinary.

He was convinced the serpents' eyes were only in the corridors. With that route blocked to him, he would have to find a different way out of the facility. Once again, he looked up to the air vent above his bed. That would be his escape. He felt certain there wouldn't be any serpents' eyes in there. Decision made, Paelen turned his attention to the handcuffs and reluctantly used his one Olympian skill.

It was incredibly painful. Starting with his right wrist, he folded his thumb in tightly and started to pull. Just like all the other times he had been chained in Olympus, Paelen was able to stretch out the bones in his hand until the metal of the cuff slid off. He repeated the process with his left hand.

With both hands free, Paelen sat up and reached for the cuffs on his ankles. He winced in pain as the bones in his feet stretched out until the cuffs simply slid away.

When he was free, he returned his shape to normal with a sigh of relief.

Paelen pressed his ear to the door and heard voices. He counted at least three men posted outside his door. They were locked in a deep conversation, talking about something called football. With their attention diverted, they would never hear him go.

Paelen climbed on his bed. Standing on his pillows, his keen eyes scanned the air vent. It would be a tight fit, even for him. But if he stretched himself out long enough, he knew he could squeeze through.

There were only four screws holding the cover to the mount. He caught hold of one of the edges and started to apply pressure. It took very little effort to pull the vent cover away from the wall. He hid it under his pillow.

Paelen stole a quick look back to the door and then reached up. He pressed his palms firmly against the inner metal walls of the duct and hauled himself up to the vent.

As he had suspected, the entrance to the air duct was brutally tight. Paelen had to painfully stretch every bone in his body to slip through. It was only then he realized his ribs weren't completely healed yet. As he moved, he felt sharp twinges of warning pain from the altered length of his ribcage.

Biting back the pain and wincing at every move, he entered the countless tunnels of ductwork. The ducts themselves were much larger than the entrance had been and he was able to return his body to its normal shape.

Crawling forward on his hands and knees, Paelen used every sense to listen for danger. When he reached a T-junction, he paused. To his left, he heard nothing. It was still very early in the morning and there weren't many people in the facility yet. But to his right, he heard voices. Paelen recognized one of the voices. It was Agent J.

What he was saying wasn't clear. But Paelen was certain he heard the word 'Pegasus'. Agent J was talking about the stallion!

Paelen followed the voices, moving as quickly and quietly as he could. Moment by moment, the agent's voice was getting louder. He approached a short tunnel and saw a light at the end shining through another vent. Through the vent, he heard Agent J speaking to two other men.

He approached the opening. Paelen discovered that if he moved his head just right, he could actually see through the louvred grill and down into the office.

Agent J was sitting at a large desk, his back to the vent. Paelen almost gasped aloud when he saw one of Mercury's sandals sitting on the desk before him. Agent J was waving the second one in the air while he spoke. Paelen looked at the other men and saw the younger one he knew as Agent O sitting before the desk. The third man seated beside Agent O was unknown to him.

'So, what do you think?' Agent J asked.

Agent O shrugged. 'I just don't know. But there are too many coincidences for it not to be true. The kid's test results and the way he sticks to the same story over and over again. Those sandals and that winged horse, Pegasus? What about those creatures in the city? I hate to admit it, but I'm beginning to believe him. I think we might actually be dealing with a bunch of Olympians and not the aliens we first thought.'

Agent J turned to the other man. 'What about you, Agent T?'

'I'm with Agent O,' he said. 'We've had hundreds of men out there combing all the boroughs for signs of a crashed or landed starship. We've contacted NORAD for satellite detection. There just aren't any traces or sightings of anything coming in from space.'

Agent J cursed. 'How the hell am I going to explain

this?' he demanded. 'Command is obsessed with finding extra-terrestrials. More importantly, their technology. Look at all the weapons developed through findings from the Roswell incident! Not to mention the more recent captures. Alien technology is invaluable, and Command expects us to provide information!'

'Calm down, sir,' Agent O said. 'You'll give yourself a stroke!'

Agent J held up a warning finger. 'Don't tell me to calm down! We are the most powerful nation on the planet! Why? Because we have the biggest weapons developed from off-world technology. How will I explain that this kid and that flying horse aren't from outside of Earth, but a bunch of old myths coming true? What's next? Vampires? Werewolves? How about some sweet little fairies riding a unicorn!'

'I know it's hard to digest,' said Agent O. 'But we'd be foolish not to consider it a possibility.'

'What about all the others?' Agent J demanded. 'Jupiter, Apollo, Cupid and all those other mythical characters. Are you suggesting they exist too? And if so, why haven't we heard from them before now?'

Paelen watched Agent O shrug. 'I don't know. Maybe they wanted to keep a low profile,' he said. 'Stay hidden in our modern world. But the myths do say that

Mercury travelled around in winged sandals. Look at what you're holding. What do our scientists say about them?'

'Nothing,' Agent J spat furiously. 'The materials are untraceable! They say these are real diamonds, rubies and sapphires sewn on to the sides. But the feathers on the wings aren't from any known bird species on Earth. Neither is the leather. They just can't tell us where they came from.'

'So our kid could in fact be Mercury?' Agent T asked.

Agent O nodded. 'He claimed that was one of his names.'

Agent J snorted. 'He also claimed to be Hercules, Jupiter and Paelen the Magnificent. I wouldn't put much stock into what he's told us so far.'

'What about the bridle?' Agent T asked.

'Same as the sandals,' Agent J answered sourly. 'Untraceable materials. Yes, it's real gold. But there's a lot more mixed in with it. They found saliva on it too. The DNA doesn't match any kind of known horse. In fact, it doesn't match anything living on this planet. Just like the kid and that creature we have down on the slab.'

'So it could belong to the real Pegasus?' said Agent O.

Agent J sighed heavily, 'Lord, I hope not. We're here to find extra-terrestrials, not Olympians! But we won't know for sure until they get here and we can test the stallion for ourselves.'

Paelen almost jumped from his skin. Had they found Pegasus?

'When should that be?' Agent O. asked.

He saw Agent J look at a small device on his wrist. 'Based on their current movements, I would imagine we'll have them captured and delivered here before noon today,' he said.

'How did you find them?' Agent T asked. 'Last I heard they were hidden in the park.'

'They left the park hours ago,' said Agent J. 'We just brought in two guys from a livery on 50th. They called the police and claimed that four people with a winged stallion broke into their stables and stole a carriage. With that, it wasn't too hard for us to locate the carriage and keep an eye on it.'

'Four people?' Agent O repeated. 'There were only two kids in the photo with Pegasus. Who are the other two?'

'The guys from the livery said one of them was a tall, super-strong woman the others called Diana. They said she carried a spear and beat them both senseless because of the way they treated their horses.'

Paelen had to cover his mouth to keep silent. Diana was in this world! If Pegasus ever told her about him stealing the bridle, he knew there would be no escaping her wrath. But to hear these people were going to bring Jupiter's daughter to this facility with Pegasus was almost too much to bear.

'The other adult with them is a New York City cop, Steve Jacobs. The girl from the picture is his thirteen-year-old daughter. What we don't know is how or why they got involved. Nor do we know who the other kid is. He may be like our Mercury or he may be human. The owners of the stable said that the monsters arrived not long after they broke into the place. I've just seen the photos our guys took of the livery. Those creatures tore through the door like it was butter.'

'What were they after?' Agent O asked.

'The stallion,' Agent J said. 'At least that's what the guys said.'

'What if they get to them before we do?' Agent T asked.

'They won't,' said Agent J confidently. 'We've already got our people in position. Pegasus and the carriage are completely surrounded on all sides. They can't make a move without us knowing it. We've got the 59th Street Bridge locked down and secure. We're just waiting for our prey to enter the trap.'

Agent O shook his head. 'Sounds a little risky to me. If we know where they are, why don't we move in now and grab them. How can you be so certain they'll try for the bridge?'

Agent J stood up. He yawned and stretched. 'Because that's what I'd do if I were them,' he said. 'Look, if we try to take them out in the open, there's a chance that stallion will fly away. We need to get them where he can't use his wings. The centre lanes of the bridge are perfect for that. The bridge itself will work as a giant cage.'

'And you're sure they are going to try to leave the city?' Agent O checked.

Agent J nodded. 'They have to get out of the city before those creatures find them again. That bridge is the closest route off Manhattan. They can't afford to waste time heading further uptown to one of the other bridges. Besides, we've got those covered too. New York City is secure. There is no way off.'

He put down the sandal. 'We've got a few hours left before we close the net. It's been a long night. I'm going to go get some rest. If they arrive here early, make sure they are all separated. I want to talk to each of them alone. Especially the kids. I have a feeling that woman with them isn't human. If she's anything like our Mercury, she won't talk. But I'm pretty certain the kids will.'

Agent T looked unconvinced. 'If Mercury hasn't talked, what makes you so sure about those kids?'

'I'm sure because we know at least one of them is human,' said Agent J. 'And unlike our strange alien or Olympian friend, I'm sure she will prove more susceptible to the persuasive powers of pain.'

Paelen listened in shock. They were planning to torture the human girl he'd seen in the picture with Pegasus. She was just a child! Yet they didn't seem to care.

The men finally left the office, closing the door behind them. Paelen waited awhile to make sure they weren't coming back. When he was certain, he reached forward and applied pressure to one side of the vent. The screws gave easily. But this time, Paelen was more careful. Instead of pushing the grate off completely, he only bent it a bit. When there was enough space, he winced in pain as he forced his bones to stretch out again.

Bit by bit, Paelen manipulated his body until he was

able to pour himself into Agent J's office. He landed softly on the floor. Without returning his body to its natural shape, he reached for Mercury's sandals. Throwing them up into the vent, Paelen quickly climbed back in after them. He secured the vent again, caught hold of the sandals and returned to his normal shape. He quickly took the tunnels back to his own quarters.

Paelen left the sandals in the vent outside his room. With another painful shape change, he slid back into his room and replaced the cover. Once he was satisfied that everything looked normal, he lay back down on the bed. He put the cuffs back on his ankles and wrists and returned to his natural shape.

It had been his plan to escape and find Pegasus. But he knew that his chances of finding the stallion in this strange world were remote at best. Hearing Agent J talking about how they were about to capture Pegasus and Diana and deliver them both to the very same facility, Paelen knew what he had to do. Nothing.

He would suffer their torture and whatever else they planned to do to him. He would not fight them. He would not try to leave. He would wait until the others were here. Then, when the time was right, he would take Mercury's sandals and help Pegasus and Diana escape.

Together they would return to the remains of Olympus.

21

As the carriage travelled slowly along 18th Street, Emily was grateful that no one was paying them much attention. Apart from the helicopters circling the city and the rotten way she was feeling, on any other day she would have enjoyed the ride. She struggled to keep her eyes open. She felt very hot and knew her fever was spiking. Diana still had her arm wrapped around her and was constantly checking her forehead.

'Hold on, child,' she coaxed. 'It will not be much longer.'

In her fevered state, Emily thought she heard her mother's voice speaking gently to her, encouraging her to go on. 'I will, Mom,' she mumbled.

Diana gave her a gentle squeeze. Dimly, Emily heard Diana speaking to her dad.

'Steve, where is Emily's mother?'

'She died three months ago,' he said sadly. 'It hit Em really hard. She and her mother were very close.'

Emily heard her father's response and felt her throat tighten. Her mother would have loved Pegasus and would have been right there fighting alongside them.

'So you are grieving,' Diana said gently. She gave Emily a comforting squeeze. 'My poor, poor child. Now I understand.'

The carriage turned up 1st Avenue. Struggling to keep awake, Emily watched the streets going by. Soon they were passing the United Nations buildings. As each block past, Emily half expected to see Nirads charging at them. But so far, it had been a blissfully quiet trip.

'Steve, do they allow carriages on the bridge?' Joel asked quietly.

'No,' he answered. 'But I've got my badge with me if anyone tries to stop us.'

Soon they were on the entrance ramp to the 59th Street Bridge.

'Here we go,' Steve called. 'Do we want to follow the route that goes under the framework of the bridge, or stay on the uncovered outside lane?'

Pegasus nickered several times and snorted.

Diana leaned forward to translate. 'He says he much prefers to stay in the open in case something should go wrong. He says his wing is feeling much recovered and should be able to carry the carriage if needs be.'

'If he's sure,' Steve said. 'Pegasus, stay to the right. That will take us to the outside uncovered lane.'

As the carriage moved into place, they found the traffic on the bridge was particularly heavy.

'It seems like a lot of other people had the same thought about leaving the city,' Joel said. 'The outside lane is bumper to bumper. Nothing is moving.'

'That area is moving over there,' Diana suggested as she pointed to the centre lanes leading under the cover of the bridge. 'We must go that way to keep moving.'

'You heard the lady, Pegasus,' Steve said. 'Take us on to the bridge and away from Manhattan.'

As the carriage joined the steady flow of traffic, they listened to the strange clip-clopping sound of the stallion's sharp golden hooves on the steel grate of the bridge. The other cars slowed as they passed, but otherwise ignored the horse-drawn carriage.

When they were just over halfway, Emily saw they were passing over Roosevelt Island. She tried to recall the last time she had been here. It had been when her mother was still alive, well over a year ago. They had taken a weekend trek out of the city. She recalled the excitement of going to Long Island and Wildwood State Park. Emily remembered how happy she'd been when they had gone swimming together and—

'Uh-oh,' Steve said. 'This isn't good.'

Drawn from her fevered memories, Emily tried to focus her attention. The traffic was slowing down to a stop.

'Look over there, it's all stopped,' Joel warned as he pointed to the other lanes going in the opposite direction.

Pegasus let out a warning whinny and started to shake his head. His ears were pricked forward and he was baring his teeth.

'What is happening?' Diana asked as she sat forward and looked around.

'I have a bad feeling about this,' Joel warned.

'So does Pegasus,' Diana agreed.

Emily sat up and gazed around the carriage. When she looked towards the back entrance of the bridge, her eyes flew wide in terror. Drawing to a stop several cars lengths back were multiple military trucks. Soldiers were pouring out of the trucks and drawing their weapons.

'Dad—'

Suddenly from both sides of the bridge, a number of armed helicopters flew down from the sky and hovered beside them. Their weapons were pointed directly at the carriage.

'It's a trap!' her father cried.

'And we're in it!' Joel shouted.

'DON'T MOVE! STAY WHERE YOU ARE!' warned a voice from one of the helicopter's loudspeakers. 'YOU ARE COMPLETELY SURROUNDED. STAY WHERE YOU ARE!'

Without pausing, Steve jumped down from the carriage. 'Joel, help me. We've got to free Pegasus!'

Emily tried to stand, but her infected leg wouldn't support her weight. She fell back down to the seat. She could no longer move. All she could do was watch as Diana stood above her and raised her spear in the air. She was preparing to take on the military.

'No, Diana!' Emily weakly reached up to catch the end of the spear. 'They'll kill you. Go with Pegs. Please, get away. Save Olympus!'

'Do not speak nonsense,' Diana shot back at her. 'I will not allow these foolish men to hurt you. If they wish to fight, I am happy to oblige.'

Everybody heard the pounding of many feet on the bridge as soldiers charged at them from all directions.

'He's free!' Steve shouted as he pulled the last of the leather straps away from Pegasus. Joel tore the blanket from his wings and smacked the stallion's rump.

'Go on, Pegasus, go!' Joel roared. 'Get out of here!

Find the Flame and save both our worlds!'

Free of the harness, Pegasus turned and ran back to the carriage. He whinnied loudly at Emily, reached forward and tried to catch her by the shirt to lift her up.

'No, Pegs, I can't move,' Emily cried as she weakly reached for the stallion. 'Please, go. Take Diana and leave here. You can't let them catch you.' Tears sprang to her eyes as she weakly shoved the stallion's head away. 'Please . . . just go!'

'Stop!' Several soldiers had drawn near and raised their weapons. 'Put your hands in the air and don't make a move!'

'Go, Pegs!' Emily shouted with all her remaining strength.

The air filled with strange popping sounds. At first Emily thought the soldiers were shooting bullets at them. But then she saw countless feathered darts strike Pegasus. Within moments, his hind quarters looked like a pin-cushion filled with the colourful darts.

'What is this insanity?' Diana called in fury as she too was struck by the tranquilizer darts. She angrily pulled them from her arms and tossed them away.

Steve and Joel were both hit by the darts. Instantly they fell to the ground, unconscious.

Because of her position, Emily hadn't been hit. But as more men descended on them, Pegasus opened his wing to cover her, taking the brunt of the darts meant for her.

'Don't worry about me, Pegs,' Emily cried. 'Please just go!'

But Pegasus refused to leave. He reared on his hind legs, threw back his head and shrieked in rage. His front legs cut through the air furiously and promised a violent death to any of the soldiers who tried to come closer. Diana joined in the battle cry, raising her spear and preparing to take on the soldiers.

Then Emily felt a sharp sting in her neck as a dart found its mark. She heard Pegasus's enraged cry and saw him lunging forward to attack the soldiers just as everything went black.

22

Emily opened her eyes. She was lying in a hospital bed in a clean white room. There was an IV in her arm, and countless bags of liquid feeding down tubes. Beside the bed was a lot of equipment that had wires attached to her head and chest. They beeped to the steady beating of her heart.

Her wounded leg was suspended in the air, wrapped in a thick layer of bandages. Despite the care, it was still pounding painfully.

'Good morning, Emily.'

A nurse rose from a chair beside the bed. 'Please don't try to move,' she said. 'I'll go get the doctor.'

Emily struggled to remember the last thing that happened. Then it all came flooding back. The bridge. Pegasus screaming. Diana holding a spear and preparing to fight. She remembered the dart hitting her in the neck and blotting out the rest of the world. The final realization put a cold shiver down her spine. The CRU.

Emily tried to rise from the bed. But pain and the fact that her leg was suspended stopped her. Panting heavily, she lay back down. She was in no condition to fight.

The nurse returned with two men. One was dressed as a doctor, but the other wore a dark suit and had a stern expression on his face. Both were middle-aged.

'Good morning, Emily,' said the doctor in a friendly tone that didn't match the coldness of his eyes. 'How are we feeling this morning?'

The other man wasn't even pretending to be nice. Suddenly Emily understood everything her father had ever told her about the secret Government agency. She was in a lot of trouble.

'We?' Emily repeated. 'I don't know about you, but I'm feeling awful.' She looked at the other man. 'Are you the CRU?'

'I work for the Central Research Unit, yes,' he said coldly. 'You may call me Agent J. I have a lot of important questions for you.' He looked at the doctor. 'You may leave us now. Emily and I are going to have a chat.'

'I really should check on my patient,' the doctor said.

'And you will, later,' Agent J said.

His tone suggested there would be no discussion, no argument. His orders were to be obeyed. Without another word, the doctor left the room.

'Where is my father?' Emily nervously asked. 'Please, may I see him?'

'I'm afraid you aren't well enough for visitors,' Agent J said. 'You've still got a very bad infection and have suffered a lot of muscle damage. Actually, you are quite fortunate the surgeons here were able to save your leg. Though I'm sorry to say you will have trouble walking from now on.'

Emily didn't feel particularly fortunate. She felt dreadful. More than that, she was terrified. Where was she? What were they doing to her father and Joel? Were they hurting Pegasus? What about Diana?

'Please tell me. Where is my father?'

'He's around.' The agent moved closer to the bed. 'Our first concern is taking care of you. Perhaps in time, if you cooperate, I will let him come in and see you.'

Emily saw the coldness of his pale eyes. 'Cooperate?'

'Yes, cooperate,' Agent J said as he sat down in the chair beside the bed. 'I have a lot of questions that need answers. And you are just the young lady to give them to me.'

'Me? But I don't know anything,' Emily said. 'I just want to see my dad.'

'First you will answer my questions. Then maybe we'll see about your father.'

Agent J pulled a small recorder from his pocket. He flicked the switch to turn it on. 'Now, I would like you to tell me what happened. Where did you find the flying horse? Where does it come from?'

'His name is Pegasus,' Emily corrected. 'And he's not a horse. He comes from Olympus. He was struck by lightning and crashed on my roof. That's all I know.'

'I'm sure you know a bit more than that,' Agent J coaxed.

'No I don't,' Emily insisted. 'Where is Pegasus? Please, I must see him. He won't understand what's happening to him. He's going to be so frightened of you.'

'The stallion is fine,' the man said. 'He gave us a great deal of trouble in the beginning and killed several of my men on the bridge. But we've managed to calm him down since then.'

Emily was puzzled by his answer. But more than that, she was frightened for Pegasus. She remembered seeing the soldiers with their guns raised on the bridge. 'You didn't shoot him, did you?'

'We had to,' Agent J said. 'He was killing my men.'

'You shot Pegasus!' Emily cried. 'Why? All he was doing was protecting us. How is he? Is he alive?'

'I told you, Emily, he is fine. His wounds have been treated and he is a lot calmer than he was.'

'Why couldn't you leave us alone?' Tears rose in Emily's eyes. 'We weren't hurting anyone. Pegasus just wants to go home.'

'Where is his home?' Agent J asked, looking alert.

'I told you already,' Emily said, sniffing. 'Olympus.'

'Yes, you told me. But where exactly is Olympus?' the agent pressed. 'How do you get there?'

'I don't know,' Emily cried. 'Please, can I see him?'

'Not yet. You are still too ill to move.'

Emily hated to agree with him, but he was right. She really was feeling awful.

'How long have we been here?'

'Four days.'

'What?' she cried as she sucked in her breath.

'I told you, Emily, you have been a very sick girl.' Agent J went on, 'You've got a raging infection. We actually thought we were going to lose you. But you've managed to come back from the brink of death. You're a very determined young lady. So now, I'll ask you again. What do you know of the flying horse? Why is he here?'

'I told you he's not a horse!' Emily shot as she sat up angrily. But just as quickly she had to lie down again as the movement threatened to make her sick. 'He is Pegasus,' she said softly. 'And he shouldn't be here. You've got to let him and Diana go.'

'Ah yes, Diana,' Agent J said. 'A very interesting woman indeed. Remarkably strong. She has managed to resist all our questions. Our scientists are still trying to figure out what she is.'

'She's the daughter of Jupiter,' Emily said, growing angry. 'That's who she is. When he finds out what you've done to her and Pegasus, he's going to be really mad!'

'Jupiter, eh?' Agent J said. 'Well, if they really do come from Olympus as you claim, why hasn't Jupiter come to see us already? What's he waiting for? I would be more than happy to discuss his daughter with him.'

Emily stared into his cold, prying eyes. Something inside warned her to say nothing more. If after four days he still wanted questions answered, it meant her father and Joel hadn't cooperated either. She quickly realized the more she said, the worse it would be for the others. She closed her eyes. 'I don't feel well. I'm so tired. Please, let me sleep.'

'In a moment,' Agent J said. 'Just tell me why Pegasus

and Diana are here.'

'I don't know,' Emily insisted. 'Why don't you ask them yourself?'

Agent J shook his head angrily. 'I did. Diana won't speak to me and I would look like a fool if I tried talking to that horse.'

'Pegasus isn't a horse!' Emily shouted. Her father had always taught her that violence wasn't a solution. But at that moment, she really wanted to smack Agent J right in the mouth. 'He's an Olympian.'

'Horse or not,' Agent J said, 'I want to know why they are here! You are going to tell me.'

'I already told you, I don't *know* why they are here. Just that you've got to let them go. They don't belong in our world.'

'What about Mercury?' Agent J asked.

'Mercury?' Emily repeated, puzzled. 'The planet?'

Agent J shook his head. 'No, not the planet,' he said irritably. 'Mercury, the messenger of Olympus. He's here as well. If their story is true, that makes at least three Olympians in my city. That doesn't even take into consideration those creatures, whatever they are called.'

'Nirads,' Emily answered without thinking.

She realized her mistake at once. Agent J had tricked

her into telling him more than she wanted.

'Nirads,' he repeated. 'Why are *they* here?'

Emily didn't want to answer any more of his questions. She was feeling too ill and making too many mistakes. Instead, she closed her eyes and lay back.

'I want to see my father.'

'Answer my question,' Agent J pressed.

Emily said nothing. With her eyes still closed, Emily could hear his breathing. He was getting angry. Suddenly she felt a searing pain in her wounded leg. Howling in agony, she opened her eyes. A cruel smile hovered on Agent J's lips as his hand pressed down on her raised leg. He was squeezing her wounds in a brutal grip.

'Why are they here?' he demanded. 'Tell me!'

The pain was blinding. Emily had never known such agony. It stole the scream from her throat and drove the wind from her lungs. Stars appeared before her eyes as the sound of water rushed in her ears. A moment later she passed out.

23

Paelen kept his hand over his mouth as he peered through the vent above the girl's bed. He knew the agent could be ruthless by his own interrogations. But he would never have imagined that Agent J could do that to a child.

As he travelled back through the vent, he was grateful that she had passed out. He doubted even he could have withstood that kind of pressure on a new wound. When this was over, Paelen promised himself that Agent J would discover that hurting the girl had been a grave mistake.

Since the others had arrived at the facility, Agents J and O seemed to have lost interest in him. They were spending less and less time trying to get him to talk. He could go a full day without seeing anyone. This gave him the time to slip out of his room to go searching for Diana and Pegasus.

But as Paelen made his way through the long maze

of ventilation ducts, he still had no clue where they were keeping the others from Olympus. He only managed to find Emily's room because it was just down the hall from his own and he'd heard the doctors speaking about her though the air vent.

In the tunnel leading to his own room, Paelen saw Mercury's sandals lying just ahead of him. He pushed them aside to get past and muttered, 'Diana, where are you? I have to find you.'

Paelen was still touching the sandals as he spoke. The tiny wings burst to life and started to flutter and move. Paelen jumped and nearly screamed in the tight confines of the air vent as they beat against his hand. He instinctively threw them away. The wings stopped moving at once and returned to their normal quiet state. Paelen reached forward and cautiously poked the nearest one. Nothing happened. He gave it a second poke. Still nothing happened. He reached forward and picked it up. The wings remained still. He then picked up the second sandal. Again, the wings remained quiet.

'Find Diana,' he said softly.

The wings started flapping wildly again as the sandals sprang to life. Paelen clutched them tightly. But he was unprepared for the sudden twisting and bending in the tight area. If he hadn't had the talent for stretching out his body, the power of the sandals would have broken his every bone as they turned him around in the tight duct area and lunged forward to obey his command.

Biting back his cries of pain and shock, Paelen was wrenched forward. Barely able to see, he was dragged noisily and uncontrollably through the long maze of ductwork in the facility. He held on for dear life. One moment they were going left. Then at another junction, they darted right. A moment later, the sandals dragged him to the edge of a long, deep drop.

'No, please wait!' Paelen cried when he saw what Mercury's sandals were intending. 'Nooooo . . .'

Without pause, the sandals drew him over the edge and plunged downward. Paelen screamed and heard the echo of his terror flooding throughout the endless tunnels. But still they would not stop. Banging his elbows, his shoulder and knees on the walls of the ductwork, they were falling.

The sandals weren't obeying his command to find Diana. They were trying to kill him!

But long before they hit bottom, the sandals changed direction again. They dashed into a new series of ducts that led away from the long drop. Finally they turned down another long tunnel that ended abruptly in an exit air vent.

'Stop, please!' Paelen begged just before they smashed into the vent cover.

They immediately obeyed his command and stopped. The sandals folded their tiny wings and became still. Paelen lay unmoving as he tried to catch his breath. That had been the worst ride of his life. Worse even than the time he'd stolen the sandals from Mercury and had tried to use them. The evil winged monsters had flown him straight into a pillar and knocked him senseless. When he finally awoke, Mercury was looming above him and furious.

But even that hadn't been like this ride of terror. As he panted heavily, Paelen was sure he was going to be sick. Rolling over on to his back, he took several deep breaths and forced his pounding heart to calm.

When he could think clearly again, he turned over on to his hands and knees. He crept forward and up to the louvred vent cover directly in front of him. He gasped when he saw Diana lying on a narrow bed. Thick, heavy chains wrapped around her waist. Other shackles bound her wrists to her waist chain. From what he could see through the vent, her ankles were also shackled to the waist chain. These chains were then secured to the wall behind her.

'I can hear you in there. Show yourself if you dare.'

Paelen paused. This was Diana, Daughter of Jupiter. She was renowned for her ferocious temper. On more than one occasion, he'd seen her bring Hercules to his knees with her biting tongue and vicious strength. Ever her uncle Neptune was frightened of her and did his best to stay on her good side. The only one who could control her was her twin brother Apollo. But Paelen had watched him die in Olympus.

Paelen himself had spent most of his life trying to avoid Diana. If she knew what he'd done to Pegasus, he doubted even those chains could restrain her.

Taking a deep breath, Paelen pushed against one edge of the vent cover. When it gave, he poked his head through cautiously. 'Diana?'

'Paelen!' Diana said furiously. 'I was told you were in this world. You stole Pegasus's bridle! You foul little thief! Do you have any idea what you have done?'

'Please, Diana, forgive me,' Paelen pleaded as, painfully, he stretched out his body to fit through the small air vent. He returned to his normal shape as he knelt before Diana's bed. 'I know it was wrong. I am so sorry. I just wanted to make a better life for myself.'

'By stealing the bridle?'

Paelen nodded. 'I thought if I took it from Pegasus, but then gave it back, he would like me. He might even let me ride him. Then everyone else in Olympus would see that I am as good as the rest of you. Perhaps you might even respect me and see me as more than a thief. I swear I meant no harm.'

'You did that to gain our respect?' Diana said incredulously.

Paelen nodded. 'I just want to be like the rest of you,' he muttered.

Diana shook her head. 'You foolish little boy. You did all of this just to prove that you are like the rest of us? Can you not see? Are you so blind? Paelen, you are an Olympian, just like me. Just like my father and just like my brother was. We are no better than you. But now, the damage you have done is immeasurable. You have single-handedly condemned us all.'

'Me? How?' Paelen cried. 'What have I done other than flee the battle and take the bridle from Pegasus?'

Diana shook her head. 'We needed that bridle to fight the Nirads.'

'I do not understand,' Paelen said helplessly. 'What can it do that Pegasus himself cannot? I have seen what his hooves did to a Nirad. They have a dead one here in this place. He died because of Pegasus, not his bridle.'

'It is not the bridle itself then, but the gold,' Diana explained. 'I did not know that Pegasus could kill them with his hooves. But back on Olympus, we discovered that the gold of his bridle was poisonous to the Nirads. One brief touch and they are weakened. Longer contact will kill them. That bridle was our only hope to make weapons against the Nirads. But now it is gone. Olympus has fallen and my father is in chains. Perhaps now, even dead.'

Paelen sat back on his heels and looked at Diana. In all their long history, he had never seen her look so defeated. As she lay there in chains, the look of despair on her face was more than he could bear.

'You are wrong, Diana. The bridle is not lost. It is here, in this strange place. I have Mercury's sandals. They can lead me to it, just as they led me to you. We can still forge those weapons and defeat the Nirads. Please, let me help. Let me prove to you and everyone else that I am more than just a thief.'

Diana shook her head sadly. 'It is too late. These people have Pegasus as well. They shot him. I saw him go down. He may be dead.'

'He is not dead,' Paelen said. He told Diana what he had heard in the vent above Emily's bed. 'Agent J insisted Pegasus is alive. I know the sandals could take me to him if we want.'

'And Emily? You have actually seen Emily?'

Paelen nodded. 'Her room is very close to mine. But she is gravely ill. Her leg has been badly wounded. Agent J said she almost died.'

'The Nirads got her,' Diana said. 'She and another boy, Joel, bravely fought them to protect Pegasus.'

'That human girl fought a Nirad?' Paelen repeated incredulously.

'She is a very special child,' said Diana. 'When we leave here, we must take her and Joel with us. We need them to save Olympus.'

'I do not understand,' Paelen said. 'How can simple humans save our home?'

'It is too complicated to explain,' Diana said. 'But we need them both if we are to succeed.'

Paelen shook his head. 'That will be difficult. The man, Agent J has already tortured her once to get her to answer questions about us. I have no doubt he will do more to get her to speak.'

'He tortured Emily?' Diana cried. 'I will kill him!' She reared up and strained against the chains that held her. 'He has no idea what he is doing. Without her and Joel, we are all doomed!'

She struggled to pull her hands free of the shackles,

but they wouldn't give. 'I have gone too long without ambrosia. I am weak and cannot break these chains.' She looked up at Paelen. 'I wish I could change my body as you do. It would be little work for you to get out of these.'

Giving up, she lay back down on the bed. 'Paelen, listen to me. If you are sincere in wanting to help, you can. You must use Mercury's sandals and find everyone. Tell Pegasus what has happened and that you wish to help. Tell him about Emily and what Agent J did to her. Then you must find Joel and her father, Steve, and tell them both what you know. We must leave here as soon as Emily is well enough to travel. There still may be time to save both our worlds. But, Paelen, you must be careful. Use all your thieving skills. Do not get caught. If you fail, we all do.'

'I will be careful,' Paelen promised as he stood up. 'I will do this for Olympus.'

Standing proudly before Diana, Paelen stretched out his bones. He tried to hide the pain it caused him so she wouldn't see his weakness.

'I will not fail,' he promised as he lifted himself back into the vent.

24

When Emily woke again, she was alone in her room. Her leg was pounding mercilessly from where that awful man had squeezed it. She remembered his prying questions and the cruel look in his eyes when he told her they'd shot Pegasus. Was he lying? Had Pegs really been shot? Was he dead? What about the others?

Worry weighed heavily on her as she lay alone in her room. The CRU were as bad as her father had told her. Worse, even. Agent J was the most evil person she'd ever met. The last thing she remembered was the cruel smile on his face and sparkle in his eyes as his hand crushed her wound.

Emily took in her surroundings. While she had been unconscious, they had disconnected her from the heart monitor and other machines. But she was still connected to the IV as several bags of fluid fed down into her arm. Whatever was in that stuff was working. She was feeling much better. Though her leg ached, her fever was down and her head was clearer.

In the silence, she became aware of odd sounds coming from above her bed. Looking up, she jumped when she saw fingers quietly pushing through the air vent. The vent came silently away from the wall and two strange long hands came through.

'Hello?' she called out.

She watched, mesmerized, as two extra long, thin arms slid out of the vent; then a mop of dark brown hair and the top of a very strangely shaped head. These were followed by painfully narrow shoulders. Moment by moment more of the snake-like thing seemed to pour itself into her room.

Emily's eyes darted to her door. She wondered if she should call out for help. Was this some new type of creature come to kill her? Had it been sent by the Nirads?

As she opened her mouth to scream, the snake-like thing spoke.

'Do not be frightened, Emily, I am here to help you.'

Biting back her cry, Emily realized it was wearing a hospital gown just like hers. But what was in the hospital gown was the strangest thing Emily had ever seen. It was almost human, with two arms and two legs and a head. But it was profoundly distorted.

The creature landed softly on her floor. Emily heard the sickening sound of cracking bones as the creature shrank back to a more human shape. A young man now stood beside her bed. He was almost handsome, in a strange kind of way. He looked a bit older than Joel but not nearly as big, with warm, smiling brown eyes. As she looked at him, Emily was certain she'd seen his face before. Then suddenly it hit her and her eyes flew wide with recognition.

'Paelen!' she said. 'You're Paelen, aren't you? I saw you steal the bridle from Pegasus. Right before you were both struck by lightning.'

A look of complete shock crossed Paelen's face. 'How do you know me?'

'Pegasus showed me,' Emily said. Then her voice grew angry. 'I saw what you did to him! He wouldn't have been hit if you hadn't stolen his bridle and attracted the lightning.'

'I know. I am very sorry,' Paelen said, dropping his head. 'But I am trying to make up for what I did. I am here to help. Listen to me please as I do not have a lot of time. I have already spoken to Diana—'

'You've seen Diana?' Emily cut in. 'Is she all right? What about Pegs? They said they'd shot him. Did they? Is he alive? I'm so frightened for him. What about my father? Have you seen him and Joel?'

Paelen held up his hands to silence the stream of questions. 'One question at a time, please. Yes, I have seen Diana. She is here in this place with us. She appears unharmed but is in chains. I have not yet seen Pegasus, but I will find him after I leave you. Nor have I seen your father or Joel.' Paelen paused and took a step closer to her. 'I just came to check on you. I was hiding up there,' he pointed up to the vent, 'and I saw what that agent did to your leg. He is a cruel and dangerous man. I have had more than one unfortunate encounter with him.'

Paelen came closer, eager to get his message across. 'Listen to me, Emily,' he said. 'When that man comes back in here, and believe me he will, tell him anything but the truth. But make your claims sound reasonable. Do not refuse to answer his questions. He will hurt you again, much worse than he already has. Diana told me what you did for Pegasus and how you were wounded trying to protect him. She says you and Joel are going to help us save Olympus. But to do that, you must get well. We cannot leave until you are ready to travel.'

'Diana told you that?' Emily said.

Paelen nodded. 'I must now find the others. Tell them what is happening. Then we will make our plans for escape. But only after you are well enough to leave.'

'I'm well enough to leave right now,' Emily said. She reached forward to undo the straps holding her wounded leg in the air. As she did, she started to feel dizzy.

'Stop, you are not well enough!' Paelen said.

'I'm all right,' Emily insisted as she forced herself to move.

'No, you are not.' Paelen said as he caught hold of her shoulders and gently made her lie down again. 'You need a bit more time to recover. I still need to find the others before we do anything. If Pegasus truly has been shot, then he too may need time to recover.'

Emily surrendered. Paelen was right. She really wasn't up to moving around just yet. 'He'll need sugar,' Emily said. 'Pegs won't eat food for horses. He needs sweet things.'

'I know.' A charming, crooked smile crossed Paelen's face. 'I am exactly the same. I do rather like chocolate.'

'Me too,' Emily agreed. 'But the people here think Pegs is a horse. They won't give him what he needs.'

'Then I will,' Paelen said. 'I promise you, Emily, Pegasus will have everything he needs to recover his strength. But what we all need right now is for you to rest. Then we can make our move.'

Emily nodded and lay back into the pillows. 'I guess

you're right. But there is one thing that may change all our plans,' she said.

'What is that?' Paelen asked.

'The Nirads. They are tracking Pegasus and me. Diana says it's because they've tasted our blood. They've been able to follow us everywhere we go,' Emily explained. 'If we've been here four days already, they might be getting really close. Because I don't know where we are, I don't know how far away they could be.'

Paelen nodded and seemed to consider her words. He rubbed his chin, thinking. 'When I was at the place they called Belleview Hospital,' he said, 'the men came to get me. They chained me down to a narrow bed and then carried me in a strange flying machine. We journeyed a short distance, to a tiny island across the water from where we were. This place is deep beneath the ground of that island. But I do not know how deep.'

'A tiny island?' Emily repeated. 'We're on an island just off Manhattan?'

Paelen shrugged. 'I guess. There was a tall statue in the water of a green woman holding a torch,' Paelen went on. 'She was looking at us.'

'A statue of a green woman?' Emily mused. Then she snapped her fingers. 'Wait, you're talking about the

Statue of Liberty! So where could we be? Roosevelt Island maybe?' Then she shook her head. 'No, wait, that's on the other side of Manhattan. Maybe Ellis Island? But does the Statue of Liberty face Ellis Island?'

Paelen looked confused. 'This is your world, not mine,' he said.

Emily nodded. 'Yes it is. But from what I can remember, I don't think Lady Liberty faces Ellis Island.' Then finally it struck Emily. *Governors Island.* When she was younger, the coastguard kids at her school had lived there until they were all moved off and relocated. As far as anyone knew, Governors Island was now empty. What better place to hide a secret Government facility than on an empty Government island?

'Paelen, I know where we are.'

'That is good.'

'No, it's not!' Emily reached out to take Paelen's hand. 'You don't understand. We're on Governors Island. It's too close to Manhattan. If the Nirads can swim, it's just a quick trip across the water and they're here.' She looked intently at him. 'Can Nirads swim?'

Paelen shook his head. 'No. They sink in water. In Olympus, it was the rivers that slowed them down until they discovered other ways of getting across.'

'Can they use boats?' Emily anxiously asked.

Paelen shrugged. 'I do not know. The truth is, I know very little about the Nirads. Until they attacked Olympus, I had never heard of them.'

'We have got to get out of here as quickly as possible. We're so close to the city. I've counted at least fourteen Nirads after us. If they steal boats at the harbour, they could sail over here. Even if we are deep beneath the ground, they are strong enough to reach us.'

'I must tell Pegasus,' Paelen said. 'And you must concentrate on getting better. If it is as you say and the Nirads are close, we must leave here soon.

'I will,' Emily agreed. 'Just find Pegs and tell him what you know,' said Emily. 'Then please find my father and Joel. They've got to know too.'

'Yes of course.' Paelen stepped back from the bed. Emily watched in gruesome fascination as he started to manipulate his body again.

'Does that hurt?' she asked, cringing at the sounds of his cracking bones.

'Yes, actually it does. Rather a lot,' Paelen answered as he finished stretching himself out. 'But it allows me to fit through tiny spaces that no one else can get past. It infuriated Jupiter when I got away from his prison.'

'Jupiter put you in prison?' Emily asked.

Paelen's snake-like head nodded. 'He caught me in

his palace stealing and had me put in prison, but I got away. Perhaps if we survive this, he will forgive me and let me remain free.'

'If we manage to survive this and save Olympus, I'm sure he'll do more than forgive you,' said Emily. 'He'll make you a hero.'

Paelen smiled brightly. 'Do you think he might?'

In his snake-like form, Paelen's smile was horrible to see. Emily averted her eyes to keep from being sick. 'I'm sure he would,' she said.

'Then I will do my best for all of us.'

When Paelen had squirmed through the vent, Emily settled back in her bed. Everything was happening so quickly she could hardly keep her thoughts straight. They were deep underground on Governors Island. Pegasus might have been shot and Diana was in chains. Her father and Joel were hidden somewhere she didn't know, and Nirads were only a short boat ride away.

Emily prayed that Paelen was telling the truth in wanting to help them. Otherwise, she couldn't see how they could get away. As she tried to figure out the best way ahead, sleep tugged at her exhausted body. Before long, she surrendered to its draw and drifted away.

25

Paelen lay in the vent wondering where he should go next. He knew it was late in the evening, as the guards had changed outside his door and activity in the building had slowed down.

He had time. No one would return to his quarters until the next morning. So, should he go to Emily's father? Joel? Or to the one he was dreading most, Pegasus? Facing Diana had been tough, but in the end, she could be reasoned with. But Pegasus would be different. There was no escaping the fact that Paelen had stolen his bridle and had intended to enslave the stallion.

He knew it, and Pegasus knew it. Would he be able to convince Pegasus that he had changed and that he wanted to help? He had to face the stallion some time. It might as well be now.

'Take me to Pegasus,' Paelen ordered.

Immediately the sandals' wings started to flap. Despite

Paelen's attempts to prepare himself to be dragged painfully through the ductwork maze within the building, it was still a rough and bruising experience.

Pegasus was being held in the very deepest part of the facility, down on the lowest level where they were holding the dead Nirad. As the sandals drew Paelen through the ventilation system, he smelled the tunnel leading to the laboratory where they were cutting up the Nirad. He was relieved that the sandals kept moving.

Finally, they started to slow down and made a turn down a duct that ended in a vent. Long before he reached the vent, Paelen smelled the sweet scent of the stallion.

'Stop,' he ordered.

He put the sandals aside and crawled the rest of the distance towards the vent. He peered through the louvers and sucked in his breath when he got his first glimpse of the stallion.

Pegasus was unrecognizable. The only remotely familiar thing about him was his wings. Those were still white, while the rest of him was a terrible combination of dull brown and black. But worse still than his colour was the state of the stallion himself.

Pegasus was lying unmoving in a bed of straw. His

chest and side were covered in thick bandages and his wings were open and held at careless angles. For a moment, Paelen feared the great stallion was dead. But as he watched, he saw Pegasus's sides moving with shallow, strained breaths.

Forcing open the vent, Paelen lowered himself into the room.

'Pegasus?' he called softly.

Nothing.

Paelen called again as he carefully approached the stallion's head. 'Please, it is I, Paelen. I have come to help you.'

When he knelt down beside Pegasus, the stallion woke. As with Diana, Paelen had never seen such pain and despair held within a pair of eyes. Tears sprang to Paelen's own eyes as he lightly stroked the stallion's face.

'I have brought this upon you,' he said miserably. 'Please, please forgive me. Had I known what would happen I would gladly have faced my own destruction in Olympus rather than see you like this.'

Pegasus made a long, deep questioning sigh.

'Emily is here,' Paelen answered as he sniffed. 'She is alive and recovering from her wounds. But she is very worried about you. I will see her later. But what must I tell her of you?'

Pegasus made several weak sounds.

'I will not tell her you are dead!' Paelen cried in horror. 'I will not tell her because you are not dead. You cannot die. You are Pegasus. You must live.'

Pegasus moaned again and tried to lift his head. He looked Paelen straight in the eye.

'Yes, I have seen Diana,' Paelen responded. 'She is here also and is unharmed. But she too is very worried about you.'

Laying his head down, Pegasus made another soft sound.

'Yes, of course we will leave here,' Paelen assured him. 'But *all* of us will go. Together. You are not remaining here, Pegasus. I will not allow it. I know you are wounded and in terrible pain. But you will recover. You just need rest and good food.'

Paelen looked around the room. Emily was right. The people here thought Pegasus was a horse. The food they had brought was not what the stallion needed. With his many wounds, without ambrosia, Pegasus was dying.

'Listen to me, Pegasus. I caused this and now I am going to mend it. Emily needs you. We all do. You will not die. I will go and get you food that will help you heal. It worked for me, it will work for you. But you must fight to live.'

Paelen climbed to his feet and looked down at the fallen stallion. 'Do not give up, Pegasus. Olympus needs you.' As he started to walk away, he called back, 'Emily cares a lot about you too. Think of her.'

Pegasus raised his head and looked at Paelen pleadingly.

'You must take care of yourself,' Paelen said. 'If you die, you will fail her and leave her to the mercy of these cruel people. Agent J has already hurt her once. He will do so again. So please hold on, she needs you. I will return shortly.'

Without further pause, Paelen folded himself into the vent. He reached for the sandals. 'I surely hope you know where to go,' he muttered. Lifting the sandals, he ordered, 'Take me to the kitchens where they prepare our food.'

Paelen had no idea how the sandals worked. But they did. Before long, they entered another tunnel. Paelen's mouth started to water at the sweet smell of sugar.

'Thank you, sandals,' he said as he approached the grill. His keen 'thief' sense listened and felt for any signs of life. There were none. He crawled through a large vent and into a spacious, kitchen. Everything seemed to be made of metal, each surface shining brightly.

The room itself was huge. It would have taken ages for him to find what he needed. But with his own deep hunger gnawing at his stomach and his nose directing him forward, it took little time for Paelen to seek out all the sweet treasures of the kitchen. He found cupboard after cupboard of sugars, sweet syrups and jellies and a huge supply of cooking chocolate. Then he nearly cried with excitement when he found a freezer filled with ice cream. It would take several trips to take it all to the stallion. But with the long night spread out before him, he had time.

Paelen found a large chef's apron. When he laid it out, he was able to fill it with several items, including the first two tubs of ice cream and tied it up into a package. Quick as he could, he climbed on the counter and shoved everything into the air vent, checking over his shoulder to ensure that he had hidden his handiwork. Satisfied that no one would notice his being here, Paelen climbed into the vent after all the food.

'Take me back to Pegasus,' he commanded the sandals, adding quickly, 'but take it slower – I am carrying precious items.'

The sandals obeyed. A short while later Paelen

was back with Pegasus, opening the apron and pulling out the food. He pulled the lid off the first tub of ice cream.

'Here, Pegasus, eat.'

Though weak and exhausted, Pegasus started to lick the melting ice cream from the tub. Before long, Paelen was opening a second. That too was quickly devoured.

When Pegasus had eaten all the ice cream, Paelen poured a bag of sugar mixed with treacle and a bit of water into one of the tubs and offered it to the stallion. Once again, Pegasus drank with relish.

While he held the tub for the stallion, Paelen bit into a bar of cooking chocolate. It was different from what he'd taken from the vending machine, but just as good. But before he was able to finish it, Pegasus reached up to take that as well.

'Of course,' Paelen said as he offered his treat to the stallion. 'You need this more than I.'

For half the night, Paelen worked to get as much as he could from the kitchen to Pegasus. The stallion was completely starved and Paelen worried that it still wouldn't be enough. But finally with less than a quarter of the supplies left, Pegasus let out a sigh and settled down in the straw.

As Paelen sat with the stallion, he apologized, once

again, for being the cause of all their problems. Just before Pegasus drifted off into a deep healing sleep, he fixed Paelen with a look that let him know that they would discuss this when he recovered.

When Pegasus finally slept, Paelen rose to his feet. He looked down on the wounded stallion and felt deep regret for trying to enslave him. He realized he had been just as guilty as the humans in the facility. He'd seen Pegasus as just a winged horse and a fast way to his own riches. He'd never really seen him for the magnificent Olympian he truly was.

'Sleep well, Pegasus,' Paelen said as he quietly walked away. 'Sleep and heal.'

26

Back in the vent, Paelen hid the remaining sugary items deep within the system of tunnels. Pegasus would need more later, and soon, unless the people here understood about their dietary requirements, Diana would be needing these supplies too.

As it was still night and Paelen knew he had time, he picked up the sandals again. 'Take me to Emily's father.'

When the sandals drew him forward, Paelen quickly discovered this was to be his worst journey yet.

It started out much the same as usual. But soon they approached the long, vertical tunnel that connected all the levels of the huge facility. Since they were at the bottom, Paelen looked up and could see countless levels rising above them.

The sandals entered the main tunnel and started to climb. Higher and higher. Paelen recognized the off-shoot that would lead to his and Emily's rooms.

The sandals quickly shot past it and kept climbing. Faster and faster they moved as they flew higher up the facility.

Paelen became aware of the curious sounds of heavy machinery. Then he heard a particularly distinctive whooping sound. Whatever it was, the sandals were drawing him straight towards it.

Paelen also noticed that the closer they came to the sound, the faster the sandals moved. Within the long, dark ventilation tunnel, Paelen couldn't clearly see where he was heading. But as he looked up, his eyes caught sight of starlight shining brightly above him.

The only trouble was the starlight seemed to flicker as though something blocked it and then moved away again. Concentrating on it, Paelen's eyes slowly adjusted to the weak light. He sucked in his breath in terror. The sandals were drawing him towards a large, spinning fan.

This was the heart of the ventilation system. This fan drew the fresh air in from the outside world and forced it down into the deep lower levels of the facility. It was about to slice Paelen to bits.

The huge cutting fan blades were getting closer. Paelen tried to order the sandals to stop, but didn't have time. They were picking up speed. All he had time to do was look up and await his death.

Closer.

Closer.

He shut his eyes and prepared for the worst. An instant later, he felt the air around him swoosh and then change abruptly. Opening his eyes, he was startled to discover that he was now outside the facility and flying higher into the night air.

'Sandals, stop!' he ordered.

Suspended in the air high above Governors Island, Paelen looked down into the wide chimney they had just flown out of. He could still see the deadly blades of the large fan turning. Somehow, the sandals had carried him between them without being hit.

With a deep shiver, Paelen looked away. The lights of Manhattan were shining brightly across the water. A little further away, he saw the same green lady holding her torch, standing in the harbour. Lady Liberty, Emily had called her. While beneath him, Paelen received the largest shock of all.

Houses! Very pretty and very non-threatening houses.

As Paelen looked again at the wide chimney, he saw that it was part of a large brick house. Out front, it had beautiful tall, white pillars, much like some of the homes in Olympus. Further down the well manicured, tree-lined street, Paelen saw a lovely yellow house, sitting amongst a group of pretty homes.

Scanning the area, Paelen couldn't take it all in. He simply couldn't understand how these lovely homes could hide such a dark and dangerous secret. There was no way anyone who looked at this pretty little island would suspect that it held such horrors as the CRU.

Now outside the facility, he wondered where Emily's father was. Just a short way away from where he was suspended, Paelen saw an ancient, squat brick building with bars on the windows. It looked just like a prison. Paelen guessed it would be as good a place as any to lock up Emily's father.

'Take me to Emily's father,' he ordered, expecting the sandals to move him towards the brick building. Instead, they drew him higher into the star-studded sky. They carried him over a large body of water and away from the island. When they finally past over land again, Paelen ordered the sandals to stop.

Wherever he was being held, Emily's father was not on Governors Island.

'Take me to Joel instead.'

They headed back towards Governors Island. Paelen

could see boats in the water, and a few lights on in the houses on the island itself. But as he looked, he didn't see anyone moving around beneath him.

'Wait,' he called. 'Take me down to the ground.'

The sandals settled Paelen gently down in the grass. As he ducked down, he listened for the sound of soldiers or anyone else moving around. All he heard were night insects on the island and the sounds rising from the huge city just across the water. He was alone.

Paelen scanned the area. He suddenly realized that if he wanted, he could simply put on the sandals and tell them to take him anywhere. He could remain in this world, or go back to what was left of Olympus. For the first time in his long life, Paelen was well and truly free.

But even as he considered leaving, he recalled the horrible sight of Pegasus lying on his side. Broken, wounded and defeated. Then there was proud Diana, chained to a wall, starved and unable to move. Finally Paelen's thoughts were drawn back to the girl, Emily, and the sounds of her agonized cries as Agent J pressed down on her wounded leg.

If he left now, he might be physically free. But he could never escape those nightmarish images. And though he may only ever be a thief, Paelen knew he

272

couldn't live with himself if he abandoned the others to the fate of the CRU.

Standing again, Paelen lifted the sandals in the air. 'Take me high enough over the island to look for Nirads.'

Obeying his commands, the sandals lifted him in the air. Paelen used all his senses to look for signs of Nirads attacking the small island. After a thorough search, he was content that there were none. Perhaps they couldn't find a way over here. As he looked out over the short stretch of water that separated them from Manhattan, he wondered if it was enough to keep the Nirads away.

'That's enough,' Paelen finally said to the sandals. 'Take me to Joel.'

27

Paelen arrived at the vent outside Joel's room, still shaking from the harrowing journey back into the facility. Getting out through the fan had been terrifying. Going back in was even worse.

Joel was being held on the same level as Diana. Paelen crawled forward and peered through the louvred grill. The boy was asleep.

'Joel,' Paelen called.

The boy in the bed stirred and moaned.

'Joel, wake up.'

More moans rose from the bed.

Paelen knew full well how brutal Agent J was. If he was capable of hurting Emily while she was wounded, he feared what he might have done to Joel.

He forced the vent open and entered Joel's room. Paelen stood beside the bed and touched the sleeping boy's shoulder. 'Joel, wake up.'

Joel opened his eyes and looked hazily at him.

'Leave me alone,' he moaned.

'Please, Joel,' Paelen whispered, 'Emily has asked me to find you.'

'Em-Emily?' Joel repeated.

'Yes, she is hurt, but recovering. I have seen Diana and Pegasus too. Please, you must wake up.'

Joel's face was bruised and swollen, his eyes bloodshot and heavy. As he pushed the covers back and struggled to sit up, Paelen saw more black bruises on the boy's neck, chest and arms. There were also marks from where the people here had injected Joel with their drugs.

'Who are you?' Joel asked as he tried to focus.

'I am Paelen.'

'Paelen!' Joel repeated. He lunged forward and caught Paelen around the neck. 'You caused this,' he roared as rage cleared his head. Springing from the bed, he slammed Paelen against the far wall.

'None of this would have happened if you hadn't taken the bridle. Pegasus wouldn't have been hit by lightning! Emily wouldn't have been hurt by the Nirads! I should kill you for what you've done!'

Paelen felt Joel's fingers around his neck, but there was no real pressure there. Joel was furious, but he was no murderer. Paelen also knew that Joel had every right to be angry. It was true. He had caused all this. So he did not fight the boy, even though he knew he was much stronger. Instead he let him rant and rage to get it out of his system.

Before long, Joel's energy ebbed and he released Paelen. 'Why?' he demanded furiously, 'why did you do it?'

Paelen saw Joel swaying on his feet. Agent J had hurt him badly. More than just the bruises showing on his arms and body, it was the way Joel was holding himself. His anger had given him strength, but the damage from their interrogation was catching up with him.

Paelen reached out and caught Joel gently by the arms. 'Please, Joel, get back into bed. You are not well.'

'I'm well enough to kick the stuffing out of you!' Joel challenged, looming a full head taller than Paelen.

Paelen smiled. Despite the dire situation, he really liked the spirit of this young human. 'Of course you are. But you should save your energy for the fight to come. Right now, Emily needs you.'

At the mention of Emily's name, Joel calmed and let Paelen lead him back to the bed. 'Where is Emily? How is she? What have they done to her?'

'She is frightened,' Paelen explained. 'She has cause to be. Agent J hurt her. Though I suspect he has hurt you more.'

'I'm fine,' Joel said defensively.

'Did they give you the drug that burns fire in your veins?'

Joel nodded, a shadow creeping across his face. 'What did they do to Emily?'

'Agent J asked her a lot of questions. When Emily refused to answer, he squeezed her wounded leg. The pain was so intense, she passed out.'

'I'm gonna kill him,' Joel spat. 'I don't care if they lock me away for life. I'm gonna kill him for hurting her.'

Paelen chuckled. 'I believe you are going to have to fight Diana and Pegasus for that privilege. You should be very proud of your friend. She told them nothing.'

'I've tried not to talk,' Joel said in a hushed whisper. 'I don't think I told them about the war in Olympus but I can't be sure. I'm so used to fighting, when they hit me, I just laughed at them. But then they used the drugs . . .'

Joel started to shake. The haunted expression was back in his eyes. Whatever they had done to him, it would have a lasting effect.

'It is going to be all right, Joel,' Paelen said softly. 'We will get out of here.'

'How?' Joel asked. 'I don't even know where we are.'

'Emily does. She said we are on Governors Island. We are deep underground, but I am free to go wherever I choose. There are serpents' eyes watching everything in the corridors, but not in the tunnels I use or in our rooms.'

'Serpents' eyes?' Joel asked.

Paelen nodded. 'Agent J says they can see everywhere in here. That is how they knew when I escaped my room. I was in the corridor and they saw me.'

'You mean cameras,' Joel said, finally understanding. He looked around his room. 'You're right. There aren't any. I guess they don't want them in the rooms in case someone made a record of the tortures they do to their prisoners.'

'Perhaps,' Paelen agreed, wondering what horrors they would have witnessed being done to Joel. 'But that leaves me free to visit all of you as long as I use the tunnels. And when Pegasus is well enough to move, we shall escape.'

'What's wrong with Pegasus?' Joel asked. 'Is it his wing again?'

Paelen dropped his eyes in shame. He explained about the stallion being shot. 'I have taken him all the food he needs, but it may be too late. He is gravely ill. I fear Pegasus might be dying.'

Joel's hands shot out and gripped Paelen's arms. 'He can't!' he cried. 'If he does, we're all dead. Pegasus is the only one who can find the Daughter of Vesta!'

Paelen frowned. 'What does Vesta have to do with Pegasus?'

'Hasn't Emily told you why Pegasus came here?'

When Paelen shook his head, Joel told him what he knew of the Daughter of Vesta and the Flame of Olympus.

Paelen started to pace. 'So this is why we were not destroyed when the Nirads extinguished the Flame in the temple,' he said. 'We must get out of this place. Pegasus must complete his mission and get the Flame back to Olympus!'

'No kidding,' Joel said sarcastically. 'What do you think we've been trying to do all this time? But now that we're here—'

'We can get out,' Paelen insisted. 'We just have to ensure that Pegasus lives.'

'You're an Olympian, right?' said Joel after a moment. 'I am.'

'Are you strong like Diana? Can you break me out of this room so we can get to Emily?'

'I am very strong,' Paelen agreed. 'And I can break down this door if needed. But now is not the time to make our move. Pegasus needs time to recover, and so do you.'

'I'm fine.' Joel rubbed his bruised chin thoughtfully. 'OK then, here's the plan. Keep feeding Pegasus sugar, lots of it. The moment he is up again, come back here and break me out. We'll free Emily and then Diana and Steve. There should be enough of us to fight our way out of here. Then we'll go get the Daughter of Vesta and Pegasus can take her back to Olympus.'

Paelen moved back to the vent. He decided not to tell the boy that Emily's father was not at this facility. Instead, he nodded. 'Very good. I will see Emily later today and tell her how you are. If they come back for you, do your best to avoid their questions. It will not be long, Joel. You will be free soon.'

28

Emily was feeling better. The antibiotics they were using were driving away the infection from the Nirad wounds, while the painkillers took the edge off the throbbing pain from her leg. Lying in her bed, she watched the nurse changing the dressing on her wound.

The nurse kept blocking her view of the actual wound.

'How bad is it?' Emily asked.

'Bad enough,' the nurse answered. 'I'm afraid there was a lot of damage. The surgeons did what they could, but the infection went very deep.'

Emily was almost afraid to ask, but had no choice. 'Will I be able to walk again?'

The nurse stopped what she was doing and turned to Emily. 'I really don't know. Possibly, but you'll need help; perhaps a cane or even a brace. But don't think about that right now. Your job is to concentrate on getting better.'

'Then what?'

The nurse stared at Emily a moment longer but then returned to the task of changing the dressing on her leg. Her silence told Emily more than she really wanted to know. The answer was simple. She had no future. When the CRU had finished with her, she would simply disappear.

'Have you seen Pegasus?' Emily finally asked.

'Your winged horse?'

Emily was fed up with correcting the people here. If they wanted to call Pegasus a horse, let them. She knew the truth, and that was enough.

'I'm not allowed to see him,' the nurse replied. 'They've had vets in, though. But from what I've heard, it's not looking too good. I'm afraid the soldiers put a lot of bullets in him. It's doubtful he'll survive.'

'Pegs is going to die?' Emily cried. She tried to climb from her bed. 'I've got to see him.'

'Emily, stop,' the nurse warned, struggling to hold her down. 'You are not strong enough. You could do more damage to your leg.'

Emily began to panic. 'You don't understand. I have to see him. He saved me from the Nirads. I can't lose him. Not now!'

As Emily fought with the nurse, she didn't hear the

code beeping at the door. Nor did she hear the two men entering her room. All she knew was she needed to get to Pegasus.

Suddenly more arms were holding her down and keeping her from leaving the bed.

'Let me go!' Emily howled. 'I have to go to Pegasus!'

'Emily, stop!' Agent J ordered.

'Leave me alone!' Emily shrieked. 'I have to go to him!'

'All right!' Agent J shouted as he and the other man overpowered her and pinned her down. 'All right, if you want to see him so badly, fine. Just stop struggling.'

Emily was panting heavily. She looked up at the agents, her eyes blurred with tears. 'Please, take me to him.'

'We will. But with one condition,' said Agent J. 'After you've seen him, you will answer all our questions. No fighting us, no lying. If you want to see Pegasus, you promise me that you will tell us everything we want to know.'

As Emily stared into his cold eyes, she recalled her conversation with Paelen and how he told her not to hold back but to tell as many lies as she could think of. She nodded. 'If you take me to him right now, I promise I'll answer all your questions. But only after I've seen him.'

Agent J turned to the second man. 'Arrange for a wheelchair, Agent O. If Emily wants to see Pegasus, she will.'

A short while later Emily was settled in a wheelchair and being pushed through the halls of the facility. She almost forgot the pain in her leg as fears for Pegasus overwhelmed her senses.

When they reached the elevator, she noted that Agent O had pressed the very last button. They were keeping Pegasus on the bottom floor.

Once there, they travelled down to a room at the end of a long corridor. As Agent J stepped up to the security lock and prepared to press the code, he looked back at Emily. 'I have your word? You will see the stallion and then answer my questions?'

Saying nothing, Emily nodded.

When Agent J entered the code, he made no attempt to block the key pad. Emily could see each number he pressed and the order in which he pressed them. As the green light flashed and door clicked, she burned the code sequence into her memory.

Agent J opened the door and Agent O pushed her

wheelchair forward. Emily peered into the room and her heart twisted in agony.

Pegasus was lying in hay in the centre of the floor. He was covered in bandages and barely breathing.

'Pegs!' Emily sprang from her chair. But her wounded leg wouldn't support her and she fell to the floor.

Agent J tried to pull her back. 'Emily stop. There's nothing you can do for him now.'

Tears filled her eyes as rage filled her heart. 'Don't touch me!' she viciously shrieked as she swatted his hand away. She ignored the searing pain from her leg and dragged herself over to Pegasus.

'Pegs,' she said softly as her trembling hand reached out to touch the stallion's dark head. 'Pegs it's me. Please, don't die. I need you.'

Emily's tears fell unchecked as she kissed his muzzle. 'Please Pegs, you can't die. You just can't.'

As she lay her head down on his thick neck and wept for the beautiful stallion, Emily heard a subtle change in the stallion's breathing. She didn't know if the others could hear or see it, but she could. Pegasus took a deep, steadying breath. He knew she was there and was responding to her.

'Emily,' Agent J said as he stepped closer. 'I've done as I promised. I've let you see him. Now it's your turn.

Come away from him and we can talk.'

In that instant, Emily somehow knew she mustn't leave him. Pegasus desperately needed her there. She could feel it. But more than that, she needed him too.

Without looking at the agent, she said, 'If you want answers to your questions, you'll get them. But I'll only answer them here. I'm not leaving Pegasus.'

'That wasn't part of the deal,' Agent J said threateningly.

'No,' Emily answered as she glared up at him coldly. 'It wasn't. But now it is. What harm can there be in letting me stay here while I answer your questions? You get what you want, and I get to stay with him.'

'It's not good for you to stay here,' Agent J said. 'What if he dies while you're with him?'

'Then someone who loves him will be the last person with him and not you!' Emily said fiercely. 'But if you try to take me back to my room, I swear I'll never speak another word, no matter what you do to me.'

Anger flashed in the agent's eyes. 'Fine,' he said at last. 'You want to stay with the dying horse while we talk, you can stay.' He loomed over her. 'I hope you appreciate how I am bending the rules for you, young lady. I will expect the same consideration from you. You will answer all my questions without hesitation and with the truth. Do you understand me?'

Emily lay pressed against the stallion's neck and continued to stroke his face. 'I understand perfectly.'

A blanket and two chairs were brought into the room. When the blanket was brought over to her, Emily felt Pegasus tense. He wasn't so far gone that he wasn't aware of what was happening around him. He didn't like the man coming near.

As the CRU agents settled in their chairs, Emily made herself comfortable in the straw. She was as close to Pegasus as she could get, curling neatly in the circle of his neck and head while she stroked his face and scratched his ears. Just being close to him was enough to make her feel better.

'All right, Emily,' Agent J said as he switched on his recording device. 'Let's take it from the very beginning. How is it you came to be with Pegasus?'

Emily took a deep breath. She knew she could never tell them why Pegasus and Diana were in New York; about the Flame or the war in Olympus. But she wanted to spend as much time as she could with the stallion. Taking Paelen's advice, Emily lied.

She began with the truth, talking about the huge storm in the city and how Pegasus was struck by lightning and crashed on her roof. But from there, the truth faded into an outrageous story that equalled the best of the Greek or Roman myths.

Agent J sat forward in his chair. 'And why were they coming here?'

'Well,' she started. 'Diana told me that back in Olympus, a thief had stolen Pegasus's golden bridle. He escaped by using the messenger's sandals.'

'So it isn't Mercury we have locked away here?'

Emily shook her head. 'He's just a thief. Diana said she and Pegasus had been chasing him across the cosmos, going from world to world and through city after city. They finally ended up here in New York. She said they were hit by lightning and got separated. Pegasus crashed on my roof and Diana fell in Central Park.'

'This thief,' Agent J asked. 'Do you know his name?'

'I can't remember,' Emily said, scratching her head. 'But I think Diana said it began with the letter P.'

'Paelen?' Agent O asked. 'Was his name Paelen?'

'Yes!' Emily agreed. 'That's it. Diana said that Paelen had also stolen a sack of gold coins from her father, Jupiter. And that she and Pegasus had come here to get it back before her father found out and lost his temper. She said when Jupiter got mad, entire worlds were destroyed.'

'If he already had the coins, why did Paelen go after Pegasus's bridle?' Agent J mused.

Emily shrugged. 'I guess he's greedy. Diana said Jupiter wouldn't care too much about the coins, but he would be furious if he found out about the bridle. So they were hoping to get it back before he noticed.'

'Gold is gold,' Agent J said lightly. 'He had enough, but wanted more.'

'Wait,' Agent O said. 'There's more to this. The myths say that whoever possesses the bridle of Pegasus can control the stallion.' He concentrated on Emily. 'Paelen wanted Pegasus, didn't he?'

This was the first Emily had heard of the myth. She shrugged. 'I don't know. Diana never said. She just told me they needed to get everything back before her father found out. But now the bridle and coins are lost, there's no telling what he'll do.'

'The bridle isn't lost,' Agent O said. 'We have it here.'

'You do?' Emily said. 'Really? Do you have the coins too?'

Agent O shook his head. 'No coins, but we had the sandals.'

'Had?' Emily said, as she continued to stroke Pegasus.

Agent J nodded. 'But it seems someone has taken them.'

Emily shrugged. 'Maybe they flew away. Diana told me the sandals have a mind of their own. Maybe they flew back to Olympus.'

'Maybe,' Agent J said, not sounding convinced. 'Or we could have a thief in our midst. So, tell me, where is Olympus?'

Emily shook her head and answered with the truth. 'I swear I don't know.' She looked down on Pegasus's closed eyes. 'Diana told me that Pegasus was her only way home. If he dies, she's going to be trapped here.'

'No, that's not right either,' Agent O said. 'The ancient myths said the Gods were always coming to Earth. There was never anything written about Diana riding Pegasus. Whenever she came here, she came of her own power. What has changed?'

'I don't know,' Emily shrugged. 'Diana doesn't talk to me much. I don't think she likes me. She's really mad at what Joel and I did to Pegasus when we dyed him these colours to keep him hidden from you. She nearly killed us when she saw him.'

'No wonder she's mad,' Agent O said. 'Look at the mess you've made of her cousin.'

'Pegs is her cousin?' Emily repeated in genuine surprise.

'Diana is the daughter of Jupiter, right?' said Agent O. When Emily nodded, he continued. 'Well, the myths say that Pegasus came from a union between Medusa and Neptune. As everyone knows, Jupiter and Neptune are brothers. So that would make Pegasus and Diana cousins.'

Emily looked at Pegasus. 'Medusa and Neptune are his parents?' she repeated. 'How is that possible?'

'You tell us,' Agent J said. 'You're the one who's claiming they all come from Olympus. You're the one who's spent time with them. Surely they must have told you this.'

'Pegasus can't talk,' Emily said. 'All I know is what Diana told me. And like I said, that hasn't been a lot. She really hates me because of what we did to Pegs.'

'From what we've seen, Diana hates everyone,' Agent J finished bitterly. 'But what did she tell you about the Nirads? Why are they here? And more over, why were they trying to kill you and Pegasus?'

Emily had been dreading this question. What could she tell them that would sound reasonable? Joel was the one who knew the Roman myths, not her. But she knew that if she didn't say something, they would take her away from Pegasus and she couldn't let that happen.

'I was hurt by accident,' she finally said. 'The Nirads weren't after me. They seemed to be after Pegasus. I was just in the wrong place at the wrong time and this one Nirad got hold of my leg.'

'But what are they?' Agent J pressed. 'Why are they here?'

'I don't know,' Emily answered honestly. 'Even Diana doesn't know. All she told me was that for some reason, they were after Pegasus. Probably because he can kill them when no one else can. She said the last time the Olympians had enemies was long ago. There had been a big war with this other race. But I can't remember their names. Maybe they sent the Nirads here to get Pegasus.'

'The Olympians were at war with the Titans,' Agent O offered.

'Yes, that was the name Diana said,' Emily quickly agreed. She looked at Agent J. 'I don't know why you are asking me all these questions when he,' she pointed at Agent O, 'seems to know all the answers.'

'I studied the myths,' Agent O responded. 'That's very different from knowing the answers to these questions. If Pegasus and the others really are from

Olympus, then the old tales may be true. But if that's the case, where have they been all this time?'

'Finally a question I can answer,' Emily said as she offered up another plausible lie. 'I asked Diana the very same thing. She said that we didn't need the Olympians any more. So they stayed in Olympus and stopped coming to our world. She said her father says it's too dangerous with all our new weapons and technology. He's actually forbidden anyone from coming here, which is why Diana and Pegasus were chasing the thief. They didn't want him captured and the secret of their existence getting out.'

'Then it seems they haven't done a very good job of it, have they?' Agent J said sarcastically. 'But that still doesn't answer the question of the Nirads. If Diana needs the stallion to fly, what means of transportation are the Nirads using?'

Emily paused. That was a good question. How were the Nirads getting to New York?

'I honestly don't know,' she said truthfully. 'Diana never told me. She said she used Pegasus and the thief used the messenger's sandals to get here. But she never did say how the Nirads were getting to New York. My dad told me that at the beginning, there were reports of four-armed demons coming out of the sewers.

But that still doesn't explain how they got here or if there are more on the way. I'm really sorry, but I just don't know.'

Agent O looked at his companion, 'I think she's telling the truth,' he said. 'She really doesn't know. We have to get these answers from Diana herself.'

'That woman is impossible,' Agent J said, looking furious. 'We stand a better chance of getting blood from a stone! Nothing works on her. Paelen's just as bad. Drugs? Torture? Threats? Nothing loosens their tongues. Emily here is our only hope of getting at the truth.'

He concentrated on Emily again. 'OK, let's try this again from the top. Tell us once more what happened on the night of the blackout?'

Emily finally settled back in her bed, wrung out and exhausted. She had no idea how long the agents had questioned her, but it had to be for most of the day. They kept repeating the same things over and over again, trying to get her to make a mistake and tell them something more.

With Pegasus lying beside her and Paelen's warning ringing in her ears, Emily had been careful not to deviate from her story. She was just grateful they'd stopped when they had. She was growing increasingly fatigued and had to concentrate harder to keep all the lies straight in her head.

When the interrogation finished, Emily begged to be allowed to stay with Pegasus. But Agent J denied her request. She could see how much pleasure it gave him to say no.

As they tried to draw her away, Emily felt Pegasus stirring. Lying against his neck throughout the long day, she'd grown aware of his pulse getting steadily stronger beneath her. He was quickly coming back to himself. But as he did, she became frightened that he might try to move against the men. If he did anything, she felt certain Agent J would have him killed so they could dissect him to see how his wings worked.

To warn the stallion, Emily threw herself across his neck and started to wail hysterically that she didn't want to go. When two orderlies came forward to drag her away, she was able quickly to whisper in the stallion's ear: 'Please don't move, Pegs. I'll be back.'

Continuing with her hysterics, Emily felt him calming. He wouldn't move. She was finally pulled away from him, settled in her wheelchair and taken back to her room.

29

Paelen spent as much of the day as he could in the ductwork outside the room where they held Pegasus. He had marvelled at the stories Emily told the men. The lies equalled anything he could have made up. For a human, she would have made a great thief.

When everyone had left, Paelen quietly entered the room and delivered more sweet food to the stallion. He was amazed at how much better Pegasus was. He knew it had something to do with Emily. Pegasus tried to hide it, but Paelen clearly saw the connection between the stallion and the girl.

After making sure Pegasus had everything he needed, Paelen headed back towards Emily's room. He arrived moments before everyone else and waited silently in the air vent. Soon he heard the lock code chiming for her door. It was the same as his.

Crouching back further in the duct, he saw the door open.

'It's been a long day,' Agent J said. 'I want you to rest. Then tomorrow we can take up where we left off.'

As the nurse and orderly lifted her into bed, Emily looked up at Agent J. 'I don't understand. I told you everything you asked me. I don't know anything more.'

'Now, that's not entirely true is it, Emily?' Agent J said suspiciously. 'I'm sure there are a few bits and pieces you've been holding back.'

'No there's not,' Emily insisted. 'You said I could see Pegasus if I told you the truth. I did. There's nothing more to tell.'

'Emily, you spent several days with the stallion,' Agent O pointed out. 'And more than enough time with Diana to know what's going on and why they are really here.'

As Emily started to protest, Paelen saw Agent J hold up a warning finger. 'Don't bother. I know you are still holding back on us. Rest tonight, because tomorrow we are going to discuss everything again.'

Without another word, they left the room. While the orderly set up her dinner tray and rolled it closer to the bed, the nurse helped Emily get her leg settled in the support strapping.

'If I were you, I'd tell them what they want to know,'

the nurse warned. 'Those agents are not nice men.'

'I've already told them everything,' Emily cried. 'What more do they want?'

'They want the truth. And one way or another, they are going to get it. But how they get it is up to you.'

'What do you mean?'

'You can give them what they want. Or believe me, they know ways you've never imagined to get everything out of you.'

Emily threw up her arms in the air. 'How can I tell them what I don't know?'

'I don't know, dear. But by morning, you'd better have more to say or tomorrow could very well be the worst day of your life.'

When she finished, the nurse and orderly left the room. Emily angrily shoved the tray table away from the bed.

'I would eat if I were you,' Paelen called softly down from the vent. 'You do not know when you might be fed again.'

Emily's eyes shot up to the vent. 'Paelen!'

The thief's fingers gently pushed the grill away from the wall. After seeing him do it yesterday, watching him stretch out his body wasn't quite as horrifying;

though the sounds of his cracking bones still set her nerves on edge.

'I'm so glad you're here,' Emily said. 'Did you hear what the nurse said to me? They're going to torture me tomorrow.'

Paelen nodded. 'I also heard what you told them today when you were with Pegasus.'

'You were there?' Emily said incredulously. 'How? I didn't hear you in the vent. Don't they miss you when you leave your room?'

'You forget I am a thief,' said Paelen. 'Keeping silent is one of my special skills. They gave up checking on me once they discovered that they can not make me speak. They leave me alone for most of the day and all night. They seem to have concentrated all their efforts on you. Though I must admit Joel has not had it easy either.'

'You've seen Joel?' Emily asked anxiously. 'How is he? How is my father?'

'Joel is relatively unharmed,' Paelen said. 'But I am sorry to say they have used violent force on him to get him to speak. Much to his credit, so far, like you, he has told them very little. But I do not know how much longer he can hold out against their torture. He is angry, but also very determined. He attacked me the first time he heard my name.'

'Sorry, that was my fault,' Emily said sheepishly. 'I told him what you'd done to Pegasus with his bridle. But Joel is really nice once you get to know him. He's angry on the outside, but really gentle on the inside.'

'He has calmed somewhat.' Paelen pushed the dinner tray back to Emily. 'Now, please eat. You will need your strength for what you are facing.' Paelen saw the fear rising in her eyes. 'Whatever happens, Emily, I will be there with you. Please don't give up.'

'I won't,' Emily said as she picked at her food. She reached for the bowl of chocolate pudding and handed it to him. 'Here, you need this more than me.'

Paelen gratefully accepted the pudding. He had been back to the kitchens several times, but most of the sugary foods he'd stolen had gone to Pegasus and Diana to build up their strength. He had kept very little for himself.

'How do you think Pegasus is doing?' Emily asked as she ate without interest.

'Recovering,' Paelen said. 'He is eating well and his strength is returning.'

'He looked dead when I first saw him today,' Emily said. Her voice shook. 'It really scared me. But then his breathing became steadier and he moved a bit.'

'Pegasus really cares about you,' Paelen told her. 'I have no doubt that seeing you today did more to help him than all the ice cream I have been taking to him.'

Emily smiled and it brightened her whole face.

'He sure does love his ice cream,' she said. Then her expression dropped. 'We've got to get him out of here. You and Diana too. You don't belong in this world. If we don't go soon, I'm afraid they will kill Pegasus just to see how he works.'

'I have a similar fear,' Paelen admitted. 'I have pushed my luck to the limit. They are furious at me for not cooperating. If I am not careful, I am sure they will try to kill me too.'

'OK,' Emily said. 'So when do we go?'

Paelen studied her in fascination. He could see the ideas spinning around in her head. 'Soon,' he answered.

'You must get Pegasus's bridle to Diana so she can make weapons with it to take back to Olympus,' Emily said. 'That's the only thing that can kill the Nirads. Then we've got to get my dad and Joel out of their rooms.'

Paelen sucked in his breath and held it. Finally he let it out slowly. 'Emily, there is something I must tell you. Your father is not here.'

A frown creased the smooth skin between her brows.

'What do you mean he's not here?' she asked. 'He has to be here.'

Paelen shook his head. 'Mercury's sandals will take me anywhere I tell them to,' he told her. 'Last night I instructed them to take me to your father. They carried me out of this place and high up into the night sky. We crossed over the water and were moving away from this small island.'

'Where is he? Where did the sandals take you?'

'I do not know,' Paelen admitted. 'I told the sandals to stop. I had them bring me back so I could help all of you.'

'Wait,' Emily said puzzled, 'so you were out of here? You were free?'

Paelen nodded.

'Why didn't you go? Diana said you were a thief that only thought of yourself. I don't understand.'

'I could have left,' Paelen said. 'I must admit, I did consider it for a moment. But then I thought of Pegasus and Diana. What would happen to them? And then I thought of you. I realized I could not leave you to the mercy of these people.'

'So you came back for us?'

'Yes,' Paelen admitted. 'I am the only one who can reach everyone. It is me who can help free all of us from this wretched place.'

Paelen saw the deepening confusion in her face. Could she really think so ill of him that she couldn't imagine he could change?

'I am so sorry I could not find your father.'

Tears were rimming Emily's eyes. 'Do you think he's dead?'

'I do not think so. The sandals were taking me to him,' Paelen pointed out. 'I doubt that they would have done so if he had died. For reasons I do not know, they are holding your father elsewhere.'

'But where?' Emily said. 'And why? What are they doing to him?'

'I am sorry, I do not know,' Paelen said softly. 'But the rest of us can get still get away. Then perhaps we can find your father and free him.'

Emily sniffed back her tears and wiped her nose. 'We still need that bridle first.'

'Then I shall go get it,' Paelen promised. 'I will bring it back here and then we can plan our escape.'

30

When Paelen was gone, Emily lay back and tried not to let fear for her father overwhelm her. But it was impossible. She had yet to meet one nice or decent CRU agent. They were all just as cruel and evil as her father had told her.

Were they torturing him right now? What were they doing? Paelen had said that they had already tortured Joel to get him to speak. What had they done to him?

As she settled, she tried to calm herself. It wasn't completely hopeless. Paelen was free to wander the facility. He was clever and agile. But more than that, he cared. With his help, they would get back down to Pegasus. Then they could free Diana and Joel and start to look for her father.

Emily replayed the events of the day in her mind. Not the questions and not the frightening faces of the agents, she thought about Pegasus. At first, he had seemed so vulnerable. But as the day progressed, she definitely felt him growing stronger. She knew he was pretending to be weaker than he was. Pegasus understood that if he made a move, he would put all of them in danger. So he did as she asked and played along.

But would Pegasus be strong enough to rise and escape with them? If he couldn't get up, would the four of them be strong enough to lift and carry him?

Emily was just starting to calm herself when loud, shrieking sirens burst through the silence of the facility. She sat up and listened to the sudden pounding of heavy footsteps and shouting in the hall outside her door. It seemed like countless people were running up and down the halls in a panic.

Paelen! she thought as fear gripped her heart. *He's been caught!* The thought tore through her brain like a bullet. All their plans for escape vanished in an instant. Paelen had been their only hope to get away. Now that was gone.

But just as despair threatened to crush her completely, Emily heard Paelen's voice calling her name urgently above the din of the angry alarms.

'Emily!' he cried through the vent.

Emily looked up and saw him shove the vent open. He cried out in pain as he stretched out his body faster than she'd ever seen before and poured himself through the vent. She saw the light glinting off the golden bridle he clutched in his hand.

'Paelen, they know you've escaped!' Emily cried. 'You must get out of here! Get the bridle to Diana and then go to Pegs. You can't get caught now.'

'It is not I who has caused this mayhem. It is the Nirads. They are here! They have come for you and Pegasus!'

'Nirads!' Emily cried. 'I thought they couldn't cross water.'

'It now appears they found a way,' Paelen said. 'I must get you out of here.' He was bending down to put on a beautiful pair of sandals. They had tiny wings and were covered in jewels. Emily gasped. Mercury's sandals!

'Paelen, look at my leg,' she said. 'I can't walk. Leave me here. You've got to free Diana and Pegs. You're their only hope. Please save them.'

'I will,' Paelen promised. 'But I just saw Pegasus. He is up and moving around. He said he would kill me if I did not bring you to him. I have betrayed him once. I will not do so again.'

Paelen threw back her covers and went to undo the support on her leg. 'I am sorry, but this may hurt.'

'I don't care about that,' Emily said. 'Just get me

306

free.' She winced while her leg was undone from the support straps. 'Have you seen the Nirads? How many are there?'

'I have not seen them,' Paelen admitted. 'But I can smell them. There are more than a few. The men of the facility are gathering to fight them. But they will fail. We do not have a lot of time before they reach us.'

Paelen handed the golden bridle to Emily. 'Here, keep hold of this. If a Nirad comes near us, hit him with it,' he said. 'But do not throw it at him. We will need it.' He turned and offered her his back. 'Climb on. These sandals can carry both faster than I can run.'

Emily held the bridle carefully and climbed on to Paelen's back. 'Am I too heavy for you?' she asked.

He turned to give her a crooked grin. 'Hardly! Now hold on.'

Paelen carried Emily over to the door and pressed the code to open the lock. As they entered the hall, the sounds of the alarms reached a terrifying pitch. Emily was shocked to see a mass of armed soldiers charging through the long corridor.

'You two, get back into your room,' ordered one of the men as he charged past.

Paelen ignored the order. 'Are you ready?' he shouted above the sirens.

'Go!' Emily shouted.

She clutched Pegasus's bridle and wrapped her arms tightly around Paelen as he shouted a string of strange words. Suddenly they were jerked up into the air.

'Get me to Diana as quickly as possible!' Paelen ordered.

When Paelen said the sandals could move faster than he could run, Emily had no idea just how fast that could be. She held on for dear life as the sandals darted them forward through the crowds of soldiers in the corridor. When they approached the stairwell, Paelen barely had time to hold out an arm to push the door open before the sandals drove them through.

They flew down the stairs at a terrifying pace, knocking soldiers out of the way as they went. When they reached Diana's level, the terrifying grunts and roars of Nirads could be heard from above.

'They're in the stairwell!' Emily called into Paelen's ear.

Paelen cursed. 'Hold on tighter, I am going to order the sandals to move faster.'

'Faster?' Emily shrieked.

In the time it would have taken for Emily to scream

in terror, the sandals tore through the stairwell doors on Diana's level and flew down the corridor, coming to an abrupt stop outside a locked door.

As the area emptied of soldiers heading towards the stairwell, Paelen lowered Emily to the floor. 'Stay well back, I am going to break it down.'

Standing on her good leg, Emily watched Paelen approach the door. 'Diana, it is I, Paelen!' he shouted through the door over the alarms. 'Get out of your chains if you can. The Nirads are here. We must go!'

He stood away from the door and looked down at the sandals. 'Lift me up,' he cried, 'and break down the door!'

Obeying the order, the sandals lifted Paelen in the air. Then as their tiny wings flapped at a speed too fast to see, Paelen let out a short cry. Emily wasn't sure whether it was a battle cry, or the sheer terror of flying feet first into a heavily secured door. Whatever it was, it rose well above the screaming alarms as he was carried forward and used as a battering ram to smash down the door like it was made of popsicle sticks.

The door exploded under the impact of Paelen's body. Emily hopped over to the threshold and peered in. Paelen was lying in an unconscious heap in the corner.

'Emily!' Diana cried, tearing away the last of the chains restraining her. 'I am so pleased to see you!' She knelt and checked Paelen for serious wounds. 'Foolish little thief,' she said gently. 'There must have been a better way for you to open the door without knocking yourself silly.'

'There wasn't time,' Emily said. 'The Nirads are in the stairwell. Soldiers are fighting them, but it won't take them long to get to Pegasus.'

'Then we must get there first,' Diana said.

She pulled Paelen into a sitting position and started to lightly slap him across the face. 'Come Paelen, wake up. Our journey is just beginning.'

Paelen let out a soft moan and slowly opened his eyes. When he saw who was supporting him, he eyes opened wider. 'Diana!' he cried in alarm.

'Do not fear me, little thief,' Diana said. 'You have earned my respect. Are you well enough to rise?'

Paelen nodded and shakily climbed to his feet. 'Nirads!' he cried. 'They are here.'

'Emily has told me,' Diana nodded. 'We must get to Pegasus.'

'And Joel,' Emily said. 'We can't forget about Joel.'

'Of course not,' Diana agreed. 'We will collect Joel first and then get to Pegasus.' Diana noticed Emily carrying the golden bridle. 'You have the bridle!'

Emily offered it to Diana, but she shook her head. 'No, child, you keep hold of it. You may need it if the Nirads reach us.'

Finally recovered, Paelen stepped to the doorway. 'Joel is being held on this level as well. He is not far from here.'

Diana helped Emily climb back on to Paelen's back. 'How is your leg?' she asked.

'Not great,' Emily admitted. 'But I won't let it slow us down.'

In a move that surprised Emily, Diana leaned forward and kissed her lightly on the cheek. 'That is my brave girl. Come now, we must go.'

Breaking down Joel's door was not quite as dramatic. With both Olympians using their superior strength, the lock could not hold, and before long it shattered and swung open.

Emily was grateful to see that Joel hadn't been chained. He was standing in the centre of the room waiting for them.

'You took your time getting back here,' he complained to Paelen. Then his eyes settled on Emily and he embraced her tightly. 'I've been so worried about you!'

'Me too!' Emily agreed, hugging him back. 'Joel, the Nirads are here. We've got to get to Pegs!'

Joel looked at the small group. 'Where's your dad?'

Emily fought down the emotions that threatened to bring tears to her eyes. 'He's not here. They've taken him somewhere else. But I don't know where.'

Joel hugged her again. 'Don't worry, Em, we'll find him.'

'We will not be finding anyone if the Nirads get us,' Paelen warned. 'We must get to Pegasus and get out of here!'

Emily was once again lifted on to Paelen's back and they made their way to the stairwell.

'They are holding Pegasus on the lowest level,' Paelen said 'Though I do not like the thought of going in the stairway again. The Nirads are coming down from above.'

'We have no choice.' Diana pushed through the doors and led the way forward. Several levels above them, everyone heard the ferocious sounds of Nirads mixed with the sound of gunfire and screaming men.

'They are getting closer,' Diana warned. 'We must move swiftly.'

They turned a corner – and came face to face with Agents J and O.

'Don't move!' Agent J ordered, drawing his weapon.

'Do not be a fool,' said Diana dismissively. 'The Nirads are here. They will kill you and everyone else in this place. They want Pegasus. If we move him, they will follow us. Your men need not die.'

'You aren't taking that horse anywhere!' Agent J said.

'Horse?' Diana roared in a fury. 'You called him a horse?'

In a move as fast as lightning, Diana charged forward. 'How dare you!' she cried as she shoved both agents against the wall with the force of a freight train. 'He is PEGASUS!'

The men didn't stand a chance against the enraged Olympian. The wind was driven from their chests with such force that they were instantly knocked out and crumpled to the ground.

Diana stepped over them. 'Consider yourselves fortunate,' she told their unconscious forms. 'Had I the time, I would show you how furious I really am for what you have done to Emily and Pegasus.'

Instead she pushed through the stairwell doors with enough pressure to wrench them off their hinges.

Emily looked over to Joel. He shrugged fearfully.

They entered Pegasus's corridor where the few soldiers they met gave them a wide birth. They had seen the stairwell doors come flying off their hinges and didn't wish to engage the angry Olympian.

'Pegasus is there at the end,' Emily said, pointing at the large door she'd been taken to. When they reached it, Paelen put Emily down and prepared to force the door open with Diana.

'Wait,' Emily said. 'I know the code. You don't have to break it down.'

Joel supported her as she hopped over to the keypad and punched in the code she'd seen Agent J use. Immediately a tiny green light flashed and the door opened.

Even before she entered, Emily heard the best sound of her life: a whinny from Pegasus. As she crossed the threshold, her heart swelled at the sight of the stallion standing.

'Pegs!' She threw her arms around his thick neck, feeling his strength. 'Oh Pegs,' she cried. 'I thought you were going to die!'

'He still might unless we get out of here,' Joel warned. 'Have we forgotten the Nirads? You know, four arms, long teeth, smelly. They're in the stairs. If we don't move now, they'll trap us down here!'

'He is right,' Diana said. She stepped up to Emily. 'May I have the bridle?'

When Emily handed it over, Diana used her amazing strength to tear the gleaming gold bridle into several large pieces. 'I am sorry we do not have time to forge better weapons,' she said as she handed everyone a piece. 'But for the moment these will have to do. If the Nirads come near you, stab them with it. The gold will kill them. Keep hold of it. It is our only defence.'

Diana handed the largest, sharpest piece to Emily.

'No, you should keep it,' Emily protested. 'You're a better fighter than me.'

'But you are more important,' Diana said.

'What?' Emily said in confusion. 'No I'm not. You and Pegasus are. You should keep it . . .' Emily saw something resting deep in Diana's eyes.

'Oh,' she said softly.

Pegasus whinnied with impatience, his ears forward and his eyes wild.

'They draw near,' Diana said. She turned to Paelen. 'Help me get Emily on Pegasus. He will take charge of her now. The rest of us will fight if we need to.'

Emily tried her best to stay quiet as they lifted her on to the stallion's back, but cried out as her wounded leg was manoeuvered into position.

'I am sorry child,' Diana said gently. 'When this is over, we shall take care of your leg.'

Tears from the pain rose in Emily's eyes, but she said nothing as the fighters fell into position. Diana took the lead. Paelen stood a pace behind her. Then Joel. Emily could see the fear in her friend's bright eyes, but there was determination in his stance. He was prepared to fight and die with the Olympians.

'All right,' Diana said. 'When we move forward, we must make for that big metal box that will transport us to the surface.'

'It's called an elevator,' Emily said. 'There's one at the other end of the corridor.' She caught hold of the stallion's mane. 'We're almost there, Pegs,' she said softly.

Pegasus stole a quick glance back to her and nickered softly.

Diana led the group forward. As they ran past the stairwell entrance, Emily noticed that Agents J and O had disappeared. The loud guttural sounds of the Nirads were getting closer. It wouldn't be long before they reached this level.

'Run!' Diana shouted. 'Get to the elevator before they reach us!'

Everyone charged forward. As they reached the freight elevator, Joel pushed the button. He bounced on his feet impatiently. 'I hope this thing is still working!'

'If it is not, we are all in trouble,' Paelen finished.

Moments before they heard the *ping* of the elevator's arrival, the first of the Nirads reached the bottom level. They charged into the corridor and faced the group. With recognition burning in their black eyes, they charged forward furiously.

'Hurry!' Joel cried. 'Please hurry!'

When the freight elevator doors opened, Emily ducked down and Pegasus entered. Joel was right behind them. But when they turned, Diana and Paelen did not follow.

'Diana, Paelen, come on!' Emily cried. 'Hurry before they get here!'

Diana shook her head. 'No child, I must stay to keep the Nirads from you.' She looked at Pegasus. 'You know what is at stake. Do not worry about me. Get the Flame to Olympus!'

Pegasus quivered. He whinnied loudly and pounded the floor with a golden hoof.

'No, I must stay,' Diana repeated. 'Tell my father what has happened. Free Olympus, Pegasus. It is up to you now.'

'Paelen, Diana, please,' Emily begged.

Just as the door started to close, Emily saw Paelen give Diana a brutal shove. She lost her balance and fell into the elevator at Pegasus's feet. As the doors closed, Emily heard Paelen cry: 'Forgive me!'

31

'Paelen!' Emily shouted. Quickly, she turned to Joel. 'Open the doors! We can't let the Nirads get him!'

'No!' Diana rose to her feet and blocked Joel's path. 'Paelen sacrificed himself for us. We must not dishonour him by failing.'

'But they'll kill him!' Emily cried.

'Yes, they will,' Diana said grimly. 'But while they do, he has given us time to escape.'

Emily felt her heart breaking at the thought of those terrible creatures tearing gentle Paelen to pieces. 'Paelen . . .' she whimpered softly as the elevator rose slowly.

When the doors opened, they were met by a terrible sight. Dead and wounded soldiers littered the floor. The sounds of moaning and crying from the injured men added to the horrible sense of loss. Emily couldn't work out where they were.

It looked like a house; a beautiful, Southern-style

house. They emerged in a large lounge. Antique furniture lined the walls and rich, deep carpet covered the floor. Surely this couldn't still be in the facility?

'Where are we?' Joel asked in equal confusion as his eyes scanned the room.

'Governors Island,' Emily said. 'But I didn't know they had houses like this here.'

'Come, we must move,' Diana warned.

They entered a grand entranceway. To the right, an elegant stairway let upwards, while around them, other halls fed into the main area. Everywhere they looked, dead soldiers lay on the fine wooden floors. A huge crystal chandelier hung from the tall ceiling. As Emily looked up at it, she shivered. There was blood splattered on the crystal teardrops.

'How many Nirads are there?' Joel asked.

'Too many,' Diana said.

Suddenly Agents J and O staggered into the entrance hall.

'I told you, you aren't going anywhere,' Agent J yelled as he raised his weapon. He glared at Diana furiously. 'Bullets may not stop you, but Emily and the boy are human. Unless you surrender right now, I swear I will kill one of them.'

Emily felt Pegasus tense beneath her. His ears

sprang forward as he threw back his head and let out a loud, ferocious shriek. The stallion rose on his hind legs and lunged forward. One golden hoof struck Agent O, leaving a deep horseshoe impression on his chest. The other hoof hit Agent J in the head with a lethal impact.

As both men fell to the ground, Pegasus turned and moved towards the front doors of the house. He reared up and kicked out at the beautiful inlaid wood of the antique doors. They both shattered under the impact of the angry stallion.

Emily was stunned to see they were now on the front porch of a large pillared house. Across the tree-lined street, by the light of the gaslights, she saw other large yellow houses. Their lights on and looking very welcoming.

'My family went to Atlanta years ago,' Joel said in hushed surprise. 'Some of the homes looked just like this. Are you sure we're on Governors?'

Emily leaned forward on Pegasus and saw the blazing lights of Manhattan rising in the distance. 'There's the City. This is Governors.'

'Where we are no longer matters,' Diana said sharply, helping to lead the stallion down the steep wooden steps. 'It is where we are going that counts. It won't take long for the Nirads to reach the surface again. We must be gone before they do.'

She looked at the stallion. 'Pegasus, are you recovered enough to carry all of us, or should I stay?'

Pegasus gently nudged his cousin and let out a soft nicker.

'Of course,' Diana said. She turned to Joel. 'Climb on, he can carry all of us.'

'What about the Daughter of Vesta?' Joel asked, as Diana helped to hoist him on to the stallion's back behind Emily. 'Will there be room for her too?'

Diana leaped up on to Pegasus, behind him. 'She is already with us,' she said softly.

'What?' Joel cried.

Emily turned in her seat. She looked at Diana. 'It is me, isn't it? I'm the Daughter of Vesta and the Flame of Olympus.'

Saying nothing, Diana nodded.

'Emily, no!' Joel hushed. 'It can't be you.'

'It's all right, Joel,' Emily said softly. 'I've suspected for a while now.'

'When did you know for certain, child?' Diana asked.

Emily patted the stallion's neck. 'It was a few things really. Back on the bridge I started to wonder. You and

Pegs should have escaped. If the Daughter of Vesta was really out there somewhere, Pegasus would have left me and gone to her. But he didn't, he fought the soldiers to protect me. Then when I heard he was dying, I knew I had to get to him. That I could somehow help. And when I touched him, I felt him react. After a few hours with me, Pegasus grew much stronger. I finally knew for sure when you said I was more important. You wouldn't have said that if it wasn't me.'

'That is correct,' Diana confirmed. 'You are more important than all of us. The Flame is burning brightly inside you now. That is why Pegasus heals so quickly when he is with you; first on your roof and then here in this place. As your feelings for him grew, so did your power to heal him. Emily, you saved Pegasus.'

'And with luck, maybe I can save Olympus too,' Emily said gravely.

'No,' Joel insisted. 'I won't let you sacrifice yourself,' he choked, staring at Emily. 'You can't die.'

Emily reached back to touch Joel's hand. 'It's all right, Joel. Believe me, it is. If I do this, Olympus will be restored and you, my dad and this whole world will be safe. I want to do it. Please, let me.'

'But Emily—' Joel dropped his head, unable to form words. He squeezed her hand and looked away. The awful sounds of Nirads filled the air. They were on the main floor of the house and heading towards the front doors.

'They're coming,' Emily said. 'Pegs, take us to Olympus.'

32

Seated right behind his wings, Emily felt the stallion's growing strength as he trotted away from the house. When they reached an open area, he turned his head towards her and whinnied.

'He says hold on,' Diana explained. 'His wing is newly healed, but untried. It may be a rough flight.'

'You can do it, Pegs,' Emily said patting his neck. 'I know you can.'

As Pegasus moved from a trot to a full gallop, he spread his massive white wings. Emily clutched his mane as he leaped confidently into the air. She felt Joel tighten his grip around her waist as Pegasus rose up and over the dark water.

Manhattan lay dead ahead. As she looked at the beautiful, sparkling lights, Emily realized this would be the last time she would ever see her home. If they made it safely to Olympus, she would die in the Temple of the Flame.

What would happen to her father? Where was he? She was going to die without his ever knowing what had happened to her. Or that she loved him and had done it for him. That pain was the worst of all.

Inhaling deeply, she looked down on New York. The city would be safe. All those millions of people in it would live and never see or hear of a Nirad again.

'Hey, wait for me!' a tiny, unsteady voice called from behind them.

'Paelen?'

Turning back, Emily and Joel saw Paelen struggling to catch up with them, limping through the dark air. Only one sandal was flapping its wings and he was covered in blood.

'Paelen!' Emily cried. 'You survived the Nirads!'

'Are you all right?' Joel called.

'No!' Paelen called back. 'But I will live. Can you please slow down so I can catch up? The Nirads wounded a sandal and only one is working.'

The stallion snorted.

'Pegasus says you may hold on to his tail,' Diana called back to Paelen. 'He can help carry you home, but we must move faster if we are to reach Olympus.'

In the night sky, it was difficult for Emily to clearly see Paelen. But as they passed over New York, the city lights revealed his deep, open wounds.

'What did they do to you?' Emily cried.

'They tried to tear me apart,' Paelen called back. 'But I was able to change my body so they could not do it. Though I have broken a lot of bones.'

'Your bravery will not go unrewarded, Paelen,' Diana promised. 'My father will know what you did for us.'

Before Paelen could respond, Pegasus whinnied to Diana.

'Emily, Joel,' she called, 'hold on. We are about to enter the Solar Stream to Olympus.'

'The Solar what?' Joel started to ask.

Suddenly they were moving at an impossible speed. The starlight around them became a blur of white light. To Emily, it looked like special effects from a science fiction movie. But this was no movie. It was very, very real.

Looking back, she saw Paelen was almost surfing the light as he struggled to cling to Pegasus's tail while the one sandal flapped its tiny wings to keep up, his terrified cries filled the air behind them.

What really surprised her was Pegasus. He was still beating his large wings. What would happen if he stopped? Emily wondered hazily. And how did Diana manage to get to Earth without wings?

As these thoughts spun through her head, Emily forgot her dark destiny for a moment. But when Pegasus slowed down and the white light faded back into simple starlight, she felt her fear return.

Not far ahead, Emily saw what looked like the top of a mountain rising in bright sunshine. They emerged from the starlight and passed into a beautiful sunny day. The sky was brilliant blue – bluer somehow than on Earth – and around them, the sky was dotted with thick fluffy white clouds. As Pegasus flew amongst them, Emily could taste their rich sweetness on her lips.

Lower and lower they went. Soon they could see lush green fields beneath them. The mountain rose from the green. Emily realized that they were heading towards it.

'Is that Mount Olympus?' Emily asked Diana.

'This is all Olympus, not just that mountain,' Diana replied. 'Though we do live at the top.'

'Just like in the myths,' Joel added, gazing around in wonder. 'Is there a Mount Helicon here where the Muses live?'

'There is,' Diana said. 'That is where the Nirads first entered our world. The Muses were the first to be captured and Helicon the first to fall.'

As they approached the mountain, Emily tried to

take in all the sights. There were huge structures of glowing white marble. But as they drew near, she could see they had been knocked over, broken and destroyed.

'Did the Nirads do this?' she asked.

'Yes, and much worse,' Diana answered.

Emily and Joel looked down on the ruins of Olympus and at last understood what they were fighting for. Before it had been destroyed by the Nirads, this world would have been the most beautiful place imaginable.

Beneath them, the amount of rubble grew in density as they entered what must have been a heavily populated area. But more than that, much to her horror, Emily started to see bodies of the dead Olympians. For as bad as seeing the men in the facility on Governors Island had been, this was so much worse. There were people of all ages, even children and strange looking animals, lying dead on the ground.

'This is all my fault,' Emily choked.

'No it's not,' Joel said, horrified. 'That's crazy talk!'

'It's not crazy, Joel. If I am the Flame, then when it became weaker in me, it became weaker here. I allowed the Nirads to attack and kill all these people.'

'No, you're wrong,' he protested. 'I won't let you blame yourself for this. The Nirads did it, not you.'

'I am sorry, Joel,' Diana corrected, 'Emily is not

entirely wrong. She is the Flame of Olympus.' Diana looked at Emily. 'But she did not cause this intentionally. I now understand what did.'

'What?' Emily asked weakly.

'Love,' Diana answered. 'The deep love you had for your mother. When she died, grief overwhelmed you. It diminished the Flame. It was not illness as I first suspected. It was grief.'

'What about now?' Emily asked in a whisper. 'Is there enough Flame left in me to save Olympus and our world?'

Diana nodded. 'Oh yes, child. Even I can feel it burning brightly in you now. You are recovering. I believe Pegasus had a great deal to do with it.'

Pegasus snorted softly. Emily felt her heart fill with emotion for the stallion. Diana was right. Meeting Pegasus and caring for him had finally dimmed the searing pain of her mother's loss.

She looked back to Diana, 'When the Temple of the Flame is lit again will you be able to save these people. Will your brother live again?'

'I hope so,' Diana said. 'Without its people, there is no Olympus.'

Pegasus started to glide in the clear air over the ruins.

'We are going down,' Diana said. 'We must all be on

our guard. We are still in grave danger. Pegasus has taken us as close to the Temple as he dares. But legions of Nirads remain here. Their one goal will be to kill Pegasus and Emily.'

'Do they know what I am?' Emily asked.

'I do not think so,' Diana answered. 'Because you were wounded before, they will think you are important enough to kill. They will chase you as much as they do Pegasus.'

'We'll be careful,' Joel said. 'If we have to fight, we fight.'

'I too am ready,' Paelen said.

Emily looked back to him and could see his deep wounds and the odd angles of his arms and legs. More than just a few of his bones were broken.

Soon Pegasus landed. Emily was shocked by the stillness of the air around them.

'Is it always this quiet?'

Diana shook her head as she climbed off the stallion's back and helped Joel down. 'No, every animal, bird and insect has fled the onslaught of the Nirads.'

As Paelen touched down, Diana directed him closer to Emily. 'Take her hand. She can help you heal.'

Emily reached down and took Paelen's hand. As she closed her fingers lightly around his wrist, she felt the bones shift and slide, slotting back together. After a few moments, Paelen could stand better and didn't look to be in as much pain.

'I do not understand,' he said as he looked at Emily in awe. 'How are you doing this to me?'

Joel put his arm around Paelen's shoulders. 'It's a long story and we just don't have the time,' he said. 'Are you feeling well enough to fight?'

Paelen gave Emily his crooked grin. 'I could take on Jupiter!' he said.

Diana actually chuckled, 'Do not let my father hear you say that.' Then she looked around. 'We must move on. The Temple is some distance away. Does everyone still have their gold?'

Emily and Joel held up their pieces of gold from Pegasus's bridle.

Paelen shook his head. 'Mine is still lodged in the head of a Nirad back on Governors Island.'

Diana reached up and took Emily's piece. She tore it in two, handing one part back to Emily and the other to Paelen. 'Do not lose this one. We need every bit of it.'

Emily remained on Pegasus as the group slowly made their way through the rubble that once was Olympus. Many times she had to avert her eyes from the horrible casualties that lay on the ground. With every nerve on edge, she strained her eyes and ears for fresh signs of the Nirads. She saw nothing but destruction and heard only the soft, empty wind. 'Where are the Nirads?'

'I do not know,' Diana answered, looking around. 'But it worries me. There were thousands here not long ago. We must be on our guard. I do not believe they have left already.'

Pressing on, they reached the spot where the worst fighting had taken place. Amongst all the ruins, Emily saw tall steps leading up to the remains of a temple. The heavy metal gates at the top were torn from their hinges and cast down on the steps.

Instinctively, Emily recognized this place.

'That is the Temple of the Flame, isn't it?' she asked, pointing to the ruins.

Diana nodded but said nothing. She was kneeling before the body of a fallen Olympian. She reached out and gently stroked dark hair from a bruised and bloodied face, silent tears trickling down her cheeks. Seeing this strong and confident woman brought to her knees weeping made Emily realize all the sacrifices that had been made already.

'Is that your brother?' Joel asked softly.

Diana sniffed, and nodded. 'It is Apollo. He was a

brave and honourable fighter. I loved him dearly.' She looked around at the other dead fighters. 'They were all brave.'

'He will be avenged,' Paelen said, determined. 'I promise you, Diana, they all will.'

The horrible cries of Nirads shattered the stillness of the area. Emily looked back and her eyes went wide at the sight of hundreds of Nirads bearing down on them from nowhere.

'We must go!' Diana cried as she rose and left her dead brother. She ran to Pegasus and Emily. 'Child, it is up to you now. You are this world's only hope. Your sacrifice could save us all. I grieve at what you must now face. But I swear your name and your gift to us will not be forgotten by any Olympian!'

She pulled Emily's face closer to her and kissed her on the cheek. 'Your mother will be very proud of you when she meets you in Elysium.'

Tears filled Emily's eyes as she realized the time of her death had come. After only thirteen short years of life, it was going to end in the agony of flames in this shattered world.

'Joel, go with Pegasus and Emily, take them to the temple,' Diana ordered. 'Paelen and I will do our best to hold back as many as we can.' She looked back up at Emily. 'Go now, child. Fulfil your destiny!'

Emily didn't even have time to say goodbye to Paelen as Pegasus darted forward. Joel struggled to keep up beside her as they ran towards the Temple of the Flame. When they reached the base of the steps, Emily looked back and saw hundreds, maybe thousands, of Nirads charging towards them. Diana threw back her head and howled the loudest battle cry Emily had ever heard. With Paelen at her side, they held up their pieces of gold bridle and charged forward into the mass of Nirads.

At the temple steps, Pegasus hesitated.

'Take me up, Pegs,' Emily said softly as tears filled her eyes. 'If I don't do this now, they'll kill you and Joel. Let me do it for you.'

Hesitantly, Pegasus started to climb the marble steps. Emily heard Joel's sniffles beside her.

'I'm not sure I can watch this,' Joel whispered.

Emily looked into her friend's red, teary eyes. 'It's all right, Joel. Really it is. But if you somehow survive this, please promise me you'll go back to Earth and find my dad. If the CRU still have him, get him away. Bring him back here. Don't let them hurt him.'

Joel looked up at her, but couldn't speak. He nodded his head weakly.

At the top of the steps, Pegasus stopped. Emily looked to Joel. 'Would you help me down?'

Joel helped her climb down from Pegasus, and steadied her on her undamaged leg.

'Do you want me to help you into the Temple?' he whispered.

Pegasus snorted and nickered softly. Emily sniffed and shook her head. 'I don't think you're allowed.' As grief overwhelmed her, Emily threw her arms around Joel's neck. She hugged him tightly. 'Please stay well,' she wept.

'I'll try,' he promised. As he broke down, he kissed Emily on the forehead. 'Thank you for being my friend, Emily.' Then, with a final backward glance, he drew out his gold piece and charged down the steps of the temple to join Diana and Paelen in their struggle against the Nirads.

'Joel, no!' Emily howled. But Joel gave no sign of hearing her as he ran screaming into the thick legion of Nirads.

'Oh Pegasus,' Emily wept.

Pegasus reached back and nudged her gently. She knew he was telling her it was time to go. She had a destiny to fulfill; Olympus to save. When he opened his newly healed wing, Emily used it to support her while she hopped the final distance into the Temple.

The ruined temple was empty except for the huge marble bowl where the Flame of Olympus had once blazed. It had been knocked off its plinth and was badly cracked.

Pegasus slowly drew her up to the bowl. It was there Emily knew she was about to die.

As she hopped forward, she came up to the stallion's head. Her tears were falling steadily and she could no longer see clearly. 'I'm glad it was me, Pegs,' she said, her voice breaking. 'I didn't want you to care for someone else. Even though I'm going to die, I know that deep in my heart, for at least a little while, you were mine. I just wish we had more time together . . .'

Emily broke down and hugged Pegasus's head as her voice finally gave out. 'I love you Pegasus.'

Letting him go, she hobbled to the large, cracked marble bowl. With a final backward glance, she saw the black and brown stallion with the brilliant white wings lowering his head and pawing the ground in grief.

'Please remember me, Pegs,' Emily said. She looked away from him and climbed into the large marble bowl.

33

The moment Emily stood upright in the bowl; she felt a searing pain in her heart. She clutched at her chest and cried out in agony. This was it. Death. She was about to be burned alive.

An instant later, huge brilliant flames burst out of her chest. The explosion of flame and energy filled the Temple with brilliant white light and spread like huge ripples on water. Flying in every direction it poured out of the Temple and throughout all Olympus. The flames were coming from each part of her, consuming her and spilling out of her every pore.

As she stood in the centre of the flames, the pain slowly ebbed and finally disappeared completely. Emily looked around. She was searching for her mother. She's always heard the moment you die, your family come for you. But where was her mother? Her grandfather, everyone she had ever lost?

All she saw was flame and brilliant light. She felt an increasing sense of peace washing over her.

Emily waited. For how long, she was uncertain. All she knew was that somehow, she was still herself. She could think, feel and hold on to all the love and memories she had. She remembered everything about her life. The happy years with her mother and father in New York. Her mother's illness and finally, death. And although there was pain at the memory, Emily knew it wasn't as bad as it had been before. But then again, she also knew her mother would be waiting for her just outside the flames.

Emily thought of Joel. Sweet, angry, hurt Joel and that first endless climb up the stairs of her building. It all seemed such a long time ago. She promised herself she would find his family and tell them what he had done for her. She recalled Paelen's crooked smile and cleverness. Then there was Diana – beautiful and strong Diana crying over the death of a New York horse and the body of her fallen brother. But most of all, Emily remembered . . . Pegasus.

Thoughts of the stallion brought a smile to her burning lips. Of all the new friends in her life, Emily knew that in death, she would miss him the most.

After the briefest of moments, or perhaps the longest of eternities, Emily felt something change. The flames were drawing back. Soon, she could see again and somehow she knew it was time to leave the flames.

A new journey spread out before her. She felt certain her mother would be there waiting for her.

As she moved to the edge of the bowl, she could see between the flickering flames. And what she saw gave her more joy than she could imagine possible . . . Pegasus

He was no longer brown and black. Pegasus was glowing brilliant white again. Not a feather stood out of place on his beautiful folded wings. Majestic and proud, he was perfect.

Emily bent down and grasped the edge of the bowl for support. When she did, she noticed the crack in the marble was gone. Not only that, but it was no longer lying on the floor of the Temple. Somehow, it was back on its tall plinth.

Crawling over the top edge, Emily lowered her good leg down to the ground. When she put her wounded leg down, she felt no pain. It was true! She thought. When you died, all the pain stopped.

But when Emily added more weight, she found her leg still would not support her. Losing her balance, she fell heavily to the marble floor.

Pegasus was instantly as her side.

'Pegs?' Emily said in confusion as she looked up into his warm brown eyes and felt his tongue on her cheek. 'Can you see me?'

'We all can, child,' Diana called.

Emily looked over and saw Diana standing at the entrance to the temple, dressed in a stunning white tunic. Another beautiful woman stood beside her. Emily felt she should know her, but she couldn't think of her name.

Diana rushed forward and helped Emily to her feet. She handed her a set of Olympian robes and hugged her tightly. 'We are all so proud of you.'

'But I died,' Emily said. 'I don't understand.'

'You have been reborn,' said the other woman. She came forward and embraced Emily. 'My beautiful child, my Flame. I am Vesta.'

Emily's eyes flew wide. 'You're Vesta? Really? And I'm alive?'

Both women smiled. Finally Diana nodded to Pegasus. 'Ask him if you do not believe me. He never left your side. He has waited here all this time for you to return to us.'

Emily turned to Pegasus and the stallion pressed

closer. She touched his glowing muzzle. 'Pegs?' she said, still hardly believing the truth. Finally she threw her arms around his neck. 'Pegs, I'm alive!'

'We all are,' Diana said, 'with grateful thanks to you. Because of what you did, your sacrifice, Olympus has been restored.'

'How?' Emily asked. 'What did I do?'

'Get dressed and come see for yourself.'

Emily pulled on the robe and tied it at the waist. She clung to Diana and Pegasus for support as they made their way to the entrance of the Temple. Behind her, the Flame continued to burn brightly on its plinth.

Emily's eyes flew wide in disbelief. Standing at the base of the temple steps were thousands of people. When they saw her emerge from the temple with Diana, Pegasus and Vesta, they raised their voices in cheers and salute.

'These are your people, Emily,' Diana said, 'All alive because of you. My brother is down there, waiting to thank you himself. Soon my father will join us and offer his gratitude.'

'*Jupiter*?' Emily gasped in shock.

Diana smiled and nodded.

It was almost too much to take in. But as Emily's

eyes scanned the huge and endless crowd, they came upon Joel and Paelen, standing side by side at the foot of the steps.

'Joel!' Emily cried as she started to wave frantically. 'Paelen!'

Both started to race up the steps to greet her. Paelen arrived first and wrapped his arms around her and gave her a brutal embrace. Joel was right behind him. With a tight hug, he swung her around in the air.

'I don't know what the heck you did in there, or how you did it,' Joel laughed as he swung Emily round again. 'But it worked!'

Emily was left speechless. 'I don't know either,' she laughed.

Pegasus nudged Emily playfully.

'He wants you to get on his back,' Diana explained. 'He is going to carry you down the steps.'

Joel helped Emily climb on to Pegasus. When she was settled, the stallion neighed gently.

'Pegasus, no,' Vesta said sternly. 'The Flame has only just emerged. She must meet her people.'

Emily looked at Diana, a thousand questions in her eyes.

Diana laughed. 'Pegasus says hold on tightly. He is going to show you Olympus his way.'

Before Vesta could protest further, Pegasus opened his wings, reared on his hind legs and threw back his head in an excited whinny as he leaped confidently off the top of the temple and into the air.

Emily's heart thrilled at the feeling of the powerful stallion beneath her. As she clung to Pegasus's mane and felt the strong beating of his wings, she was part of him. They were one. Emily threw back her own head and whooped in pure joy.

Pegasus made a full circle of the top of the Temple. Then, with Emily still safely secured on his back, he flapped his massive wings and took her away over the heads of the cheering crowds. Emily waved at the people as she passed, still hardly believing what was happening. Beneath her, the scars of the war were being healed as workers rebuilt the beautiful buildings.

There was only one thing missing. Her father. He was still a prisoner of the CRU. But as she soared on the bare back of Pegasus, feeling a joy unmatched, Emily knew it wouldn't be long before he was to be freed and they were reunited. Whatever came next, as long as Pegasus was with her, Emily knew everything would be all right.

Q&A with Kate O'Hearn

Q) When did you first get the idea to write about Pegasus?

A) The idea came to me a couple of years ago, and all by accident. A friend asked me if I would ever write a book about horses. I responded, 'No, not unless it was Pegasus, as he's my favourite stallion in the world.' After that, the idea just spread like wildfire until it became *Pegasus and the Flame*. I think I owe that friend a big Thank You! (And maybe a huge box of chocolates.)

Q) In this book, Emily and Joel are very normal teens, who become heroes. Do you believe that ordinary people can make a difference?

A) Absolutely! I have always believed that it is the ordinary people who make all the difference in the world! They are the best heroes. How often have we heard stories of ordinary people doing extraordinary things? Most of the time they don't even want thanks. They are just everyday, generous and wonderful people. So I believe that each and every person – you, me, anyone – can make a phenomenal difference to this world if we try.

Q) Was it a challenge to mix mythology and the modern world?

A) It was amazing and so much fun. I grew up with the myths and have always loved them. Even before I started writing the book, I felt I already knew the characters so well – it was like revisiting old friends. But what really excited me was to put those great Olympians in our modern world and imagine how hard it would be for them to fit in. I mean, hiding Pegasus in the middle of New York City? It doesn't get better than that!

Q) *Pegasus and the Flame* was compared to the Percy Jackson books by Rick Riordan. Have you ever met Rick Riordan and has he influenced you?

A) I haven't met Rick Riordan, but I really want to! I have read the Percy Jackson books and love how he mixes the myths with reality. We are so different in our approach to our stories, but I can tell he cares for the myths just as much as I do! I'm such a big fan of his. I can just imagine the fun we would have debating the difference between the Greek and Roman myths! I hope that one day I may have the opportunity to meet him and personally thank him for writing such fantastic books and for being so generous in writing his great review of my book.